Suicide Tuesday

J. Cerrone

Written & Edited by J. Cerrone Smith

Book Design & Cover by Kyn Mixson

ISBN 978-0-9898111-6-3

Paper-Chase Publications LLC

Philadelphia, PA

Intro . . .

Message:

First, I would like to thank all my readers and supporters.

"Molly" is the street name for the illicit drug "MDMA," which is the active ingredient in the popular party drug "Ecstasy." In line with the other literary works I have released thus far, "Suicide Tuesday" is a story which brings to light the harsh realities of everyday life, specifically in the urban community, and shows the realistic consequences of certain actions rather than glorifying them. Although the drugs "Ecstasy" and "Molly" are often glorified and promoted as mostly harmless "party drugs" when obtained from a "trusted" source and taken in moderation, there are hidden dangers associated with them. "Suicide Tuesday" explores some of these hidden dangers and how they affected the main character and those around him.

The last two letters ("M-A") in the acronym "MDMA," represent "methamphetamine." This is the same active ingredient in the notorious street drug often referred to as "crystal meth." With that being said, please be mindful of who you associate with and cultivate relationships with. Please also be very careful when making decisions about what you allow into your personal space and what you put into your body. Just because something looks or feels good *does not* mean it is good for you.

I hope this story serves its intended purpose of entertaining and enlightening its readers. Enjoy!

J. Cerrone

Please be Advised: This story is a work of fiction. Any likeness to any person, living or deceased, is purely coincidental.

Friday . . .

September 11, 2015

Chapter 1

"Yo cuz! Long time, no see! What's good with you?" Raheem asked as he approached another young man while exiting the 69th Street Terminal in Upper Darby, Pennsylvania; a small, bustling city on the outskirts of West Philadelphia. "Where you been, dog?"

"Oh shit! What's good with you Heem?" Taj excitedly exclaimed as he turned around to greet his older cousin. They shook hands and hugged. "Man, I just got out the County. I was in that bitch for the past six months!"

"Damn, bro. You got locked up again? You were up State Road?"

"Naw man, I was in the nut-ass jawn out here – George Hill," Taj replied. "I got booked on some nut-ass robbery charge. Some bitch-ass nigga lied and told the law I robbed him. He found out I was knocking his baby-mom off and I guess he was too pussy to confront me about it like a man. I beat that case though. Niggas know my record, man. I hustle – I don't rob niggas! My mom didn't tell y'all I was down?"

"Naw, you know how my people are," Raheem sighed. "They don't fuck with me like that ever since they converted to Christianity. Even if your mom told them, they never told me."

"I already know," Taj admitted, dejected. "They don't really fuck with none of the family anymore. My mother gets real upset when she talks about how her and Uncle Has used to be so close until y'all changed religions a few years back. She's always talking about how she misses hanging out as a family and going to the mosque together."

"I feel you. But don't say 'y'all,' though," Raheem objected. "That's my parents' religion! I can't get down with their church. You know I can't pray to a white Jesus! I really just been on some trying to be spiritual in general, 'at one with the Universe,' without organized religion-type mentality the last few years. I've just been playing my position since they let me and Kim move in before the baby was born. What you doing up this way anyway?"

"I'm out here selling loosies, getting this money! You know how I do," Taj bragged. "There's too many niggas doing the same shit out Fifty-Second Street, so I figured I'd slide over here real quick and off these jawns. I'm about to be done though. What you getting into?"

"On my way back to the crib from work. I don't even really feel like going to the crib right now, though. I'm not trying to deal with the nut shit with my people. I had a rough day."

"You still working at UPS?" Taj asked his cousin. "You smell like it – all sweaty and stinking!"

"Yeah, man," Raheem laughed. "They're still working me like a dog! I'm trying to get a promotion and a raise or some shit, but you know how they do. Working my ass off ain't enough for them. You gotta be cool with the right people and I'm not about to be all joe, kissing people's asses. I'm tired of taking SEPTA all the way out Willow Grove for this nut-ass nine dollars an hour too. I'm about to get out on the block with you!"

"Naw, nigga," Taj objected. "You don't need to do that. I already have a record and it's just me I have to worry about. You got a whole wife and newborn at home. You don't need to get booked or choked out by the law for selling loosies on some Eric Garner shit."

"I feel you, but I'm tired of dealing with the nut shit," Raheem complained. "I'm sick of breaking my back for pennies and coming home to get treated like trash by my own family. Kim been acting nutty since the baby was born too!"

"Damn, cousin," Taj shook his head. "That's drawing. Why don't you slide through the crib with me so you can see my mom and we can put one in the air? I'll drop you back off at your crib when we're done."

"That'll work."

The two young men walked across the street and down the block to Taj's vehicle which was parked on a side street near the historic Tower Theatre. Taj started his car, lit a cigarette and turned his sound system all the way up before pulling away from the curb. The young men made the short trip to his West Philadelphia neighborhood while blasting a new Dark Lo mixtape.

"Is that my nephew?" Taj's mother smiled and waved from the porch of her Lancaster Avenue rowhome as Taj and Raheem exited the vehicle.

"Hey Aunt Kareemah," Raheem greeted Taj's mother as he walked up the steps to her porch and embraced her. "How you been?"

"I'm blessed, thank you," Kareemah replied. "More importantly, how are your beautiful wife and daughter? I haven't had the chance to see them since the baby was born. Every time I call my brother to try to figure out when I can stop by he's always talking about how busy everybody is; like y'all the only people who have things to do! I can never seem to get him to commit to a time for me to come by."

"I know. I'm sorry Auntie. You know how my father has been acting ever since they stopped going to the mosque. Kim and the baby are good, though. I want to bring them to see you but it's hard between working and not having a car."

"I understand baby," Kareemah replied as she gave her nephew another hug. "Don't even stress about it. Just do what you need to do and everything will work out eventually – Insha Allah. Maybe your cousin can give y'all a ride over here one of these days so I can see my great-niece."

"You stay volunteering me to drive somebody somewhere! I'm about to start hacking," Taj chuckled.

"That would be better than what you've been doing for money," Kareemah exclaimed as she rolled her eyes at her son. "I already know y'all are probably about to go in the basement and get high, so I hope you ain't complaining about bringing your cousins over here to do something productive!"

"Here we go! Naw, ma, I'm not complaining at all," Taj replied, defeated. "I'm just saying…"

"And I'm just saying, as long as you live here rent-free, you shouldn't have nothing negative to say when I suggest you do a favor for your cousin," Kareemah interjected.

7

"You right," Taj acquiesced. "Let's go in this basement and smoke before my mother decides to beat me upside my head with the Qur'an!"

"I ain't no hater, but I've always been kind of jealous of the relationship you have with your mother," Raheem confessed to his cousin as they sat in the basement.

"Jealous? Of what?" Taj asked, surprised.

"Y'all just have a really open relationship and she treats you like an adult."

"Yeah, when she feels like it," Taj replied coolly. "But you saw that shit, though. I'm twenty-two years old and she's telling me what to do with my car! She didn't buy that jawn and she damn-sure doesn't pay my insurance or put gas in it!"

"I feel you," Raheem admitted. "But nigga, I'm twenty-five with a whole wife and baby and my parents treat me like I'm a young-boy! At least Aunt Kareemah ain't on your top about everything you do. She let you turn the basement into a studio, she lets you come and go as you please and can do damn-near whatever you want in this jawn. You just came home and she let you come back and get right back to it. If I ever got locked up my parents would leave me hanging for sure!"

"You ain't never lied, fam," Taj admitted as he lit the blunt. "I guess we're at that age where we can't really expect to be treated like adults if we still live at home. My mom has always been cool like that, though. I remember your pops was always strict, even when they were still Muslim. What the fuck made them change religions anyway?"

"On some real shit, cuz," Raheem began, "This shit has been a long-time-coming. My mother was born and raised Baptist. From what I hear, my other grandparents were never happy about her converting to Islam when her and my father started dating seriously. There was always a lot of tension in the family behind that, which is why I was never close with them growing up. My father took it real hard when Grandma died. He was having issues with his faith and really started losing it on the low. Plus, there was some beef with how the mosque handled the Janazah. After the funeral, my mother and my other grandparents started pressuring him about the religion and I guess they finally broke him. It was really bad at first. My parents almost split up over the shit. That's the *real* reason why they moved out of West Philly."

"Oh snap. I didn't even know all that," Taj exclaimed as he passed the blunt to his cousin. "That makes sense though. Grandma was the truth! I know Grandma and Uncle Has were even closer than her and my mom were. I miss her like crazy. It fucked my head up when my mother told me she passed while I was locked up that first time."

"Yeah, man, the shit was totally unexpected. You should be happy you were booked at the time. There was a lot of drama in the family when Grandma passed. You know how that shit goes. Everything had died down by the time you got out. Now we're back to dealing with the usual bullshit!"

"Ha-ha! You ain't never lied," Taj agreed. "Our family is crazy!"

"Yeah, but whose family isn't these days? I just hope niggas can fix their issues before my daughter is old enough to start picking up on the family's bad habits," Raheem confessed as he exhaled a mouth full of marijuana smoke and passed the cigar back to his cousin.

"I feel you cuz! That's why I'm glad I ain't get none of these jawns pregnant out here," Taj replied. "I got enough of my own problems without having to deal with having a kid and all the bullshit that comes with baby-mothers! What's up with wifey though? Everything good with y'all? You said she's been acting nutty?"

"Pshhhh," Raheem sighed heavily. "She's been on some nut shit for real, dog!"

"What you mean?"

"So, you know how strict and controlling my parents have always been?"

"Do I? Nigga, why you think I never wanted to spend the night over your crib growing up?" Taj laughed. "Your pop was always so strict. No disrespect, but if I didn't know any better I would think Uncle Has was the third coming of the prophet Muhammed! Real rap!"

"Pretty much," Raheem agreed. "But check it, that's another reason why it was so wild when my parents converted. Not only did they change religions; my father took all that enthusiasm he raised me with for Islam and transferred it to the new religion. Then he expected me to just fall in line even though I was already grown! We were beefing all crazy about it after Grandma died. I was about to get married anyway, so I just moved out and got a crib with Kim. Him and my mom were mad how I just dipped and kept it moving with wifey. It was all good between me and her until she got pregnant. Then I guess my mother got in her head. Kim started pressuring me to move back in with my people so we could save money. I wasn't with it at first, but we were kind of struggling financially, so I finally agreed. When we moved in a few months before the baby was born, all of a sudden Kim wanted to start going to church with my parents. She started pressuring me so much that my parents don't really have to say much directly to me about it. We've been beefing about it ever since. I won't front like I was going to the mosque regularly anyway, but I damn sure ain't trying to go to church!"

"For real? I didn't know you were going through all of that, fam."

"Yeah, that ain't even the half," Raheem continued. "The past couple weeks my pop started threatening to kick me out if I don't start going to church with them. I've been wanting to move back out for a minute, but ever since I lost my other job I don't make enough bread to handle everything I need to handle. I'm broke as fuck between all the expenses for the baby, paying a few hundred dollars in rent to my parents every month and paying for these damn SEPTA passes. Not to mention the way Kim spends money on nut shit like take-out, constantly getting her hair and nails done and buying new clothes every time she loses more of the pregnancy weight!"

"See, that's why I'm glad I don't have no baby and no girlfriend," Taj shook his head. "I don't know how you do it!"

"I ain't even gonna hold you, dog. I love Kim and my daughter to death, but I don't know how I keep dealing with this shit either," Raheem confided in his cousin. "What makes it even worse is that every time I talk to her about cutting back on spending and saving money so we can get a wheel and move out, Kim takes my parents' side, talking about, 'you need to be thankful they let us stay here. I'm not tryna be broke just so we can have our own place again. Why don't you just do what they tell you to do?'

We actually just had a crazy argument last night because she told me if my parents kick me out she's gonna stay at my people's crib with the baby!"

"Stop playing cuz! That's outta pocket!"

"I know right? She's my wife! How the fuck is she gonna take sides with my parents?" Raheem continued venting. "We have our own family and she'd rather be comfortable living with them than to be a grown woman and grind it out with me! She goes to church with them all the time and she is always pressuring me to go. It's like my mother is using her as a puppet to try to control me. I swear some of the shit Kim says to me sounds like my mother wrote it down for her and made her rehearse! I never expected things to be like this between me and Kim. I don't think she was ready to get married. I don't even know how much longer I can take this shit."

"Damn, dog… I'm sorry to hear that. I'm sure everything will be cool sooner or later," Taj reassured his cousin. "But if shit gets too hectic at the crib you can always stay here for a while. You know you're always welcome. You can sleep on this futon. You know we wouldn't mind."

"That's love, my nigga. I appreciate that. But your mother and my father already have enough tension in their relationship. I'm not trying to cause any more drama… I know my pop would be pissed if they kick me out and your mom let me stay here. I'll be cool. I'll figure something out soon. Speaking of which, I should probably get back to the crib. You ready to give me a ride?"

As the young men crossed 63rd Street onto Marshall Road – leaving Philadelphia City limits and entering Upper Darby, Taj decided he wanted to stop and buy some more cigarettes while he was in the suburbs. The City of Philadelphia had implemented a relatively new tax on cigarettes which did not apply to the surrounding counties, so buying packs and cartons in the city cut into Taj's profits when he sold loose cigarettes ("loosies"). They pulled up in front of a beer distributor not far from Raheem's parents' house and both of the young men exited the vehicle and walked into the store.

"Hey Raheem," a shapely young woman greeted Raheem as he walked into the store.

"Oh, hey what's going on Sarah?" Raheem quickly replied, careful not to maintain eye-contact with the attractive young lady.

"Not much. Just running errands for my nigga, as usual," Sarah replied as she smiled and rolled her eyes. "He always has me doing wifey shit but he still hasn't put a ring on it!"

"Ha-ha! I'm sure he will soon," Raheem replied nervously. "I'm sure he wants to keep you around."

"Shit.... I know I would," Taj interjected.

"Y'all silly," Sarah smiled bashfully. "Well, it was good seeing you Raheem. Tell your family I said hi."

"You already know," Raheem replied as Sarah exited the store and Taj stood in line to buy cigarettes.

"Who the fuck was that?" Taj enthusiastically inquired.

"Just some jawn from around here," Raheem replied nonchalantly.

"*Nigga*! Don't you mean 'just some bad jawn' who is on your top?"

"Don't even start that shit," Raheem objected. "She ain't hardly on my top. Her parents live next door to us and she visits them a few times a week, so I see her around. I think she lives on the other side, though. Her parents go to church with my people. Besides, I'm married. And she fucks with some get-money, hustling-ass nigga."

"I respect you talking all that, 'I'm married' shit… that's what you're supposed to say," Taj laughed. "But I'm your cousin, nigga! I've known you my whole life! She bad as hell and thicker than a motherfucking snicker! I know that's your twist! And she was all in your face, joe as shit! She obviously isn't too worried about her dude. And you just finished telling me how unhappy you are at home. Bitches can sense that shit. Maybe she wants to be your side jawn. She can be your little escape every now and then when you don't feel like dealing with the bullshit at the crib."

"I'm cool, bro," Raheem objected. "No bullshit – she is bad as fuck! But that wouldn't be cool. I married Kim and vowed not to fuck with any other women. Besides, I don't need any more drama in my life. I'm already having a hard-enough time getting along with Kim and my parents without spending extra time outside the crib creeping with a side jawn. Not to mention, if I got caught it would be a wrap for my marriage and it would probably lead to beef with her nigga. It ain't worth it."

"That's why you gotta do like Jeezy said: 'don't get caught!'" Taj laughed as the pair exited the store and entered his vehicle.

"You're a wild dude, cuz!"

"I'm just speaking facts," Taj stated seriously as he drove away from the store and turned onto his cousin's block.

"Good looking on the smoke and the ride, cuz," Raheem thanked Taj as he shook his hand after they pulled up in front of Raheem's parents' house. "You wanna come in and holla at everybody and see the baby?"

"Maybe next time when I'm sober, man," Taj declined. "I'm high as fuck and based on what you told me, this is probably not the best time. I'm not tryna get preached to and have Uncle Has blow my high!"

"Say less," Raheem agreed. "I'll holla at you."

Chapter 2

"You're home later than usual Raheem," Raheem's mother sternly greeted him the moment he walked through the front door. She had been sitting on the living room sofa and saw him approaching through the front window. "Who dropped you off?"

"Oh, hey Ma," Raheem softly replied. "I saw Taj when I got off the train at 69th Street and he gave me a ride."

"So, shouldn't you have been back sooner if he gave you a ride?" Mrs. Brown asked skeptically.

"We went to his house first so I could see Aunt Kareemah, then he stopped at the store before he dropped me off," Raheem answered gruffly. He grew agitated upon being questioned by his mother. He had just walked into the house and she was already giving him the third-degree as if he wasn't a grown man who had just worked all day. She hadn't even said "hello," before she started her inquisition.

"Oh, well, you know how we feel about you hanging with that thug," Mrs. Brown continued. "If Kareemah had been more worried about being his mother instead of being his friend, then maybe that boy would know how to act instead of being in and out of jail all the time!"

"For real, though, ma? You really feel the need to do this right now?" Raheem sighed, frustrated. "I literally *just* walked in the house from work. I'm still dirty and sweaty. Can I at least take a shower before you hit me with all that?"

"I really don't like your attitude," Mrs. Brown snapped. "I don't care how grown you think you are... I'm still your mother! I carried you for nine months and I raised you. I think that gives me the right to correct you when you need correcting. You seem to feel real comfortable getting smart with me considering the circumstances."

"What circumstances are those, ma?" Raheem asked sarcastically.

"The fact that I've been watching *your* baby all afternoon so *your* wife can get some rest and you walk into *my* house later than expected. *Those* circumstances," Raheem's mother fired back. "Not to mention the fact that you smell like weed!"

"Well, you just mentioned it," Raheem muttered under his breath as he walked up the stairs and into the bedroom he shared with his wife.

"Boy, you better watch your mouth!" Mrs. Brown called out to her son. "Walking around this house like you own something. Lord Jesus, give me the strength!"

"Oh my God," Raheem exclaimed as he closed the bedroom door behind him. "I'm tired of this shit!"

"Damn, baby! Why you gotta be so loud? I was having a good dream," Kim complained. The commotion Raheem caused as he entered the room had interrupted his wife's nap.

"My fault baby," Raheem apologized as he leaned over the bed and kissed his wife on her forehead. "I just walked in the door to my mother's usual nagging. How was your day?"

"It was okay," Kim replied as she sat up in the bed. "Chanel wouldn't take a nap for me though. I didn't even have a chance to take a shower. I crashed when your mom got home from work and offered to watch her for me."

"Well, at least you and the baby have a good relationship with my mother," Raheem replied sullenly. "That must be nice…"

"Well, you already know what your parents' issue with you is. We've been living here for almost a year and you're still acting surprised?"

"I'm not surprised, but that doesn't mean I like it," Raheem answered his wife curtly as he retrieved clean underwear from his dresser. "That's why we need to move the fuck up outta here. But I'm not even trying to get into all this with you again right now. I need to wash my ass. I'm about to hop in the shower."

"Oh, but wait," Kim objected. "I just told you I didn't get to take a shower yet today. Can I take one real quick first?"

15

"Baby, you know I just got home from work. I'm sweating and stinking. I need to hop up under this water with a quickness."

"I know, but I've been needing to take a shower all day. I didn't have a chance because I've been taking care of *our* child all day. I crashed as soon as your mom gave me a break," Kim complained.

"I understand that Kim, but why don't you just go back to sleep while I'm in the bathroom? Can't you take a shower when I'm done?" Raheem attempted to negotiate with his wife.

"I *was* taking a nap until you came in here being all loud," Kim snapped. "Now I'm up because of you and I would like to take a shower before the baby wakes up."

"I'll be real quick so you can get in there right after me," Raheem replied. "Besides, I haven't seen my baby-girl all day, so I want to spend time with her anyway. I'll take care of her when she wakes up after I finish in the shower. You can relax for the rest of the evening."

"Why does everything always have to be on your schedule, Raheem?" Kim whined. "You *always* get your way! What about what *I* want?"

"What? Are you being serious right now Kim?"

"Yes, I'm dead-serious," Kim continued. "I get up with the baby, I'm here all day with her. I never get to do anything for myself or get to hang out with my friends ever since she was born. All I'm asking is for you to let me take a shower first and you won't even let me do that! It's not fair!"

"Wow." Raheem sighed. "First of all, welcome to parenthood! Our lives don't revolve around us anymore, they revolve around Chanel. You're not the only one who doesn't ever get to have fun. I work all day, then I gotta come home to the bullshit with my parents. I agreed to move here so we didn't have to stress as much about money since you insisted on it. My parents stress me out enough. I don't need this shit from you too."

"You claim you don't get to have fun but you smell like weed right now, so I guess you found some time to have fun before you came home," Kim retorted. "You're so selfish sometimes Raheem!"

"You know what, Kim... just take a shower. Go ahead. It's not that deep."

"Thanks love!" Kim's mood automatically improved. She smiled as she hopped out of bed, grabbed her robe, towel and washcloth before leaving the bedroom. Raheem shook his head in frustration as he watched his young wife exit their small bedroom.

"My family is gonna be the death of me," Raheem sighed as he sat on the bedroom floor so as not to contaminate his bed with his dirty clothes. He unlocked the screen on his cellular phone and scrolled through his social media accounts to temporarily distract himself from the stressful events of the day. Thirty-five minutes later, Kim finally re-entered the bedroom, bringing with her the fresh scent of the body-wash she used in the shower. "So much for a quick shower," Raheem thought to himself.

"Damn baby... you're smelling and looking like a snack," Raheem greeted his wife as he rose from the floor and groped her behind.

"Boy, if you don't get your dirty hands off me and take a shower," Kim scolded her husband.

"They wouldn't be dirty if you would've let me take a shower first," Raheem laughed, assuming his wife was only half-serious. "I'm on your top when I get out the shower though. You've been warned!"

"Yeah, we'll see," Kim replied half-heartedly. "Maybe we can *try* to do something if I'm not tired, if the baby is still asleep and if your parents aren't upstairs by the time you're done."

"Girl, please! Miss me with that 'try' shit! 'Trying' is why we haven't had sex in so long," Raheem complained. "I got a whole three weeks' worth of pent up frustration to bust off!"

"You're doing all this talking and you could have already been in the shower! You're wasting time!"

"Yeah, alright," Raheem shook his head as he made his way to the bathroom. As soon as he had stripped off his clothes and turned on the shower, Raheem's father, Hassan, hastily entered the front door of the house. He ran up the stairs and began frantically banging on the bathroom door.

"Who's in the bathroom?" Mr. Brown asked aggressively.

"Pop, it's me," Raheem called out. "I just got home from work. I'm about to take a shower."

"I just got home from work and I need to get in there. Come on out so I can pee!"

"Can you just wait a second please?" Raheem asked respectfully. "I'm not dressed and I'm about to hop in the shower. Give me a second and you can just come in and do your thing."

"Or, you can just do what I said and come out so I can use *my* bathroom," Mr. Brown demanded.

"Goddamn. I guess he can't even ask nicely. Always with the nut shit," Raheem cursed under his breath. "Okay, let me put my drawers back on!"

Raheem quickly slipped his underwear on and exited the bathroom as his father rushed by him without a word. He patiently waited in the hallway for more than five minutes as his father used the bathroom. When Mr. Brown finally opened the door to exit the restroom, Raheem was blasted in the face by the pungent odor of fresh feces.

"Dag, Pop! I didn't know you were gonna blow that jawn up like that before I took a shower," Raheem attempted to joke with his father.

"Yeah, well, I had to cover up that strong marijuana smell you have consuming the bathroom," Mr. Brown huffed. "I *know* you haven't been smoking in *my* house! Is that your clothes smelling like that?"

"Yeah, sorry Pop. It's my clothes," Raheem replied passively. "I wouldn't smoke in your house. I'm not gonna disrespect your crib like that after you invited us to live here."

"Yeah, alright," Hassan casually replied. "That's what I thought."

Raheem walked into the bathroom, shaking his head. He didn't understand why everybody in the house seemed to want to start arguments with him. As he had discussed with Taj and Kim, he understood his parents were upset that he had not converted to Christianity like they had, but it had been years. He thought they would have accepted it by now. In

18

addition to that, they knew before they offered repeatedly for him and Kim to move in that he hadn't changed his views on religion. They hadn't been quite so aggressive with him about their feelings before he had moved back home. He felt like he had been set up to either "get with the program" or be punished on a daily basis. It was like an unspoken ultimatum. He felt he was being treated unfairly and he was growing tired of biting his tongue about the matter.

"Is there a problem, boy?" Mr. Brown asked aggressively as his son walked past him, shaking his head. Raheem chose to ignore his father's comment and closed the door as if he hadn't heard what his father had said. He turned the shower back on, started playing music on his phone and finally began to shower. "Hurry up too! I gotta clean the bathroom!"

"These people are crazy," Raheem said out loud to himself as he let the warm water cascade over his body. "They're doing too much! I can't keep dealing with this. I'm about to snap."

Raheem made his way to his bedroom upon exiting the bathroom, anticipating much needed intercourse with his wife. To his surprise, she was not there. He put basketball shorts and a t-shirt on, then proceeded down the stairs and into the kitchen where he saw his mother and his wife conversing. Their moods shifted when they noticed he had entered the room.

"So, I guess y'all were talking about me based on how y'all switched up when I came in here, huh?"

"You're so paranoid sometimes Raheem! Ain't nobody talking about you," Kim objected. "You act like nobody has anything better to do than to talk about you!"

"Damn, wife! It's like that?" Raheem was unable to hide the hurt in his voice. His wife was unnecessarily abrasive far too often. "Oh, alright... say less. Well, I was tryna see if we were gonna handle what we talked about before I got in the shower."

"I was telling your wife that your sister and her new man are coming over for dinner tonight," Mrs. Brown interjected. "Your father said she told him they're getting pretty serious so he wants to get to know him better."

"Seriously?" Raheem asked incredulously. "The ink on her divorce ain't even dry yet! How serious can they be? That girl doesn't learn."

Raheem's older sister, Sharika, had been married for less than a year to her child's father. They had married less than ten months after they met and had a child roughly eight months later. Within six months of the birth of Raheem's nephew, Sharika and her husband separated and he had not even been around to see his son since they split. They had finalized their divorce about a year later. Now she was already talking about being serious with her new boyfriend of three months.

"Serious enough for her to tell your father that they're serious," Mrs. Brown replied pragmatically. "Let he who is without sin be the first to cast a stone."

"What does that even mean?" Raheem asked his mother as he glanced at his wife.

"Don't play stupid Raheem. You know *exactly* what it means!"

"Yeah, Ma... I know what it means," Raheem replied, attempting not to betray his growing frustration. "I'm just asking what that has to do with what we were talking about."

"You shouldn't be up here talking about how your sister doesn't learn when you're the most hard-headed person I know," Raheem's mother chastised him.

"Are you serious? How did this conversation get turned around to talk about what you think I'm doing wrong? I swear to God!"

"You better watch your mouth, boy! Don't be taking up the Lord's name in vain in my house," Mrs. Brown shrieked.

"Wow... you're really tripping with this whole Christian, holy-roller, Bible-thumper thing," Raheem complained. "You ain't quote the Qur'an half as much my whole life as you have quoted the Bible these past three years! Besides, you don't even mess with Sharika like that! I'm your blood and she's your step-daughter but all of a sudden, you're real quick to defend her! Is that because she converted to Christianity too just to make

Pop happy? Or is that only because you can use it as an excuse to come at my neck?"

"Heem," Kim interjected. "Don't disrespect your mother, baby. Let's just go upstairs before this goes all the way south."

"Sounds like a good idea," Raheem agreed as he exited the kitchen and began climbing the stairs, Kim walking behind him.

"Yeah, I agree. Get that boy out my face before I have to remind him where he is," Mrs. Brown jeered. Raheem immediately stopped mid-stride and cut his eyes at his mother. Kim placed her hand on her husband's back and gently pushed Raheem to encourage him to continue to walk up the stairs to their bedroom.

"Don't even entertain it baby," she whispered. "I'll make you feel better when we get upstairs."

They entered their room and Raheem laid on their bed covering his face with his hands. His wife closed the door behind them and laid next to her husband, embracing him.

"What the fuck is wrong with my parents?" Raheem exhaled, fighting back tears of frustration. "They really want beef with me or some shit!"

"I know, I'm sorry baby," Kim attempted to console her husband. "Try not to worry about it, though."

"It's kind of hard not worrying about it when I deal with it damn-near every time I see or speak with them! I told you this was the main reason I didn't wanna move back in here! I knew they were gonna act like this!"

"Yeah, I know… you were right," Kim admitted. "But it's not that bad all the time baby. You gotta look at the positive side of things."

"That's easy for you to say," Raheem retorted. "They're nicer to you than they are to me and they're not even your parents!"

"I'm sorry baby. I don't know why. I can help you feel better though."

21

Kim smiled seductively at her husband as she slipped her hand down his shorts and began to rub his manhood while kissing his neck. Raheem let out a sigh as he relaxed from his wife's touch. It had been too long since they had been intimate. He knew his unsatisfied sexual urges were partially responsible for his pent-up aggression and his decreased ability to handle the mistreatment from his family. Between Raheem's work schedule, the baby's sleep schedule, their limited privacy because of living with his parents and Kim's lack of energy, it had become difficult for them to be spontaneous. It was almost as if they needed to schedule time to be intimate and it had not been working out recently. They hadn't had sex in almost a month. He was elated to finally be able to do what they were supposed to be able to do as a young, married couple.

After a minute of enjoying his wife's touch, Raheem engaged Kim; pulling his shorts down, opening his wife's robe and pulling her on top of him. He groped her and began to kiss her passionately before pulling her panties down. By the time she had adjusted her position while straddling him in order to fully remove her underwear, a loud shriek was relayed over the baby monitor positioned on their nightstand. Baby Chanel, who had been napping in her grandparents' room, had awakened from her slumber.

"You gotta be fucking kidding me," Raheem uttered as he tried to assist his wife up from her position on top of him.

"Real quick Heem," Kim whispered as she gently nibbled on Raheem's earlobe and placed all her body weight on her husband to resist being moved. "There's formula in the fridge. Let your mom handle it until we're done. She already agreed to watch her."

"Yeah, I wish," Raheem sighed. "She said that earlier so you could get some rest; *not* so you could get some dick! You know if neither one of us comes out there, they're gonna start talking shit! Besides, I haven't seen my baby-girl awake since late last night!" Raheem picked his wife up and laid her gently on the bed beside him. He put his shorts back on as she crossed her arms, pouted and sighed dramatically. "I'm just as upset as you are, if not more! Don't worry, I'll blow your back out later after Chanel goes to bed."

"Yeah, I guess so," Kim replied sullenly. "That's if I still have the energy by the time she goes to bed and your sister and her boyfriend leave."

"I'll just have to go to the *papi* store and get you an energy drink then," Raheem said half-jokingly as he rushed out the bedroom to retrieve the crying infant. Raheem's mother had just walked up the stairs and followed behind him as he entered his parents' bedroom.

"I was just about to come grab her," Mrs. Brown informed her son as he picked his daughter up from the playpen in his parents' room and consoled her.

"Thanks Ma, it's all good though. I got her," Raheem softly replied as he walked back out of his parents' room and past the bathroom where his father was cleaning in preparation for Sharika's arrival.

"Yeah, well, I thought maybe you were so busy complaining to your wife about me that you didn't hear your baby crying," Mrs. Brown replied sarcastically as she followed her son downstairs into the kitchen.

"For real, Ma? Why you always got something negative to say to me?" Raheem asked without turning to look at his mother. He was cradling his daughter in one arm while retrieving a bottle of formula from the refrigerator.

"You don't like when people tell you the truth, so you get upset," the older woman fired back. "But I'ma tell you like it is! I know that's what you went upstairs to do!"

"Actually, naw, Ma. You're mistaken," Raheem gently corrected his mother as he warmed up the bottle of formula. "I wasn't even worried about that by the time Chanel started crying."

"Well, if you're saying what I think you're saying, then I'm glad the baby started crying," Raheem's mother stated smugly. "Lord knows y'all definitely don't need to be making any more babies when you can barely take care of the one you have!"

"What did you just say to me?" Raheem said as he jerked his head around to glare at his mother.

"You heard me!"

23

"I feel like I heard you wrong," Raheem repeated. His voice was calm, but his mother observed her son's intense facial expression and noticed the vein protruding from his forehead. "What did you say to me Mommy?"

"I said you better learn how to be more responsible before you bring any more children into this world," Mrs. Brown re-worded her hurtful comment, realizing she had finally struck a nerve. She couldn't remember the last time her son had referred to her as "Mommy," and it was strange for her to hear him call her that after all the years that had passed since he started referring to her as "Ma."

Mrs. Brown did, however, remember the last time, more recently, when she had noticed Raheem's veins protruding from his forehead. Her most recent memory of this occurring was before Raheem's older sister's and her ex-husband separated. Sharika had accused her then-husband of physically abusing her. As she relayed the story to the family, Raheem sat quietly, but the veins had begun to swell from his forehead. The next conversation Sharika had with her husband was when he was calling to complain about how Raheem had stopped by the house while she was gone, kicked the front door in and beat him until his mouth and nose were leaking blood. Veins bulging from Raheem's forehead was a foreboding sign.

"That's *not* what you said, Mommy. Would you please say it the same way you said it before? Matter-of-fact... Kim!" Raheem called up the steps to his wife as he tested the temperature of the formula on his inner wrist before proceeding to feed his daughter. "Kim, come to the kitchen please!"

"What's up Heem?" Kim called out as she slowly made her way down the steps. Raheem felt his blood boiling and passed their daughter, along with her bottle to his wife once she entered the kitchen. He then leaned his back against the counter, folded his arms and took a deep breath before proceeding.

"Go ahead Mommy," he motioned towards his mother with his hand. "Please repeat what you said to me for your daughter-in-law."

"I said that *you*, Raheem, personally need to learn some responsibility because I feel like you're not handling certain affairs in the most mature way," Mrs. Brown stuttered.

"So, you're gonna sit up here and act like that's really what you just said to me when we first came into the kitchen?"

"That *is* what I said," Raheem's mother replied coolly.

"Let's be real, Mommy," the vein in Raheem's head was pulsating as he attempted to maintain his composure. "Maybe that's what you meant to say, but that *is **not*** what you said."

"Well, not verbatim, but that's basically what I said," Mrs. Brown reaffirmed.

"Naw… it's *not at all* what you said. Tell Kim what you said about us."

"First of all, this is my house!" Mrs. Brown yelled. "You're not gonna sit up here and twist my words to make me look bad in front of your wife!"

"Hmmmm…" Raheem took another deep breath. He felt himself about to lose control of his temper. "I'm not twisting your words to make you look bad. You are twisting your own words to make yourself sound better. You changed what you said three times already. And I'm also trying to figure out why you're raising your voice at me."

"What, boy? Who do you think you're talking to?" Mrs. Brown shrieked. "You're not gonna tell me how to talk and what to say in *my* house! I can raise my voice if I want to. I'm the parent – you're the child! I ain't got no reason to lie to you!"

"Then why don't you just repeat what you said the first time instead of misdirecting the conversation?" Raheem asked in an unusually calm manner.

"Baby," Kim interjected. "What is the whole point of this?"

"Because my mother was talking crazy when I got Chanel out of their room," Raheem snapped. "Then she followed me into the kitchen saying how she knew I was talking trash about her upstairs. When I told her I wasn't worried about it, she said she was glad the baby started crying so we wouldn't have any more children because we can barely take care of Chanel!"

"I *did not* say that," Misses Brown objected. Raheem's mother was a relatively fair-skinned, melanated woman. Her face was getting flushed and her eyes were welling up with tears.

"Stop lying!" Raheem roared, finally losing control of his temper. "She *did* say that disrespectful shit! And you're cool with living here, dealing with this bullshit? It ain't even just about me anymore. That's how she feels about all three of us – me, you *and* the baby!"

"Calm down Raheem," Kim protested. "You're gonna upset the baby!"

At that very moment, Raheem's father, Hassan rushed down the stairs. He had overheard the yelling as he finished cleaning the bathroom. He was already perturbed because his wife had not assisted in cooking, cleaning or preparing for Sharika and her boyfriend's arrival. He was accustomed to doing the bulk of the cooking and cleaning by himself, especially when they were having company. The only person who consistently helped with household chores over the years had been Raheem.

"Are you down here yelling at your mother?" Mr. Brown asked aggressively, glaring down at his son once he reached the bottom of the stairs and entered the kitchen.

"You didn't hear what your wife said to me about me, my wife and my baby," Raheem attempted to explain.

"I didn't say anything that wasn't true," Mrs. Brown protested. "This boy just doesn't like hearing the truth! He wants to do whatever he wants and expects nobody to say anything about it!"

"What are you even talking about?" Raheem screamed. "Why do you keep lying? I can't stand that shit!"

"Cuss in my house again, Raheem, and we're gonna have a major problem!" Mr. Brown threatened as he stepped into his son's personal space.

"First of all," Raheem stood his ground, "I'm not trying to disrespect anybody in this house but y'all seem to be determined to disrespect me every chance y'all get! Why did you insist we move here knowing y'all were planning on treating me like this? That's real dirty!"

"I'm just saying, you better watch your mouth in my house," Mr. Brown reiterated menacingly.

"How about you check your wife?" Raheem snapped. "I ain't never disrespected you or stepped to you a day in my life Pop, but this is about *my* family and *my* child now! Mommy is being totally disrespectful and you're basically co-signing it by not checking her!"

"Boy, you better watch your mouth," Mr. Brown threatened as he stepped closer and shoved his son.

At that moment, Raheem momentarily lost every ounce of self-control, threw his fists up and lunged at his father for the first and only time in his twenty-five years on the planet. Immediately, both Kim, who was holding their baby, and Mrs. Brown, simultaneously jumped in between the men. Seeing his wife and daughter in his path of attack quickly brought Raheem back to reality and he stopped in mid-attack.

"I'm not with this bullshit anymore y'all!" Raheem screamed, unsuccessfully attempting to hold back the tears of hurt and frustration which had formed in his eyes. "All the times you put hands on me my whole life and been disrespecting me since we moved back in and I keep taking that shit on the chin out of love and respect for you as my father. I'm done!"

"Get your stuff, and get out of my house! Now!"

"You're just gonna kick us and your newborn grandchild out after y'all insisted on us moving here so you could 'help us' save money?" Raheem asked in disbelief.

"I didn't say *they* need to leave," Hassan corrected his son. "I said *you* need to leave!"

"For real?" Raheem's voice cracked. He looked at Kim who was standing a few feet from him, holding their daughter. He could tell she was purposely avoiding making direct eye-contact with him. "Y'all really gonna do me like that?"

"You did yourself like that," Raheem's mother haughtily replied, devoid of any real empathy for her only biological child.

"It's whatever, yo," Raheem snapped as he finally broke down in tears. His already raspy voice was breaking and cracking as he continued to yell while he walked upstairs to the bedroom he shared with his wife and daughter. His wife followed him into the room, their daughter crying in her arms. Kim said nothing, however. Raheem didn't speak to his wife either. He already knew how she felt about the situation based on their conversation the previous night. He felt betrayed, nonetheless, that she hadn't come to his defense or even asked his parents to reconsider. Raheem quickly packed a bag and kissed his daughter on her cheek without even acknowledging his wife who was still holding her. As he walked back down the steps, his older sister had just happened to walk in the front door along with her boyfriend.

"I don't know why y'all didn't just abort me since y'all obviously didn't want me," Raheem roared, still attempting to hold back tears. "I can't stand y'all! And Pop, I swear to God, if you ever put your hands on me again I'll put you in the fucking hospital! Fuck y'all!"

Raheem stormed out the front door into the cool fall air. He was alone, emotionally devastated and had no idea where he would go and what he would do. This was not at all how he anticipated he would spend his Friday evening.

Chapter 3

Raheem slammed the door and walked down the front steps onto the sidewalk. He was an emotional wreck. He started breathing deliberately to calm himself down and stop crying. The young man had no idea what he was going to do. Should he get a hotel room? He walked to the mini-market and beer store to buy some Black and Mild cigars to smoke while he calculated his next move.

Raheem had calmed down to the point where he had completely stopped crying by the time he had walked the block and a half to the mini-market. He went in, bought a few cigars, exited the store and lit one. As he inhaled deeply, his inner cheeks, lungs and blood quickly absorbed the tobacco and sent a calming sensation through his veins. He stretched and glanced around, looking for a place to sit so he could search for nearby hotel accommodations on his phone. A familiar car caught his eye in the store's parking lot on Marshall Road, roughly twenty-five feet away. The headlights of the vehicle shone brightly in the night. It appeared to be his neighbor's daughter, Sarah's car. Raheem had just seen her when he was with Taj at the same store earlier that day. Raheem decided to continue to walk in that direction. As he approached the vehicle, he noticed Sarah in the driver's seat, with her head in her hands.

"Yo, Sarah," Raheem called out so she could hear him through her closed car window. Sarah looked up suddenly, obviously startled. Raheem waved to her. "You cool?"

"Just a second," Sarah replied, holding up one finger and frantically searching for more tissue. She wiped her eyes, blew her nose and then rolled down her window. "Hey Raheem," Sarah sniffled. "You caught me at a bad time."

"Yeah, I'm sorry," Raheem replied bashfully. "It seems like that's going around today. I saw you looking like you were going through it so I decided to come check on you. You headed to your parents' crib?"

"Thanks for checking on me Heem! You're so sweet," Sarah replied, smiling from ear to ear as tears sporadically streamed down her face. "I was about to go over there, but I have to calm down first. I can't let my father see me like this. I really don't even want you to see me like this!"

"Oh please, girl! You're still beautiful." It was the first time Raheem had complimented Sarah, or any other young woman besides his wife, on her appearance since he had been married. "Are your parents okay?"

"Um, yeah, thank you," Sarah stuttered. She was taken off guard by the compliment. She never even thought Raheem viewed her as attractive. He had never flirted with her or even complimented her before, and he had lived next door to her parents for almost a year. Sarah knew Raheem was married with a baby girl, so she actually respected the fact that he had never flirted with her. She was surprised when he complimented her for the first time. What had made him change? "Yeah, my parents are okay, thank you for asking."

"So, what's wrong, if you don't mind me asking?"

"Um… well," Sarah hesitated as she looked around and over her shoulders before continuing. "What you about to do?"

"Good question," Raheem sighed. "Today has been the Friday from Hell!"

"Oh, you too, huh?" Sarah sniffed and wiped her nose. "I need to fix my face and my hair if I'm gonna keep sitting here talking to you. You wanna get in?"

"Say less," Raheem immediately replied, walked around the car and entered the passenger's side. He opened the passenger's side door, placed his duffle bag on the floor, sat down and closed the door. Sarah, who was fixing her hair while looking in the visor mirror, paused and looked down at Raheem's duffle bag.

"I thought you were a regular, working brother," Sarah started. "You out here making moves in these streets now, Heem?"

"Um, well, I guess you could say that," Raheem stuttered. "I'm about to figure out where I'm about to stay. Me and my wife and parents just got into it real crazy, so I left. I'm making moves 'cause I gotta move out the crib! Ha-ha!"

"You're silly," Sarah giggled as she rubbed hand sanitizer between her palms and fingers after blowing her nose one final time. "That's messed up. I'm sorry. At least you can joke about it though. Where's Kim and the baby?"

"Pshhh," Raheem sighed. "I think it's a wrap for me and Kim! I gotta figure out where I'ma live and then figure out getting my daughter… but I think my marriage is over."

"Oh no! I'm so sorry," Sarah frowned, covering her mouth in shock. She rubbed Raheem's shoulder compassionately. "Are you okay?"

"Not really, but it is what it is at this point," Raheem coolly replied. "Me and Kim have been having issues since before we moved over here. It's just gotten worse since we've been living here. Her and my parents are always ganging up on me. They won't let me live! But never mind all that. What's going on with you?"

"Boy," Sarah shrieked. "So, you know how I was in the store earlier buying shit for my nigga? He was busy handling shit so he called and asked me to pick up some liquor, wraps and cigarettes for him. He was supposed to be going to deejay and sell molly at some bachelor party in A.C. So, I get home from the store and he's already home, taking a shower. I went on the laptop and I guess he forgot to log out of Facebook. This message came through on Facebook Messenger from some bitch. She was sending him hotel confirmation for the room they're staying in this weekend! I start scrolling… come to find out this nigga been fucking with this bitch for like six months! I just moved in about a year ago! Two years of my life – wasted! I'm pushing thirty Raheem! I'm trying to settle down, you know?"

"Yeah, I feel you," Raheem sympathized. "You're tryna settle down and I'm getting unsettled! You're still young and attractive and got a good personality. A nigga would be lucky to have you on his team!"

"Oh, stop it, Raheem!" Sarah blushed, grinning widely. "You're gonna give me a big head!" Sarah was now convinced that Raheem was flirting with her. Her interest was piqued. She had been physically attracted to him since she met him. Seeing that he seemed to be a responsible, consistent, working, young, married Black man attracted her to him as well. The fact that he honored his marriage to Kim and was never inappropriate when he and Sarah spoke was also very intriguing to her. Now Raheem was in her car, flirting with her after she had just discovered her boyfriend was cheating. It seemed like perfect timing, considering the circumstances. "Do you need a ride somewhere? You said you're gonna stay in a hotel tonight? Which one?"

"I actually didn't even get a chance to look yet," Raheem replied. "I literally just came out the crib from the beef, went to the store and saw you. I'm about to search on my phone now."

"Um... you wanna come over until you figure it out?" Sarah asked timidly.

"What about your dude? I'm not trying to be all up in another man's crib..."

"That trifling-ass nigga is in A.C. with his other bitch," Sarah snapped. "Or should I say his *new* bitch, 'cause I'm done with him! My name is on the lease so it's just as much my place as it is his! But all his shit will be in the hallway by the time he comes back from Atlantic City!"

"I mean, if you say so," Raheem agreed. "I definitely want to chill with you, but I don't need any more drama tonight if he comes back early."

"Oh, trust me... neither do I," Sarah insisted. "I got a bottle for myself when I was at the store earlier. Do you drink apple E&J?"

"You already know," Raheem chuckled. "I got some tree with me. Do you blow?"

"Yeah, every now and then. Usually on special occasions." Sarah smiled as she gazed into Raheem's eyes. "I would like to smoke with you. I didn't even know you smoked. Let me find out!"

"Yeah... I'm full of surprises," Raheem said slyly as he placed his hand on Sarah's thigh.

Sarah shifted her car into gear and made the short trip to her apartment complex a couple blocks away from the intersection of Long

Lane and Marshall Road. They walked up the steps and entered the apartment. Sarah turned on the living room light and hung her jacket in the closet.

"Make yourself comfortable," Sarah warmly instructed. "You want me to put your stuff in the closet until you figure out what you're doing?"

"Uh, yeah," Raheem hesitated. "Let me get my tree and wraps out first though." Raheem sat down on the sofa and placed his duffle bag in his lap. He looked to his right as he unzipped his bag and paused when he noticed a picture of Sarah and her boyfriend on the coffee table next to the sofa.

"Oh, sorry." Sarah quickly rushed over and turned the picture face down. "I don't want to see that shit either. Do you know him?"

"Naw, not really," Raheem confessed. "I've seen him in traffic but I don't really chill with niggas out here. I'm from out West. Since I've been living over here I just work, take care of my family and stay out the way." Raheem quickly retrieved the marijuana and cigars from his duffle bag and handed the bag to Sarah.

"That's good, though," Sarah commended Raheem. "Yeah, I sensed that from the times we spoke since we first met. You seem like a good dude."

"Thanks ma. I'm far from perfect, but I try."

Raheem and Sarah sat on the sofa, smoked several blunts, drank shots of vodka and talked for over two hours. They had good chemistry and the conversation was natural and fluid. They quickly lost track of time. Sarah excused herself to use the restroom, so Raheem reached for his phone to search for hotel rooms for the night. His stomach growled and he realized he was hungry. He called out to Sarah when he heard her opening the bathroom door.

"Yo, Sarah! You hungry, ma? I'm starving and I was gonna order something."

"Yeah, I can eat," Sarah called back out from the rear of the apartment. "What you wanna order?"

"You ever eat from that curry spot on Marshall Road?"

"Yeah, that sounds good, thanks. What are you gonna order," Sarah asked as she entered the living room and sat down on the sofa, close to Raheem, leaning on him slightly.

"Yeah, I'm not sure. I'm pulling up the menu on my phone right now. Do you know what you want?"

"I want some of this," Sarah grinned slyly as she held up a bag containing a crystallized, powdery substance. "You ever try this before?"

"Naw," Raheem replied honestly as he looked up from his phone and quickly examined the bag Sarah held in front of him. "That's that molly shit your dude sells?"

"My *ex-dude*, but yeah," Sarah rolled her eyes and smiled. "I have only done it about a dozen times, but it's dope as fuck. You wanna try it?"

"Isn't that the same shit that had niggas running around naked in the streets last summer?" Raheem asked warily. "I ain't tryna go viral on the Gram or WorldStar, snapping out on molly! I already have enough problems!"

"Ha-ha! Boy, you're crazy," Sarah giggled. "That was some bullshit molly that had people acting like that. This nigga has the real thing. He sells it at the parties, weddings and clubs he deejays at – especially to the rich white people! That's why he makes so much money with it. This ain't no ghetto-ass, ratchet molly! I haven't done it in almost six months, though. You should do it with me!" Sarah sat up on her knees, leaning into Raheem's face with her hands clasped in anticipation.

"I don't know, sexy," Raheem was hesitant. "I'm not tryna get fucked up off that shit. I usually stick to my weed and liquor."

"I understand, but this is quality shit," Sarah reiterated. "I don't put just anything in my body either! I promise you'll be fine. "It'll be fun!"

Sarah leaned in even closer, pursed her lips and quickly pecked Raheem on his lips. She stayed close and stared into his eyes as she rested the palms of her hands in his lap, inches from his manhood. He gazed back into Sarah's eyes for a moment before replying.

"Alright ma. I'll do it with you this *one time*," Raheem agreed. "But how do you do that shit anyway? I'm not snorting that shit!"

"Aw, hell naw!" Sarah protested. "I'm not putting that shit my nose! I'm not a fiend, Raheem! I just swallow it when I do it."

"Oh, so you swallow it, huh?" Raheem smiled devilishly.

"Boy, you're so nasty! I'm talking about the molly," Sarah laughed and gently pinched Raheem's cheek as she clarified. "You gotta drink *a lot* of water when you are on this shit so you don't get dehydrated, though. I actually do something called 'parachuting' it."

"I ain't even gonna hold you ma... that sounds kind of suspect to me!"

"Oh please, Raheem! Stop being so dramatic," Sarah teased as she jumped up from the sofa and skipped to the rear of the apartment. "I'll show you. I'll be right back."

Sarah scurried to the bathroom and came back carrying a fresh roll of toilet paper. She stopped in the kitchen on her way back into the living room and retrieved a bottle of water from the refrigerator for each of them. The attractive, young woman excitedly skipped back into the living room and plopped down on the sofa next to Raheem. After handing him a bottle of water, she picked up a DVD case, placed it in her lap and intently tore a single sheet of toilet paper from the roll. She then cautiously separated the ply of the toilet paper until she was holding a thin piece, half the thickness of the original square. Sarah meticulously tore the remaining sheet in half, length-wise. She smiled gleefully the entire time.

"I'm so excited," Sarah continued, crossing her legs in her lap as she smiled up at Raheem. He was gazing up at her adoringly, with his arm resting across the top of the sofa behind her. "Are you ready?"

"Yeah, ma... I'm ready for whatever," Raheem replied, looking at Sarah longingly. "What are we about to do?"

"We're about to parachute this molly!"

Sarah carefully took the two small pieces of toilet paper and placed them flat on the DVD case in her lap. She slowly poured a small amount of the crystalline drug onto the toilet paper and closed the bag containing the molly. Raheem watched intently as his beautiful hostess skillfully took each fragile piece of toilet paper along with the molly and twisted the toilet paper into two small balls with tails on top. They resembled two small tadpoles. Sarah handed one to her new romantic interest and held hers in the air next to Raheem. She picked up her water bottle with her other hand and held it in the air as well.

"Cheers," Sarah sang as she and Raheem touched bottles and molly "parachutes" in the air before consuming them. Sarah then leaned over and passionately kissed Raheem while rubbing his leg. After approximately thirty seconds, she stopped abruptly and hopped up from the sofa. "I'm about to put on some music. I need to find the remote. You want me to make you a drink while I'm up?"

"Yeah, good looking out, sexy." Raheem was having an extremely good time with Sarah so far. He was still distressed about what had transpired between him and his family earlier. If it was going to happen on any day, at least it happened at a time when Sarah was ready and willing to spend time with him to take her mind away from her own worries.

"What you wanna listen to?" Sarah asked as she located the remote control and turned on her smart television. She logged into her music streaming account and scrolled through the artists and albums. "Rap? R&B? Neo-Soul?"

"You got any Metallica?" Raheem asked, smiling at the attractive young woman. Sarah whipped her head around from looking at the screen. She paused and looked at Raheem skeptically. "Sike, naw! I'm just fucking with you! I wanted to see what you would say," Raheem laughed.

"I was about to say... Let me find out you're an Oreo!" Sarah laughed.

"Me? An Oreo? You're the one who has me up here taking white people drugs," Raheem teased. "Naw, but we can listen to whatever, ma. I'm just enjoying chilling with you."

"Oh, so you got bars, huh, Raheem?" Sarah smiled. "You running game on me now? I never knew you were such a player!"

Suicide Tuesday   J. Cerrone

"Naw, I'm not a player," Raheem objected. "I'm real loyal, actually. I've been noticing you since we met when I first moved out here. I just would never say anything because I'm married. But now, that's a wrap and me and you happened to link up at the same time when you and your dude are going through something. I feel like the Universe made this happen."

"Hmmmm…" Sarah hesitated as she scrolled through the list in her music account, selected the Kendrick Lamar album entitled "Good Kid, M.A.A.D. City." and pressed "play." "I can see that," she replied, nodding her head. "You want a chaser with this E&J?"

"Naw, I'm good thanks. I'll take it straight."

"Okay gangsta!" Sarah giggled as she handed the remote to Raheem and made her way to the kitchen. "I'm gonna grab us more water too. We gotta stay hydrated, especially since we're about to drink more liquor. We should start rolling soon."

"Oh, you want to smoke some more? I'll roll up now." Raheem walked to the closet and retrieved some more marijuana and another wrap from his duffle bag.

"Oh," Sarah peeked her head from behind the refrigerator door and called back to Raheem. "We can smoke again if you want to, but when I said, 'rolling,' I was talking about the molly. That's what they call it when you start to get high off it."

"Ha-ha! Oh, okay! What else you need to school me on?"

"Oh… I'm not sure." Sarah shrugged as she strutted back into the living room with two bottles of water in each hand. She switched her hips dramatically as she approached Raheem and bent over placing her cleavage within inches of his mouth. As he exhaled, she felt his warm breath on the exposed part of her breast and she gently placed the four cold water bottles in his lap. "I might have to tell you about how good it is to come while you're rolling," Sarah said while licking her lips before turning around and walking back into the kitchen.

"Shit! You can *show* me better than you can tell me," Raheem replied matter-of-factly as he felt blood rush to his manhood. He watched Sarah closely as she glided back into the living room carrying two glasses

37

of liquor and handed him one. "Thanks ma." Raheem took a gulp of his glass of liquor and quickly swallowed it before leaning over to tongue kiss Sarah.

"Ooh boy," Sarah exhaled deeply after they had kissed passionately and groped each other again for several minutes. "You're welcome! You got me dripping down there. Thank you for that!"

"You ain't seen nothing yet," Raheem stated confidently as he leaned back in for another kiss.

"Oh, so you bragging now, huh?" Sarah smiled as she gently grabbed Raheem's chin hairs between her thumb and forefinger and gave him several long pecks on his lips. "Slow down soldier! Let's not rush. I want to wait until we're feeling the molly. Are you feeling it already?"

"Naw, I don't think so," Raheem confessed. "But I'm definitely feeling you! What is this molly high supposed to feel like?"

"Like ecstasy – *literally*," Sarah exclaimed. "You'll know when it hits you. You'll just feel so happy and all the positive feelings and good sensations are magnified like a thousand percent! It's basically the same drug as E-pills but it's the main ingredient in its purest form so it's even better. Let me look at your eyes."

"Oh, for real?" Raheem nodded his head as Sarah directed his chin so she could look into his eyes. "That sounds decent. What you looking all up in my eyes for? They're just regular, brown eyes!"

"Boy, hush," Sarah playfully scolded Raheem. "I'm looking to see if your pupils are dilated yet or not. They don't look like it though."

"What are you, a doctor now?"

"Ooh, you irking! No, cornball! When the molly starts hitting you, your pupils will start dilating. That's one reason why people wear sunglasses in the club and at night, 'cause they're rolling off that 'E' or molly. Look at my eyes. Are my pupils dilated? I think I'm starting to feel it a little bit already."

"Maybe a little. I can't really tell to be honest," Raheem confessed as he examined Sarah's pupils to the best of his ability.

"Aye! This is my shit!" Sarah jumped up, grabbed the remote and turned the volume all the way up when the song entitled "Backseat Freestyle" from the Kendrick Lamar album started to play. "All my life I want money and power…" Sarah sung along as she snapped her fingers, danced and gyrated her hips while standing directly in front of Raheem, who was still seated on the couch. He watched her dance; her waist-length braids flowing back and forth as she bobbed her head to the beat and shook her behind mere inches from his face. His passion grew stronger by the second. He used all the restraint he could muster to refrain from pulling her onto his lap. She had already told him she wanted to wait until they were both feeling the effects of the party drug. Just then, Sarah snapped her head around and took a break from singing. "You're not feeling it yet? I'm feeling it!"

"Come here, yo." Raheem took Sarah' question as an indication that she was ready to be intimate. He grabbed her hips and gently pulled her back until she was sitting on his lap, still facing away from him. He kissed and licked the side and back of her neck as she gyrated her hips, grinding her behind against his pelvis. Raheem slowly placed his left hand up the inside of the front of Sarah's shirt while simultaneously placing his right hand down the front of her leggings. Sarah moaned as Raheem caressed her nipple, gently rubbed her clitoris and sucked on her neck. As time passed and their passion escalated, she grinded her rear end against his pelvis harder and faster as her vaginal juices began to flow more abundantly. Sarah grabbed Raheem's hand and pushed his forefinger and his middle finger directly into her soaking wet sexual organ. She let out an intense, primal moan. The young woman's body jerked as her vagina exploded and overflowed with sexual fluid. She grabbed Raheem's hand and held it still as she shivered sporadically for another minute. Sarah then lifted Raheem's hand as she stood up, turned around and sat back down on his lap, straddling him. She looked into his eyes seductively, slowly placed his fingers in her mouth and began sucking on them as she caressed his private area with her other hand. The beautiful temptress slowly removed Raheem's fingers from her mouth and slid down to her knees, simultaneously pulling Raheem's pants down and putting his member in her mouth. She used just the appropriate amount of saliva to lubricate Raheem. He watched in sheer pleasure as the beautiful young woman he had been secretly admiring for almost a year pleasured him with her warm, wet mouth. Raheem moaned deeply as her head bobbed up and down until he erupted.

Sarah looked up at Raheem with one hand covering her mouth and the other hand signaling a "thumbs up" once Raheem's body relaxed and his legs had completely stopped shaking. She quickly got up and ran to the bathroom. A few minutes later, she reentered the living room with a wet rag and sat next to Raheem.

"Sorry it took so long. I had to brush my teeth real quick," Sarah apologized as she gently wiped the remainder of the bodily fluids from Raheem's crotch.

"Shit… you ain't got nothing to apologize for!"

"It's been a minute, huh?" Sarah asked. "It seemed like your body had a lot it needed to let out!"

"Yeah," Raheem acknowledged. "I told you me and Kim been going through it."

"Wow," Sarah sighed as she looked up at him, her head laying on his chest. "So, you really never cheated on your wife?"

"Well… never before tonight." Raheem sensed Sarah grow tense when the words left his mouth. "Look, it is what it is. I told you I don't get down like that, but me and her are over. You don't even have to worry about that right now."

"Yeah, Heem," Sarah replied as cheerfully as she could. "You say that now. In the morning you'll be probably go right back home to her."

"Naw, I doubt it. But why you focusing on that bullshit anyway? You're gonna blow your own high! You wanna do another hit of that molly?"

"Damn, boy," Sarah exclaimed. "You hooked already? I'm still just starting to really get on."

"Actually, naw," Raheem replied coolly. "I might be hooked on you already after that brain you just gave me, but I'm really not feeling the molly like that yet, to be honest."

"What? Really? But, wait… we were supposed to wait until we were *both* rolling," Sarah whined.

"It's all good, ma. I was feeling it a little bit by the time you started going down," Raheem confessed. "It was the best nut I ever had from getting head. But you said I would know when I'm really 'rolling' and I feel like it hasn't fully kicked in yet."

"You really wanna do another hit? For real? I think I'm cool for now. I'm still on my way up. I can make you another parachute if you want me to. We should drink some more water first though."

"Naw, it's cool. You don't have to make me another parachute. I got something else in mind." Raheem quickly chugged his entire bottle of water and waited for Sarah to finish drinking hers. "You good now, sexy?"

"Yeah, I'm good now," Sarah smiled as she held her chest and took a deep breath upon drinking half of her water bottle. "So… what do you have in mind with the molly?"

"Let me see it real quick."

Sarah handed Raheem the bag containing the drug. He took it and leaned into her, backing her down onto the sofa as they entangled tongues and he gripped her exposed breast with his free hand. Raheem pulled away and began licking Sarah's neck, down to her chest. He worked his way down, caressing her flat stomach with his tongue and slowly pulled her leggings down with his free hand as he kissed around her navel, then the top of her pelvis. He skipped over her private parts, licking her inner thighs as he pulled her leggings down to her feet. Sarah bent one knee at a time to make it easier for Raheem to remove her pants as she shivered in anticipation. Raheem then worked his way back up Sarah's firm, but shapely legs with his tongue. As his face neared her private parts once again, he took the bag of molly and opened it ever so slightly as he kissed her southernmost lips. Sarah looked down as she heard the plastic.

"What you doing, daddy?" she moaned.

"Don't worry about it. I'm doing some more molly."

Raheem sprinkled some of the drug on Sarah's lower pelvis and spread it into an outline around her vagina. He then rubbed it into her vaginal lips with his finger and licked and sucked on her as he simultaneously stimulated her with his fingers. Sarah once again began to move her waist around wildly as she moaned louder and louder. Her eyes rolled back into her head and she arched her back as Raheem devoured her with his mouth. Raheem penetrated Sarah with one hand and reached upward, lightly gripping her neck with his other hand. The pleasure was too much for Sarah to contain. She let out a moan so loud but simultaneously weak that it sounded like she was about to cry. She arched her back sharply, causing Raheem's face to sink deeper into her pelvic area. Sarah grabbed the back of Raheem's head and held it in between her legs as she shook and quivered violently and moaned until her voice cracked and her moans were so faint they became almost inaudible.

"Fuck me Heem!" Sarah suddenly groaned.

Sarah pulled Raheem's head from her crotch and gently, but firmly pulled his face up towards hers. Raheem complied, met Sarah face-to-face and began sucking on her luscious lips as she pulled his mouth to hers. Raheem took his boxers off with rushed assistance from his new lover. He paused momentarily and thought about how it was wrong for him to be with Sarah. Raheem quickly imagined how sex might have been with Kim if they had done molly together for the first time. Maybe it would have rekindled their sex life and perhaps helped preserve their marriage. Oh well, he would never know. Kim had made her decision about their marriage. She had sided with his parents against him and sealed his fate, making it impossible for them to keep their young family united. For now, Raheem decided he was going to make the most of his opportunity with Sarah.

Raheem pushed all thoughts of his wife, his parents and even his daughter out of his mind for the time being. He immediately pushed every inch of his manhood into Sarah's warm, soft, soaking wet vagina. He simultaneously felt a blast of energy and a warm, tingling feeling surging throughout his body. It was unlike any other feeling he had before, even from the best sexual encounters he had in the past. He felt as if he was jumping out of his skin, but in a delightful way. It was as if every atom and molecule in Raheem's body was dancing and vibrating in sync with every molecule in Sarah's body. It was as if he could smell, taste and feel her sexual energy with his entire being. He felt as if their bodies, genitals and all, had merged to form the perfect hybrid organism built strictly for sexual pleasure.

Both bodies pulsated and generated heat as the young man lay on top of the young woman pumping his waist back and forth as he gripped her bare buttocks while she grinded against him in perfect harmony with his rhythm. Raheem opened his eyes for a moment and looked down at Sarah, who was moaning loudly, her eyes rapidly blinking as they rolled back into her head while she bit her lip. She was lost in the feeling. Raheem was turned on even more by the sights and sounds of his new sexual partner. As he pumped his pelvis into hers, Raheem felt his manhood swell more than he ever had in his entire repertoire of sexual encounters. Sarah's moans grew more sensual as her lower regions spilled natural lubricant all over Raheem's unprotected manhood and onto her sofa. Raheem felt his heart race and his skin heat up as he began to reach his climax along with Sarah. He closed his eyes and saw darkness scattered with flashes of lights that were only visible behind his closed eyelids. He was aware of nothing but the way his skin felt against Sarah's and the noises she made as he repeatedly penetrated her while she sucked and bit his neck and chest and dug her nails into his back. They both sweated, panted and groaned; bodies quivering against each other as their mutual climax seemed to last for hours. They exploded simultaneously and Raheem held himself up on his elbows as Sarah held his waist, holding him inside of her as she panted and kissed his neck. The pair had reached their intended destination – pure ecstasy. They were officially rolling.

Chapter 4

"Damn, Heem," Sarah panted as she smiled from ear to ear, "You really put your thing down!"

"Oh, you liked that, huh?" Raheem replied smugly as he looked into Sarah's eyes. He was still laying on top of her, still inside of her. "I already told you I was *that nigga!*"

"I'll give you that," Sarah conceded as she rubbed Raheem's back and kissed his neck and chest. "That was literally ***the best*** sex I've ever had – even on molly!"

"Aw shit… now you're just tryna gas my head up!"

"No, real shit Raheem," Sarah reiterated. "That was *so* good. I'm so wet, it's ridiculous! You feel that?"

"That's what's up! I'm glad I wasn't a waste of your time," Raheem slyly replied. "That ain't all you down there, though. Speaking of which… I'm trying to figure out how I'm gonna get up without making too much of a mess."

"Hold up," Sarah hesitated. "You didn't strap up?"

"Um… naw," Raheem confessed. "I mean, I was kind of caught up. Between the molly, drinking, smoking and your fine ass twerking all up on me! I'm just a man, baby!"

"Don't start trying to sweet-talk me to get yourself out of trouble," Sarah laughed. "It was our first time together so I just really wish you would've worn a condom."

"Yeah, I feel you. But let's be real… I've been married almost three years. When is the last time you think I used, or even bought condoms?"

"Ugh! Don't remind me," Sarah sighed. "I guess you're right though. I'm so used to these trifling-ass niggas, like my ex. I assume every nigga is out here sexing multiple women all the time, whether they're married or not! I guess I'll just have to get the Plan B in the morning."

"Yeah, I'll pay for half of it," Raheem volunteered. "But after what you just said, I was just thinking. You said your dude has been cheating on you, right?"

"You mean my *ex*-dude?" Sarah rolled her eyes. "What time is it?" Sarah squinted and glanced over at the cable box. "One-thirty? Yeah... that nigga is probably in A.C. getting head in the DJ booth from the bitch right now!"

"Were y'all using protection, though?"

"Not since we moved in together." Sarah paused and then placed her face in her hands as she lay her head back on the sofa's armrest. She was still laying on her back and Raheem was still on top of her, supporting himself on his elbows. "Aw shit! *This nigga* probably been dingy-dicking me this whole time after being out fucking his side-hoe! I'm gonna be sick..."

"I'm sure you're okay ma," Raheem kissed Sarah on her forehead. He was trying to comfort and reassure her, but he was also attempting to do the same for himself. He imagined that would be the worst possible outcome – for him to catch a sexually transmitted disease at twenty-five years old after having sex with somebody other than Kim for the first time in years. "I'm about to get up though, sexy."

"Mmm-Hmmmm," Sarah rolled her eyes as Raheem slowly backed up while cupping his hand under his crotch and standing up from the sofa. "We were chilling all comfortable all this time. Now you all in a rush to get up off me? That was perfect timing, huh?"

"It ain't even like that, baby," Raheem protested. "I gotta pee. I'll be right back."

"Oh alright. Can you bring me a towel back please? They're in the bathroom closet."

"I got you ma," Raheem quickly made several long strides to the bathroom, his hand still cupped below his manhood in an attempt to prevent leaking any residual emissions onto the apartment floor. He entered the bathroom, closed the door behind him and turned the hot water faucet on in the sink. He then pulled back the shower curtain, retrieved the bar of soap and began lathering it between his hands under the hot, running water before proceeding to wash his face and genitals in the sink. Upon rinsing, washing his hands and returning the soap to the shower; Raheem grabbed a towel for himself from the narrow linen closet inside the bathroom. After drying his lower body, he paused and looked at himself in the mirror. He was irritated with himself.

"Fuck is wrong with you, nigga? What are you doing?" Raheem cursed at his reflection. "Didn't Snoop say, 'ain't no pussy good enough to burnt while I'm up in it?' You better hope you didn't catch nothing from this jawn! Oh well... it is what it is at this point! She *is* bad as shit!" Raheem shrugged at his reflection before searching under the sink to see if there was any mouthwash in the bathroom. Upon locating it, he poured some directly into his mouth without touching his lips to the container, swished and gargled vigorously for a while, then spit into the sink. He leaned in close to the mirror and examined his eyes. His pupils were dramatically dilated. They had grown to resemble large black saucers. It was as if Raheem's eyeballs had been replaced with two solar eclipses. He laughed out loud at his own reflection before grabbing a towel for Sarah and exiting the bathroom.

"Damn, boy," Sarah exclaimed, wide-eyed as Raheem handed her the towel. "Boing! Boing!" She simultaneously laughed and licked her lips as she gently tapped his manhood downward twice, making it bounce like a diving board. "You're still ready to go, huh?"

"You already know! I ain't even gonna hold you... that molly is the truth! You ready to get it in again?"

"Yeah, I definitely want to have sex again, but give me a minute," Sarah replied as she finished using the towel to wipe her private parts dry. "I'm still having aftershocks down here!"

"She wasn't ready!" Raheem joked, impersonating a popular routine from Philadelphia comedian, Kevin Hart. They both laughed.

"See, now you're feeling yourself," Sarah joked back, giggling. "It's all good though! You should be!"

"Why, thank you! Let me know when you're ready to go again."

"Okay, I will. I'm gonna go wash up real quick. I didn't even finish my drink. I should be ready by the time I finish this E&J!" Sarah scurried to the bathroom.

The Kendrick Lamar album finished playing as Raheem put his boxers back on before sitting back down on the sofa. He crushed up some more marijuana and rolled another blunt. Before lighting it, he grabbed the remote and scrolled through the list of music until he found an album he hadn't listened to in a while. He selected the Young Jeezy album entitled "TM:103" and pressed the "play" button on the remote. The young man lit the marijuana-filled cigar, inhaled deeply and looked around the room as he exhaled the weed smoke. It was a very nice apartment. He could tell Sarah had decorated it, but it wasn't too feminine. He could picture himself spending a lot of time in the apartment if Sarah was really done with her boyfriend and planned on kicking him out like she claimed.

"We shall see. You know how these women be lying," Raheem said out loud to no one in particular as he took another drag of the blunt.

"Who you talking to?" Raheem was so deep in thought, so high from the synergy of liquor, marijuana, molly and sexual energy that he had not noticed Sarah reenter the room. "I'm gonna grab us some more water. You want me to make you another drink?"

"Yeah. Good looking ma," Raheem replied, snapping out of his trance. "I see you're really on point with drinking all this water!"

"Yeah, well, like I said; it's really important to stay hydrated when you're on this shit," Sarah called out as she diverted her path to the kitchen and retrieved two more bottles of water and the entire bottle of brown liquor. "People really get dehydrated and pass out from this shit if they're not careful."

"Oh yeah?"

"I wouldn't lie to you just to make you drink up all my water," Sarah laughed as she handed Raheem the bottled water. She picked up

Raheem's empty cup from the coffee table and poured more liquor into it. "So, what were you talking about when I walked in the room? You seemed like you were saying some heavy shit!"

"Oh, nothing," Raheem shrugged. "I was just thinking out loud."

"Oh no! Please don't tell me you're gonna start acting crazy as soon as you finish fucking me good enough to make me fall in love! I *knew* it was too good to be true! I knew there *had* to be something wrong with you!"

"That isn't even funny," Raheem grimaced, trying to laugh at Sarah's joke. "Naw, I'm no crazier than the average Black man living in America!"

"Oh, okay... If you say so! You did tell me you're 'full of surprises.' Let me find out! Six months from now you're gonna be like 'surprise! I'm shot out!' Ha-ha!"

"Yeah, whatever," Raheem chuckled. "I'm worried about *you* being crazy! It's a scientific fact that *all* the best-looking women are totally throwed off!" He laughed and took a sip of his drink.

"Bye boy! Whatever!" Sarah leaned over to lay on Raheem's lap as they drank and he smoked. "I do really like you though."

"I really like you too, Sarah." Raheem looked down at the beautiful, young woman gazing up at him. He admired her flawless, chocolate-colored skin and full, soft lips. Her large, dark brown eyes were framed by unusually long eyelashes. "Are those fake eyelashes?"

"Boy, bye! Are those fake muscles?"

"Do they feel fake?"

"Do my eyelashes look fake?" Sarah snapped back as she sat up and stared at Raheem, wearing a half-perturbed smile. "Don't come for me Raheem!"

"Damn, sexy! Chill," Raheem laughed as he put his hand up defensively. "I'm just saying... you got really, nice, long eyelashes and most of the females I know with eyelashes that long wear fake ones."

48

"So now you're comparing me to 'most females?'"

"Aw shit... here we go," Raheem exhaled. "It was supposed to be a compliment! You sure you're not the crazy one?"

"My bad, you caught me slipping into crazy-chick mode! You can't give me amazing sex the first time and expect me not to act a little crazy!" They both laughed.

"It's all good." Raheem paused before continuing. "You said 'six months from now' though. You think you're still gonna wanna mess with me six months from now?"

"I mean... I dunno," Sarah stuttered. "I was just saying... We'll see though. I do really like you and you always seemed nice. I love me a fine, strong, hard-working, Black man. But you are married with a baby. I guess we gotta wait and see what happens."

"Yeah, that makes sense."

"Is this that old Jeezy jawn?" Sarah abruptly changed the subject. "I haven't listened to this in a while."

"Yeah, me neither. That's why I played it when I saw it in the list." Raheem took another sip from his cup and a long drag of the marijuana before offering it to Sarah.

"I'm high as shit," Sarah declined, raising her hand in objection. "I'ma just drink this E&J and enjoy this molly-high until I'm ready to ride you!"

"Sounds like a plan." Raheem winked at his female companion and rubbed her thigh and behind as she lay on him. He couldn't help but feel like the events of the day had occurred when and how they had for a reason. He felt almost as if it was predestined. He had declined moving in with his parents on several occasions before Kim had finally talked him into it. Before moving there, he had never spent much time in Upper Darby other than occasional shopping or going to the movie theatre on 69th Street. Things had already been strained in his relationship with Kim, even before they found out she was pregnant. He hoped agreeing to move in with his parents would alleviate financial stress and make it easier for he and his wife to get along, but things had not worked out that way. After a relatively short time, things had actually grown worse between the young, married couple. Approximately a month after moving, Sarah's mother introduced her to Raheem and his wife when they were all outside while Sarah was visiting. Who would have predicted less than a year later he would get kicked out of his parents' house, he and Kim would be separated and he would be in Sarah's apartment drinking, smoking, doing molly, having sex and vibing with arguably the coolest, most attractive woman he had been intimate with in his adult life? Despite his anguish over the rift in his family, Raheem could not help but feel like the whole situation was meant to be. "So, what do you plan on doing when your dude gets home?"

"I really don't want to think about it right now," Sarah confessed. "I think I'm gonna wake up early and put his stuff in the hallway. I gotta go to the hardware store and get new locks and figure out how to change them. I know the landlord won't do it without that cheating-ass, no-good nigga's permission since his name is on the lease too."

"Oh shit," Raheem gasped. "You're not playing?"

"Not at all! Fuck that nigga! He did the wrong bitch dirty!"

"I feel you," Raheem agreed. "His loss, my gain though! Don't worry, I'll help you change the locks if you want me to. I just don't want you to have any unnecessary drama when this nigga comes home to see his shit outside and his key doesn't work!"

"If he was that worried about it he would have taken his shit before he left for A.C. to go be with that bitch!"

"Facts!" Raheem concurred.

"That's actually the part that pisses me off," Sarah explained. "I mean, getting cheated on hurts like a bitch. But on top of that, the nigga is really just gonna leave and do whatever anyway? I understand he has to make money deejaying, but goddamn! Like, this nigga really just said, 'fuck the fact that I just hurt the only girl who is down for me and helps me with my daughter every other weekend, fuck the fact that I just got caught cheating red-handed, fuck this argument!' This nigga really left like he was gonna come back like everything is cool. I mean… what do I look like? He's got the wrong bitch!"

"Yeah, that's drawing…"

"I'm not usually a vindictive bitch, but he got me wanting to..." Sarah stopped herself in mid-sentence.

"He got you wanting to do what?" Raheem inquired as he stamped the marijuana roach in the ash tray, his curiosity piqued.

"I mean," Sarah hesitated before continuing. "I'm talking all this gangster shit about putting his stuff out and changing the locks but I know it's not going to be so simple. He's not just going to let it rock if I do that, you know?"

"Yeah, I feel you," Raheem nodded. "I would be pissed if that happened to me, but I don't really know anything about your dude, so I can't really guess how he would react. What do you think will happen?"

"Well, he's a street-nigga, but he's a smart dude," Sarah explained. "I know he's gonna get real mad and probably want to kick the door down. I mean, I'm not trying to make him seem like he's abusive because he's never even threatened to put his hands on me. I'm just saying..."

"What are you saying, ma?"

"I can show you better than I can tell you..." Sara jumped up from the sofa, walked over to the living room closet and opened the door. She stretched on the tips of her toes and reached up to retrieve a sneaker box from the shelf above the hangers. She carefully walked over to the sofa, the box secured between her hands and slowly sat down next to Raheem before opening the box.

"Oh shit!" Raheem was both surprised and impressed by the large, shiny forty-five caliber handgun. He also noticed a zipper-bag half-full of what appeared to be more molly. "I didn't know your dude was holding like that!"

"That ain't the half," Sarah vented. "He has two more guns he keeps on him – another big one like this he keeps in his glove compartment of his truck and a small one he keeps in a holster on his ankle!"

"Oh okay! I see that nigga ain't playing out here in these streets!"

"Naw, not at all," Sarah shook her head. "He's kind of a pretty-boy and real laid-back. Most people know him as a DJ and that he gets at a dollar so they think it's sweet because he's so cool and doesn't walk around trying to act tough. Even the niggas who know he hustles don't give him the same respect because he sells a 'rich, white-people drug!' People try him sometimes. He tries to stay away from beef and drama, but he has a temper and will get it popping if he feels he needs to. I've seen it. I just don't know what he might do if he comes home to all his stuff outside and the locks changed. He's smart, so he might just try to handle it through the courts and sue me or something. But then again, we were already beefing earlier so he might snap out and do something reckless. I'm not sure and I really don't want to risk bringing the worst out of him."

"Damn, ma. That's wild. So, what you think you're gonna do?"

"Well, I was thinking," Sarah started. "I was thinking I could pack my stuff and move back in with my parents until I find a new place. But before I leave I want to make him pay. I want to take some of his shit and sell it to the pawn shop or whatever. You know, his jewelry, electronics – shit that would hurt his pockets since that's all he seems to care about." Sarah frowned.

"Yeah, but that nigga will wile out when he comes back and sees you gone and all his shit is missing. He'll probably come to your parents' crib on some rowdy shit, looking for you."

"Naw, he's smarter than that," Sarah objected. "If I'm not here he'll have time to figure out how to handle it to try to get his money back. He'll probably sue me for the value of the shit, but I'm not worried about it. We live together, both our names are on the lease and he won't be able to prove he bought the shit."

"Wow, shorty," Raheem exclaimed. "Remind me to make sure I *never* hurt your feelings! You came up with that scheme with a quickness!"

"Ha-ha…" Sarah laughed mockingly. "First of all, I didn't come up with the plan that fast. I was actually thinking about it before you walked up on me in the parking lot! Second of all; why do you need extra motivation *not* to hurt me, Raheem?"

"Aw shit, I put my foot in my mouth again! Naw, sexy," Raheem protested as he removed the box containing the gun and drugs from Sarah's lap, placed it on the coffee table and leaned in, stroking her inner thigh. "I would *never* hurt you! Not unless I accidentally hurt you when I beat the pussy up!"

"Oh, yeah? All that talk," Sarah snickered. "I don't see you doing nothing though!"

"Say less."

Raheem quickly lifted the petite but shapely young woman off the sofa and placed her in his lap until she was straddling him. He caressed her breasts with both hands as he passionately licked her neck. Sarah let out an erotic sigh and gently tilted her head into his face as his beard tickled her skin. The sensation of Raheem's tongue against her neck stimulated her love below. Her nipples quickly hardened at the same time Raheem's manhood rose to the occasion. They wasted no time as Sarah arched her back and Raheem released her breasts, placed both hands on the small of her back alongside her hips and firmly pulled her pelvis into his. Her juices flowed into his lap and she moaned when Raheem entered her. They gyrated in sync and gradually increased their pace until they were rapidly grinding against each other and beads of sweat formed on both their foreheads. Sarah threw her head back and growled passionately as Raheem gently bit her shoulder and rapidly slapped her rear-end. They continued to increase the pace until their body-heat, moans and various other elements of the sexual soundtrack consumed the living room. After what seemed like hours they both climaxed long and hard. Sarah collapsed, letting out one last provocative moan and laid her head on Raheem's shoulder.

"It gets better every time," Sarah smiled and kissed Raheem on his cheek as she grasped a section of his long beard from his chin and swirled it between her fingers. "I think I'm hooked!"

"I know *I* am," Raheem sincerely agreed, trying to sound cool. He didn't want to seem like he was too into Sarah during their first time hanging out on the same day they had both experienced relationship crises. "I'm really feeling you Sarah."

"Awwww... I'm really feeling you too, love," Sarah wrapped her arms around the back of Raheem's neck and kissed him on his lips.

"Let me know when you're ready to go again!"

"Damn baby! I guess you really *are* hooked," Sarah exclaimed as she turned around to check the time on the cable box. "It's almost three in the morning, baby! You're not tired?"

"Naw, not really," Raheem informed her matter-of-factly.

"I'm starting to get sleepy," Sarah confessed as she leaned back, stretched her arms wide and then rubbed her eyes with both hands. "I think you sexed me so good that all the molly dripped out of me! You're still feeling it?"

"Naw, not really. A little bit. I just don't really need much sleep anyway. Besides, it's been a long time since I had sex before tonight. You're so sexy and I've been wanting you for so long. I guess I can't get enough of you!" Raheem smiled as he smacked Sarah's bare bottom again. "Why don't you take some more molly?"

"Oh... naw, I'm good," Sarah declined. "I need to get some rest. It's been a long day and I need to get up early and figure out exactly what I'm doing before he starts making his way back from A.C. I'm trying to be long gone before he gets here."

"I feel you."

"I'll be right back. I need to use the ladies' room again. You want me to bring you a water on the way back?"

"Yes, please. Thanks ma."

Raheem stared at Sarah's naked body as she slowly got up from his lap and walked down the hallway towards the bathroom. As she disappeared behind the closed door, he thought to himself at how fortunate he was to go from arguing with his parents, separating from his wife and not knowing where he was going to stay that night to being alone with Sarah and having earth-shattering, almost tantric sex with her multiple times a few short hours later. Based on their conversation Raheem was starting to feel like he may have already found his replacement girl. He once again concluded that the Universe must have aligned events to occur the way they had.

"You're always in deep thought." Sarah interrupted Raheem from his contemplation as she handed him a bottle of water.

"Yeah, my fault sexy. I over-think shit sometimes."

"So… what were you over-thinking about?" Sarah innocently inquired.

"I was just thinking of a way to help you with the situation with dude that may work out for both of us."

"Oh yeah? You're so sweet for trying to help me," Sarah replied softly as she bent over and kissed Raheem on the side of his face. She took a sip of her water before continuing. "Can we talk about it after I sleep? I'm about to pass out all of a sudden. I think I'm crashing from that molly wearing off."

"Yeah, of course. That's cool. I'm trying to figure out what I'm about to do."

"You can make yourself at home since you're not ready to sleep. You have the remote. You have to change the input to 'AV1' if you want to watch cable. When you get tired you can come in the room and get in bed with me."

"You want me to sleep in the bed with you? In *there*?" Raheem was shocked that Sarah invited him to sleep in the bed she shared with her "ex."

"Yeah, why not?" Sarah shrugged. "Whichever one of us winds up moving out, we're through! One thing is for sure – I'm not ever sleeping in that, or any other bed, with *that nigga* again. Don't worry; I already changed the sheets after he left. Ain't no telling who else that nigga had up in here!" Sarah shook her head and kissed Raheem on the lips once more before walking away. "Who knows… if we're up early enough, maybe we can have morning sex!"

"That's a bet!" Raheem heartily replied. Sarah turned and blew a kiss at him before closing the bedroom door behind her.

Raheem sat in silence for a moment, once again pondering the events of the day and evening. The Young Jeezy album had concluded but he was not in the mood to watch television. Raheem picked up the remote and scrolled through the list of available music. He stopped when he came to the Prodigy "H.N.I.C. 2" album – another solo project released by the front-man of the popular hip-hop duo, Mobb Deep. As the album began to play, Raheem rose from the sofa, walked to the kitchen and poured himself another glass of E&J.

He retrieved some more marijuana from his duffle bag and rolled up the last of his marijuana in his last cigar. As he sat, smoked, drank and zoned out to the music, the events of the day replayed over and over in Raheem's consciousness. After roughly ten minutes his blunt was almost gone and so were the most potent effects of the molly. He felt himself coming down and his mood regressed to a more negative state. As he continued to dwell on the negative events of the day, he began to think if he should have handled the situation with his wife and parents differently. Raheem began to feel increasingly guilty about the role he played in escalating the situation. Even more damaging was how he was beginning to be consumed with guilt for having sex with Sarah. What if she was right? What if he and Kim eventually reconciled? He hadn't even spoken to her since he left. As the thought crossed his mind, he picked his pants up from the floor, pulled out his phone and unlocked it. Raheem's wife had not even called him or sent him a text message to check on him since he left!

"Fuck Kim!" Raheem huffed to himself. "She don't give a fuck about me! That's why I'm here in the first place! I don't have shit to feel guilty about," he tried to convince himself.

Raheem did, however, feel guilty. Not only that, but he thought about how much more difficult his life was going to become now that he had to find a new place to live, get a divorce and figure out how he was going to be able to spend time with his daughter now that he and Kim were no longer together as a couple. He became overwhelmed with emotion. He and Taj had just spoken of those types of situations – "baby-mama drama" – earlier in the day. Kim wasn't his "baby-mama," though. She was his *wife*. He never anticipated things turning out this way for their family. Raheem grew anxious just thinking about it all. He did not like how he was feeling. He was growing rapidly depressed, which was the polar opposite of how he had been feeling a few short minutes before. Raheem had absolutely zero desire to continue to feel depressed and he wasn't in the least bit tired. He would have to stay awake and suffer if he wasn't able to find a way to get his mind off his family and marital issues. Sarah was sleeping, so he couldn't use sex with her as a distraction until she woke up.

Raheem glanced over at the shoebox containing the gun and molly, still sitting on the coffee table directly next to him. He glared at it for a few minutes, contemplating whether more molly was the answer to his current dilemma. It wasn't his molly, so he didn't want to steal it. He reasoned that Sarah likely would not mind if he had some more; especially since it was her boyfriend's and she planned on robbing him anyway.

Raheem decided to take another dose of molly in an attempt to quickly improve his mood. He reasoned he couldn't possibly be productive and come up with a feasible plan of action while he was feeling so down. Considering the circumstances, he was on a strict timeline to come up with a plan. He figured the chemical boost the molly would give his brain was exactly what he needed at the moment.

Raheem grabbed the roll of toilet paper Sarah had brought into the living room hours beforehand. He followed the same steps he had observed Sarah follow when she made their molly "parachutes" and made two for himself. He walked to the kitchen, grabbed two more bottles of water and consumed the first parachute, chasing it with an entire bottle of water. He then did the same with the second. He plopped back down onto the sofa and sipped his liquor. He laid his head against the back of the sofa, closed his eyes and listened to the Prodigy album as it delved into issues of political corruption, social programming and manipulation, science and environmental disaster; laced with his usual hardcore, violent narrative. After three more songs had played in full, Raheem felt a surge of adrenaline flow throughout his veins into his extremities – from the tips of his toes, to the tips of his fingertips, up to the top of his head and everything in between. He felt as if his skin was jumping. The vibrations throughout his frame were so strong he felt as if his teeth and hair follicles were trembling.

"There you go," Raheem smiled to himself in satisfaction. He quickly jumped up from the sofa and began pacing back and forth in the living room as he nodded his head to the music and rapped along with the lyrics he had memorized. He murmured to himself out loud as he paced. He began to devise a plan on how to help Sarah out of her difficult predicament while simultaneously helping himself with his own.

"Yeah... that'll work," he assured himself out loud as he smiled hard, laughed and clapped his hands together as if he was sharing good news with a friend. "Yeah... that's right! Everything is going to work out!"

Saturday . . .

September 12, 2015

Chapter 5

Sarah stirred in her bed as the sweet aroma of cinnamon infiltrated her nostrils, waking her from her slumber. Her eyes half-closed, she reached across her bed to retrieve her cellular phone from the night-stand, as was her daily custom upon waking up. She entered her security code into her phone, unlocking it to check the time and to see if she had received any text messages, phone calls or social media notifications.

"Figures this nigga didn't even text me," Sarah huffed under her breath. Her first instinct upon waking was to see if her boyfriend had tried to contact her. "Oh… it's 7:11," she said to herself, smiling when she noticed the time. "Maybe it's a sign." The beautiful, young woman rose from bed when she heard the noise of two metal surfaces colliding reverberate from the kitchen. She realized that Raheem must have been cooking breakfast. The magnetic perfume of sweet cinnamon emanating from the kitchen had resurrected her from her drug, alcohol and sex-induced coma. She inhaled through her nostrils deeply as she stretched from head-to-toe – her perfectly toned, brown body flexing in the rays of early morning sunlight peeking through the vertical blinds.

"Hey daddy," Sarah wrapped her arms around Raheem's waist as she approached him from behind, hugged him and rested her head between his shoulder blades. "Thanks for making breakfast! It smells good!"

"Hey sexy." Raheem turned slightly, holding the handle of the skillet in his left hand and a spatula in his right. He kissed Sarah on her forehead before turning back around to attend to the stove. "Yeah, I'm just making a little something-something. French toast and scrambled eggs. I would have made meat but you don't have any beef or even turkey."

"Yeah sorry… when I do buy bacon, it's usually pork! I didn't know you could cook, though. I'm impressed!"

"I told you I'm full of surprises," Raheem smirked. "But don't be impressed until you taste it! You might not like it!"

"If it tastes as good as it smells, I know I'll love it," Sarah smiled.

"That's the same way I felt about you last night," Raheem replied coolly as he turned around to look at Sarah.

"You're smooth as butter, baby!" Sarah smiled as she sat, facing Raheem, on the chair next to the small kitchen table. She crossed her bare legs. She was wearing only a bra and panties and Raheem gazed at her longingly for a moment before turning back to flip the French toast. "You didn't come into the bed with me last night? Or was I sleeping so deeply that I didn't even notice?"

"Naw, I didn't come in there last night." Raheem cracked six eggs into a bowl and rapidly whipped them with a fork.

"Why not? What happened? Did you pass out on the sofa?"

"Naw." Raheem concisely replied as he mixed seasonings, two slices of cheese and a small amount of milk into the eggs and stirred the mixture.

"What's wrong?" Sarah asked, concerned, as she stood up and approached Raheem. "You didn't feel comfortable coming into the bedroom?"

"Oh, naw," Raheem chuckled. "I'm good. I'm just focused on this cooking. But naw, I didn't come in there because I never went to sleep and I didn't want to disturb you."

"What do you mean, you 'never went to sleep?'" Sarah gasped.

"I mean, I haven't slept yet," Raheem shrugged. "I wasn't tired."

"That's not good, Raheem," Sarah shook her head in disappointment.

"It's not even that deep. Remember I told you I don't sleep much anyway. Especially when I'm stressing and going through shit."

"Yeah, I guess so," Sarah sighed before looking back up at Raheem. She paused. "I guess it's even harder to sleep when you do molly for the first time. You did a lot of it too! Are you still high? Let me see your eyes."

61

"I'm cool Sarah." Raheem side-stepped the young woman as she tried to angle her body to look directly into his eyes to see if his pupils were still dilated. "I'm trying to make us breakfast and you're gonna fuck around and make me burn these eggs!"

"Yeah, alright," Sarah replied abruptly before turning around to walk back to her chair.

"I'm trying to hurry up and finish this so we can eat and get into that morning sex you promised me last night!" Raheem quickly turned around and smacked the left cheek of Sarah's perfectly shaped behind. She skipped upon the impact, giggled and quickly sat down.

"You stay on 'go' huh, Raheem?" Sarah smiled seductively as she watched him resume cooking. "You're like, too good to be true! You're a sexy, hard-working Black man, the sex is amazing *and* you cook! What's the catch? Oh yeah… you're married!" Sarah's smile quickly vanished as the words left her mouth.

"Come on Sarah," Raheem sighed. "I already told you what's up. That's a wrap. You don't have to worry about that. Anyway, the real 'catch' is that I'm crazy, remember? You said that last night!" Raheem forced a laugh, attempting to ease the tension.

"I'm serious Raheem," Sarah whined. "I don't want to get too attached to you just for you and your wife to get back together as soon as I catch feelings for you."

"I keep trying to tell you not to worry about that. I'm not gonna play games with you and I'm not gonna hurt you. Besides, you're acting like you don't have a nigga with two straps on him about to come back here in a few hours! Let's just enjoy our time together. We'll eat this food and then I'm gonna bust that ass again! We'll talk about the serious shit later."

Raheem and Sarah engaged in casual conversation as they sat and ate the breakfast Raheem had prepared. Upon finishing, Sarah washed the dishes and cleaned the kitchen while Raheem took a shower. He felt so uncomfortable showering in another man's home that he hurried and was finished in the bathroom before Sarah had completed cleaning the kitchen. He walked past Sarah and told her he would wait for her in the living room. She commented on how quickly he had finished in the bathroom and told him she would join him momentarily.

Raheem glanced around the living room as he waited on the sofa. As his gaze drifted, the zipper-bag containing the euphoria-inducing molly drew his attention. He hesitated only momentarily before grabbing the bag with one hand and the toilet paper with the other. He quickly made two molly "parachutes" – one for himself and one for Sarah.

"Yo, sexy," Raheem called out to Sarah. "Would you please bring a couple bottles of water with you when you finish?"

"Yes, love. Here I come now. I'm just washing my hands."

Sarah entered the living room and approached the sofa holding a bottle of water in each hand. Raheem held up the toilet-paper wrapped molly and extended one of the parachutes to Sarah. Her face lit up in surprise and her mouth formed into a half-smile. Sarah leaned in closer and looked directly into Raheem's eyes.

"You wanna do more molly, Heem? Are you already high?" Sarah asked in shock, giggling.

"Naw, I'm not still high," Raheem lied. "But I'm trying to do more molly before we get it popping!"

"I don't know," Sarah hesitated. "I'm not trying to have either one of us getting addicted to this shit. It's all good every now and then, but we already did a lot last night. Plus, that nigga is coming back and he's already going to trip when he sees some is gone. He's definitely about his money!"

"Fuck that nigga! I thought you said you were gonna take all his valuable shit anyway," Raheem retorted. "Plus, we don't know when we're going to have to another chance to do molly again, so we might as well go out with a bang! You said he's going to be back this afternoon, so it might help you be in a better mood and be more motivated to do what you have to do without getting too stressed."

"Uh… Hmmm," Sarah sighed as she eyed the parachute Raheem was holding near her face. She then shrugged her shoulders before exchanging one bottle of water for a molly parachute. "Fuck it… bottom's up!"

Raheem and Sarah both swallowed the drugs, guzzled their bottles of water and immediately began kissing and groping each other passionately. After several minutes Sarah stepped off the sofa, stooped to her knees and aggressively tugged Raheem's sweatpants and boxer shorts down. Raheem firmly but gently placed the palm of one of his hands on the back of Sarah's head as he placed the other hand down the front of her bra and caressed her breast. She moaned softly and Raheem let out a loud sigh as he rested the back of his head on the sofa. Suddenly Sarah stopped the act of fellatio, jumped to her feet and ran over to the living room window.

"Damn, ma," Raheem gasped. "What the fuck is wrong? Why did you stop?"

"You hear that loud-ass music? That sounds like his truck," Sarah explained as she peeked through the blinds and discreetly scanned the small parking lot.

"What time is it – eight-thirty?" Raheem responded. "Have you heard from him? I thought you said he wouldn't be back until later."

"Oh my god!" Sarah gasped, ignoring Raheem's statement. "It *is* him! He's here! What the fuck?"

"Stop playing and get your sexy ass back over here," Raheem chuckled as he glanced over at Sarah. But as his eyes met hers, the terror he saw in her panicked expression made him realize she was not joking at all. He immediately rose to his feet and pulled up his pants. "He's here for real? What is that nigga doing back so early?"

"I don't know, but we don't have time for this," Sarah snapped, her voice trembling. "You gotta get out of here Raheem! I don't know what he might do if he catches you here!"

"I ain't scared of that nigga! I don't run from niggas," Raheem replied aggressively. "Plus, I gotta get all my shit out of here anyway."

"Then I need you to get the rest of your shit and take it in the closet, like *now*! He just got out of his truck! He's on his way up here," Sarah gasped as she began to hyperventilate.

"I'm not hiding from your dude, Sarah," Raheem refused.

"I don't have time for this macho shit right now, Raheem! Please just do it for me until he goes in the back room or leaves. I don't want any drama," Sarah pleaded.

"Alright," Raheem huffed as he begrudgingly gathered his belongings. "I'll do it for you."

Raheem closed himself inside the living room closet and shook his head in disappointment as he watched Sarah pace the living room frantically for a moment. She dropped to the sofa and played with her hair as she tried to calm herself down. Moments after Sarah sat down, the sound of keys in the doorknob evoked an increasing level of anxiety in the young woman. Her palms and armpits became saturated and beads of sweat formed on her forehead as she crossed her arms and tried to regain some level of composure. Sarah's boyfriend – a tall, light-skinned man with an athletic build, opened the door and entered the apartment. He walked past the closet and stood in front of the sofa looking at Sarah, waiting for her to meet his gaze. She resisted and continued to stare at the floor, her arms crossed, resting under her bosom.

"So, you're not even going to speak to your man when I walk into the crib after working all night?" her boyfriend asked slyly.

"Oh, please, Marcus," Sarah snickered, still not making eye contact with the man. "Didn't you mean to say, 'fucking random whores all night?'"

"Why you always tripping?" Marcus smiled as he sat on the sofa next to Sarah, placing his arm around her. "You know I was spinning records, selling that work and getting that paper so I can take care of you!"

"First of all, Marcus," Sarah objected, pointing her finger in the man's face, "I don't need you or anybody else to take care of me! Secondly, if you weren't out fucking bitches why didn't I hear from you all night? You didn't feel the need to reach out to me all night after how things were when you left?"

Raheem rolled his eyes as he listened to the conversation from inside the living room closet. "She isn't done with this nigga," he thought as he sat uncomfortably on the closet floor, hanging jackets brushing against his face.

"Look, baby," Marcus began. "You already know I had to take that long-ass drive to A.C. and I had work in the truck. I was running late because of arguing with you, so I just needed to focus and get there without getting pulled over. I needed to calm down so I could concentrate on work. I figured you could use some time to cool off too. By the time I got there I had to set up and start working. It was lit in there too, so I was so busy between spinning records, selling molly and all that, I didn't even take any videos to post on social media. When it was over, I had more moves to make with the molly. The sun was coming up by the time I was done and went to the diner to eat, so I didn't want to call and wake you. I ate and came straight home."

"You're such a liar! I don't believe any of that! I really just think you should leave."

"Leave *where*?" Marcus chuckled. "I know you ain't talking about *me* leaving *my* crib that *I* moved *you* into?"

"Here you go with that 'my crib' shit again," Sarah sighed. "I knew I should have never gave up my apartment and moved in with you!"

"Honestly, I don't even know why you're acting like you really wanna break up," Marcus replied coolly. "Why don't you just do what you usually do and go stay at your parents' crib for a couple nights until you love me again?"

"Wow," Raheem thought to himself upon hearing Marcus' comments. "He's a vicious dude! That nigga is a straight asshole for real!"

"Shut up Marcus," Sarah whimpered as she attempted to hold back her tears.

"You know you love me," Marcus grinned devilishly. "Look... you can put on your usual little show to make yourself feel better. You know you're stuck with me anyway, so when you snap out of your little mood and you're ready to fuck and be friends again just let me know. Or if you'd rather move back out, start over again and find another apartment and another nigga, be my guest. But if you do move out, don't come running back to me when the next nigga break ups with you or whoops your ass when he finds out you have herpes! Alright?!"

"Shut up! I fucking hate you Marcus!" Sarah wailed as she burst into tears.

"Hey, don't shoot the messenger," Marcus laughed sadistically. "You know it's the truth! Besides, you keep acting all shocked, but how many times have we gone through this since the doctor told you six months ago? You try to act all innocent, but how am I supposed to know I'm the one who burnt you and it wasn't the other way around? I don't know what you really do when I'm working or when you're at the 'happy hours' for your job or when you stay at your 'parents' house' days at a time when you're mad at me for whatever random reason! You weren't a virgin when we met, so stop trying to act like you're some type of angel. You're just an extra-pretty smut with a decent job who knows how to ride dick! You definitely need to work on giving head, though. I really don't even know why I let you stay around so long. As a matter of fact, maybe you should move out after all..."

"Shut up! Just shut up! You're so fucking evil," Sarah cried, stuttering and hyperventilating. "I have done nothing but show you love and had your back since day one. You convinced me to move in with you, that you loved me and wanted to have a life together and then started treating me so dirty when I finally did! You're a piece of shit! I hate you!"

Raheem's head began to spin as he listened from inside the closet. His worst fear from the previous night had become a harsh reality. He had sex with a woman other than Kim for the first time in years and she was infected with a sexually transmitted disease. He would have to get tested. He hoped and silently prayed that he hadn't been infected. He realized that the chances that he had avoided being infected were slim because of how much unprotected sex they had that night. Raheem cursed himself, Sarah, Marcus and even Kim and his parents under his breath. He blamed everybody involved for putting him in the position to be exposed to the incurable disease.

"Yeah, yeah... I love you too," Marcus laughed maniacally as he stood up from the sofa and looked back at his hysterical girlfriend. "But I'm about to take a shower and get some sleep. I gotta go back out tonight so I need some rest. But if you wanna wake me up to practice giving me head later, that would be love."

"You're such an arrogant dickhead! This conversation is not over Marcus! I'm not done with you!"

"Whatever, yo," Marcus replied nonchalantly. "That's funny you said the conversation isn't over 'cause I'm done talking about it. You can talk to yourself or do whatever you want. It doesn't matter to me. I'm going to take a shower and a nap."

"What did I do to deserve this shit?" Sarah moaned.

"For real, though... stop being dramatic! You're going to upset the neighbors and I don't need them calling the law," Marcus said coldly as he turned around and looked at Sarah in disgust. He turned to walk to the bathroom before pausing. "Wait a minute. Why is my shoebox out with my burner and the work?"

"Oh... um," Sarah stuttered.

"You were dipping in my work?" Marcus asked calmly but aggressively as he walked past Sarah and approached the coffee table. He picked up the zipper-bag containing the molly and eyed it for several seconds. He then noticed the roll of toilet paper on the table. "You turning into a junkie now, bitch? Where the fuck did all my work go? I'm missing at least an eighth out this jawn!"

"Wait... what? No way," Sarah protested as she timidly looked up at the man.

"Don't lie to me, you dumb bitch!" Marcus' tone was calm, but his words were searing and his eyes lit up in a controlled rage. "This is what I do! You know I can eyeball this shit in the dark!"

"I did some, but not that much," the scared young woman admitted.

"Not that much? I can't tell! Look at this shit!" Marcus leaned over Sarah menacingly as he held the bag directly in front of her face.

"Oh shit," Sarah gasped as her eyes widened in disbelief. "How much did he do while I was asleep?" The words left Sarah's mouth before she realized she had uttered them verbally instead of thinking them.

"What? What the fuck did you just say? Who the fuck is 'he?'"

"Oh, no... I didn't mean that," Sarah replied frantically, her body trembling in fear.

"You had a nigga in my crib where I lay my head, around my guns, fucking with my work while I was gone? You stupid bitch! I swear to god I should kill your dumb-ass!"

"Marcus, it wasn't even like that –"

"Shut the fuck up with the weak-ass lies," Marcus roared as he smacked his girlfriend across her face for the first time in their two years of dating. "I should whoop your ass!"

Raheem flinched as he heard the sound of Marcus's hand striking Sarah. He was filled with rage as he thought of that no-good man striking her angelic face. As he listened to Sarah sob while Marcus continued to scream at her, Raheem's blood ran thick through his veins. He sensed the feeling and pictured his blood cells fighting to burst through his skin. His chest became heavy and his stomach flipped as he tried to control the compulsion to burst out of the closet and pounce on Marcus to protect Sarah.

"Stop bitching! You bought that! You know how much of my money you just fucked up?" Marcus continued to scream. "And with some random nigga too? You outta pocket shorty!"

"But Marcus, it wasn't –"

Smack!

"I guess you didn't learn the first time," Marcus growled as he slapped Sarah across her face once more. "Stop fucking lying to me! Now tell me who the nigga is unless you want to take twice the ass-whooping for you *and* him!"

Raheem had heard enough. He immediately lunged from the closet and jumped onto an unsuspecting Marcus. Raheem grabbed the back of Marcus' shirt and pulled him from his position standing over Sarah. Before Marcus was aware of what was happening, he had been slammed onto his back in his own living room and was being pummeled in his face by a man he did not even know. Sarah screamed as Raheem viciously punished Marcus' face with both of his fists. He began to sweat as his body heat rose dramatically as if lava was flowing through his veins. He physically vented all his frustrations from the previous twenty-four hours as he savagely struck Marcus over and over. Raheem became so engrossed in the beating that he was unaware of his surroundings and did not hear Sarah repeatedly screaming for him to stop.

"Oh my god! That's enough Raheem! You're gonna kill him," Sarah screamed as she placed the barrel of the gun that had been sitting in the shoe box on the coffee table to the back of Raheem's head. The feeling of cold, hard steel against his hair momentarily snapped Raheem out of his rage. He jerked his head around to look at Sarah. She was standing with her knees slightly bent, pointing the gun at Raheem. "Thank you for protecting me, but he's done. He's knocked out. He's not even moving Raheem!"

"You're gonna point at gun at *me*, though? You let this nigga smack the shit out of you and didn't do shit, but you're gonna point a gun at me for having your back?"

"Raheem... I'm sorry, I didn't know what to do," Sarah sobbed. "I kept asking you to stop but it was like you didn't even hear me. It's like you blacked out. I just don't want you to kill him."

"Fuck him," Raheem said coldly as he released his grip on Marcus' shirt and slowly rose from his position kneeling over the unconscious, bloody man. "You actually still care about this dickhead after what he did to you?"

"I mean, no," Sarah sniffled. "I just don't want you to go to jail for no good reason."

"I ain't worried about that shit," Raheem rebuffed. "Now are you gonna get that gun out of my face?"

"Oh yeah. I'm sorry." Sarah stuttered as she backed away and placed the gun back onto the coffee table next to the sofa. "This is just too much for me. See... this is what I was talking about when I said I didn't want drama. I don't know what to do."

"Well, you need to pack your shit so we can get the fuck up out of here," Raheem huffed in frustration as he plopped his body onto the sofa.

"You know the neighbors heard that shit. They might fuck around and call the law. You better hurry up!"

"Well, I can't just leave him here all bloody and fucked up like this."

"For real Sarah? Are you serious? Niggas get trashed every day, B. He'll be alright! He's tough, right? Cam'ron voice!" Raheem chuckled.

"Oh my goodness Raheem," Sarah shook her head. "That's not even funny! You *are* crazy!"

"If you say so," Raheem glared at the woman as he felt the passion and infatuation he felt for her leave his soul more quickly than it had entered.

"I'm gonna go pack some shit real quick so we can figure out what we're doing." Sarah quickly left the living room and scurried to her bedroom. As Raheem waited, he lit a black and mild cigar and took a few swigs from the bottle of E&J. It had been sitting out all night and the sweet liquor was room temperature. The slight burn Raheem felt in his chest as he drank was exactly the sensation he was in need of. He looked down at Marcus's still body and sighed.

"Maybe this wasn't what the Universe had planned for me after all," he thought to himself. A few minutes later, Sarah reappeared with a medium-sized designer duffle bag in tow.

"I got some shit. We can go. I just gotta figure out when and how I'm gonna get the rest of my shit, but I'll worry about that later," Sarah stated hurriedly. She then looked down at Marcus. "You beat him bad Raheem. He's fucked up."

"Yeah, well, better him than you," Raheem replied, devoid of emotion as he rose from the sofa and retrieved his own duffle bag.

"I'm surprised he didn't even start to wake up yet." Sarah looked concerned as she walked over to where her ex-boyfriend lay. "He doesn't even look like he's breathing." Sarah knelt beside Marcus and held a finger to his neck for half-a-minute. Raheem noticed as panic and terror filled the beautiful young woman's face. "He's dead!"

"Stop playing," Raheem casually replied. "Let's go. He'll eventually wake up and go to the hospital. We'll be long gone by then."

"No, Raheem! He's dead," Sarah started to sob.

"What are you talking about Sarah? I just beat his bitch-ass up real good. He's probably not used to getting hands put on him like that. What makes you think he's dead?"

"I'm a fucking CNA, Raheem! I just took his pulse and he doesn't have one," Sarah bawled. "What the fuck did you do? We have to call 9-1-1!"

"First of all, what the fuck do you mean, 'what did I do?' I was riding for you! That's what the fuck I did," Raheem growled angrily. "Plus, what the fuck you think is gonna happen if you call the police! I'm not getting locked up for this shit!"

"So, we're supposed to just leave his body here and go," Sarah's voice cracked as tears streamed down her face.

"That's the only option I can think of," Raheem answered matter-of-factly. "He has drugs and guns here, so when somebody finds him and calls the cops they'll think it's drug-related."

"Um, no Raheem," Sarah objected. "My name is on the lease and I'm sure the neighbors heard us arguing. The cops are gonna come looking for me!"

"Well, then, we're just going to have to do what you were talking about last night and take all the valuables and the molly and sell them on the streets," Raheem proposed. "We can take the money and run away somewhere."

"What? What are you talking about Raheem?" Sarah gasped, crying even more hysterically than she already had been. "You work at UPS – where is all this shit coming from? We're not about to be on some Bonnie and Clyde shit! I'm not living my life like that! Besides, we can't just leave him here. It wouldn't be right!"

"But I guess not telling me that you already knew you had herpes for six months and then acting like you were upset at the thought that he might have burnt you was 'right?'"

72

"Wait a second, Raheem," Sarah interjected. "You gotta listen to me..."

"Listen to what? I would have listened last night," Raheem snapped. "This ain't even cool, though. I ride out for you and protect you even after I find out you intentionally burnt me and now you wanna get me locked up? I'm willing to leave my family and my daughter and runaway with you because of this shit and you want to preach to me about right and wrong? I didn't ask for none of this shit! You got me fucked up Sarah. Your nigga was right – you *are* just an extra-pretty smut with a good job and good pussy!"

"Ugh! You know what? Fuck you Raheem," Sarah sobbed in disgust. "I'm not gonna let some nine-dollar an hour, UPS nigga talk to me like that!"

"Oh, so that's why you put up with this nigga's shit all this time, huh?" Raheem sneered. "It's all about money, huh? Y'all bitches are all the same. Y'all all ain't shit. My mother, my wife *and* you... Fuck you Sarah. At least my wife didn't fucking burn me!"

"Eat a dick, Raheem! I'm not going to keep arguing with you! I'm calling the cops!"

Sarah sobbed as she ran to the kitchen. As soon as she grabbed the cordless house phone Raheem was upon her.

"Let me go!" Sarah screamed as Raheem attempted to wrestle the phone from her hands. Sarah gripped the phone tightly with both hands and kicked Raheem.

"Lower your voice Sarah," Raheem commanded. "Give me the fucking phone and let's go! I'm not getting locked up over this shit! You're not calling the cops!"

"Oh, yes I am! I'm not going anywhere with your crazy-ass! Let go!"

Raheem instantly felt his body go numb and his consciousness transform into a state he had only experienced while he was beating Marcus.

73

Minutes later, Raheem snapped out of the dream-like state. He drove down Marshall Road, across Cobbs Creek Parkway and onto Spruce Street. His mind raced as he drove without a specific destination in mind. He saw signs for Interstate 76 and took the exit onto the highway.

"I guess I'll hop on 95 and get a hotel near the airport until I figure out what the fuck I'm doing," Raheem said to himself aloud as he lit a black and mild and turned on the radio. "Hold up! I don't even have a car. Whose truck am I driving?"

Chapter 6

Raheem drove down a long driveway on Industrial Highway in Essington, Pennsylvania, a short distance from the Philadelphia International Airport. The driveway was the entrance to a chain restaurant and an independently owned and operated motel. Raheem parked and turned the truck's engine off. He sat in silence for several minutes, attempting to gain his bearings. Raheem's head spun as he struggled to remember the events of the night and where he had obtained the truck he was driving as if it were his own. His head pulsated and he began sweating profusely. Raheem's chest grew heavy with the anxiety which overwhelmed him when he came to the realization that he could not recollect anything that transpired after the first time he had sex with Sarah. He slammed his hands on the steering wheel in frustration. He gripped opposing sides near the top of the steering wheel until his knuckles transitioned to a much lighter shade of his brown complexion. As he exhaled and dropped his head in anguish, he noticed the Cadillac symbol in the center of the steering wheel. Raheem sat back in the leather seat and looked around the interior of the luxury vehicle.

"This jawn is tough," Raheem nodded his head in approval, removing the key from the ignition, admiring the pristine leather seats, polished wood grain accents and sleek console display. The young man slowly exited the vehicle and raised the rear door of the truck, revealing his own duffle bag and a shoebox resting atop high-end turntables, speakers an amplifier and other DJ equipment. "What the hell is all this?"

A puzzled Raheem took the shoebox in hand and removed the lid, quickly replacing it and looking around the parking lot suspiciously when he saw is contents.

"Oh shit! A burner, molly and bread," Raheem gasped to himself. He quickly and discreetly tucked the shoebox under his arm, lowered the rear door of the Cadillac and reentered the driver's side of the vehicle. The confused young man removed the lid of the shoebox once more and examined the contents of the box as he was now shielded from potential onlookers by the dark tints of the truck's windows. He racked his brain in an attempt to add the pieces of the puzzle together to determine what exactly was going on. To say his memories of the previous night's events were a blur would have been an understatement. He had absolutely no recollection of anything that occurred after he and Sarah had taken their first dose of molly and had sex for the first time. He checked his watch and saw that it was almost ten in the morning. "Molly, a gun and DJ equipment in the back of the truck? This must be Sarah's dude's shit. But why do I have it?"

Raheem could not make sense of the situation and he was growing extremely frustrated with himself due to his inability to recall the events of the previous eight hours. He concluded that sitting in the truck, doing nothing was not going to help him remember, so he counted the money which was neatly, tightly wrapped in a rubber band.

"Twelve hundred? That's what's up," Raheem exclaimed to himself. He folded and rolled the bills and proceeded to wrap the rubber band around them before shoving the knot in his pocket. He then placed the zipper-bag of molly in his other pocket, tucked the shoebox containing the firearm under the driver's seat and exited the vehicle. Raheem then made his way into the lobby of the motel.

"Hey what's going on?" Raheem greeted the clerk.

"What do you need?" the haggard, middle-aged white woman asked abruptly.

"A room," Raheem answered sarcastically. Why else would he be in the lobby of a motel?

"Check-in isn't until noon."

"You don't have anything available right now?"

"Check-in isn't until noon," the woman repeated robotically.

"Whatever. I'll be back." Raheem quickly exited the small lobby and sat in the truck contemplating his next move. "Nut-ass bitch," he sighed to himself. "It's not my fault she doesn't like her job. I don't need to deal with her fucking attitude."

Raheem retrieved the bag of molly from his pocket and examined it. He was sober for the first time since the previous night. He grew melancholy as he replayed the argument between himself and his family in his mind. He then checked his cell phone to see if he had received any messages or missed calls from his parents or his wife. Nothing.

"Fuck them," Raheem growled under his breath. A mental image of his wife holding their baby daughter caused Raheem to become overwhelmed with emotion as he thought about how all their lives would be forever changed based on the previous day's events. Raheem felt himself slipping into a state of deep sadness and he was opposed to allowing himself to be overwhelmed by negative emotions. He eyed the bag of molly and decided he would take another dose. His only problem was that he did not have any toilet paper or water to assist in constructing and ingesting a molly "parachute." Raheem paused and contemplated how he was going to take more of the drug as soon as possible before he slipped into a deep depression. Raheem had previously confided in his wife and father how he had been battling bouts of severe depression for the previous two years. The thought of how insolently they had treated him even though they knew he was struggling with his mental health made him resent them even more. As the anger grew inside his heart, he decided he needed to take more molly to snap out of his negative mood as quickly as possible.

"Fuck it," Raheem sighed to himself as he retrieved his pocket knife, inserted it into the bag of crystalline powder, carefully held the tip of the blade to his nostril and inhaled deeply, snorting the molly into his nasal cavity. "Oh shit!"

Unlike the night before, Raheem felt an immediate surge of adrenaline flow through his veins. The desired affect only took moments to engulf his mind, body and spirit. He instantly felt his mood elevate. The euphoric young man placed the bag of molly in his pocket, inserted the key into the ignition of the vehicle, turned on the radio and closed his eyes as he leaned back in the soft, leather seat and allowed the molly-induced euphoria to take control of his body. As he sat in the truck only half-listening to the radio commercials, the sensation of his spirit leaving his body sent a delightful tingle up his spine, through his extremities and into his scalp. Raheem smiled to himself as the newly familiar feeling of the molly-high encompassed him. The only difference was the feeling was more intense now than he remembered it feeling the night before. Raheem assumed the fact that he had snorted the drug instead of parachuting it was responsible for the quicker, stronger impact of the substance. His smile quickly turned to a grimace when the radio station's commercial break ended and a Bryson Tiller song entitled "Exchange" began to resonate from the truck's powerful speakers.

"This what happens when I think 'bout you. I get in my feelings, girl. I start reminiscing, girl. Next time around, fuck, I want it to be different girl…"

"Aw, hell naw!" Raheem quickly turned off the radio as the lyrics instantly caused the image of his newly estranged wife to appear in his mind. "Bryson, my nigga… I fucks with you, but why you trying to kill my vibe?" Raheem chuckled to himself.

As the young man gazed through the truck's windshield he noticed a voluptuous, attractive, exotic-looking young woman standing near the entrance of the motel approximately twenty-feet from the truck. He had never seen a woman who looked like her before and he squinted to get a better look. Her skin was so fair that from a distance he mistook her for a white woman at first but was confused by the texture of her hair and how curvy her frame was.

"Excuse me," Raheem said softly as he exited the vehicle and slowly approached the attractive young woman. "Can I talk to you for a minute, ma?"

"Sure. What's up?" The beautiful young woman smiled as she turned and met Raheem's gaze. He was immediately enchanted by her smile and grayish-blue colored eyes. He paused mid-stride and quickly admired her. She was voluptuous indeed. Upon closer examination, Raheem realized that she was a Black woman with albinism. Her shoulder-length hair was sandy-brown, almost blonde. Pinkish-red lipstick evenly coated and glistened on her full lips.

"My name is Raheem."

"I'm Crystal. Nice to meet you." The young woman smiled bashfully as she extended her hand and shook Raheem's hand.

"Nice to meet you too," Raheem replied with a large smile, as he was even more sociable than usual due to the drugs in his system. "Are you staying here?"

"I'm not sure what I'm doing, to tell the truth," Crystal admitted. "I'm kinda lost in the sauce right now. I just got here from out of town."

"Yeah I'm kind of lost in the sauce my damn self. I was about to check in but the lady said I have to wait until noon," Raheem informed his new acquaintance. "Maybe we can keep each other company for a while. You want to get some breakfast? There's a Denny's right there."

"You don't waste any time," the young woman grinned. "Are you asking me out on a date, Raheem?"

"Hey, if that's what you want to call it, then that's what it will be!"

"That's what it is then," Crystal smiled as she winked at Raheem. His heart fluttered as the attractive young woman hypnotically stared into his eyes. "You ready?"

"You already know."

Raheem used the Cadillac's remote to lock the doors and arm the security system as the new acquaintances began the short walk from the hotel parking lot to the front door of the neighboring restaurant.

"That's a very nice truck," Crystal complimented Raheem when she heard the beeping sound indicating the vehicle's security system had been activated.

"Um, thanks," Raheem reluctantly replied.

"What? You don't like it?"

"Naw, I like it a lot. It's just that..."

"What's wrong, then? Why did you say, 'thanks' like that?" Crystal inquired.

"I mean," Raheem hesitated as he opened the door to the entrance of the restaurant and held it open so Crystal could enter. "It's nothing. Let's just go in here and get a table."

"Okay. If you say so," Crystal complied.

"Good morning! Will it be just you dining with us today or will there be others joining you today?" A cheerful hostess greeted Raheem as he approached. The hostess retrieved a menu from behind the counter as she smiled widely, revealing a mouth full of large, white, perfectly straight teeth.

"Yeah, just the two of us," Raheem casually replied. The friendly hostess paused and looked at Raheem incredulously before retrieving a second menu from behind the counter.

"You can follow me," the hostess smiled as she led the way to a booth and placed the menus on opposite sides of the table. "Your server will be with you shortly. Do you want any coffee while you wait?"

"I'm good, thanks. I don't drink coffee. How about you?" Raheem asked while looking at Crystal, who shook her head "no." "Naw, we're good, thanks."

"Oh… okay," the hostess replied nervously with a goofy grin plastered across her young face. "Well, enjoy your meal!"

The young woman scurried away and returned to her station, posted in the front of the restaurant.

"Did you see that? She was acting funny as hell," Raheem sighed. "What was that about?"

"Yeah, I noticed," Crystal acknowledged. "Who knows? People are weird!"

"You ain't never lied, ma," Raheem chuckled as he opened his menu and scanned its contents. "I'm getting tired of dealing with funny-acting people! I think I need a vacation from society in general!"

"Yeah, I feel you on that," Crystal chuckled. "Is that why you were checking into the hotel? You need a break from people?"

"Something like that," Raheem hesitated. "Do you know what you want to order," the young man asked, changing the subject.

"I'm not sure," Crystal admitted. "What about you?"

"I think I'ma get the Grand Slam breakfast."

"Somebody must be extra hungry," Crystal grinned.

"Yeah, I'm pretty hungry," Raheem acknowledged. "It's a lot of food and I probably won't finish it all. It's worth it for the price though."

"I'm not that hungry, so maybe that's why I can't figure out what I want to eat."

"Oh. Well, we didn't have to come here if you aren't that hungry," Raheem passively replied.

"To be honest, Raheem," Crystal began, "I would have gone *anywhere* with you! I was kind of hoping you said something to me. I saw you when you pulled up and noticed how handsome you are, but I'm too shy to approach a man. You could have asked me to go fishing, clean and cook the fish for breakfast and I still would have said yes!"

"Aw shit," Raheem laughed. "You're feeling a nigga like that?"

"Um… yeah," Crystal bashfully replied. "Like I said, I just got into town. I was supposed to meet up with somebody, but they left me hanging so I wasn't really sure what I was going to do. It's like you pulled up just in time. I think maybe the Universe maneuvered events so we met. I try not to ignore signs like that."

"For real?" Raheem asked in shock "You actually sound like you're on the same type of time I'm on. Maybe you're right! Maybe we were supposed to meet…"

"I think so, but I guess we'll find out for sure…"

"Well, do you want to share my Grand Slam breakfast since you're not really hungry and I probably won't finish the whole thing?"

"Are you sure you're okay with that, Raheem," Crystal asked shyly. "I know most men don't like sharing their meal with their girlfriend, let alone some random girl they just met!"

"Yeah, well, I guess I'm not like most men! Yeah, I'm sure," Raheem confirmed. "I invited you and I was going to pay for your meal anyway. You'll be saving me money!"

81

"Okay, that works. Thanks Raheem!"

"No problem, beautiful," Raheem smiled as he gazed into the albino woman's crystal-colored, almost transparent eyes.

"Good morning," a young woman exclaimed warmly as she approached the table. "My name is Jennifer. I'll be your server this morning. Have you decided what you would like to order?"

"Yeah, thanks," Raheem began. "Can I get the Grand Slam breakfast with half turkey sausage and half turkey bacon? Eggs scrambled, no cheese. Can I also get an extra plate and another set of silverware? The hostess only gave us one set."

"Um, yes. That's not a problem," Jennifer discreetly cut her eyes in Raheem's direction as she slowly replied while rapidly writing the order in her pad. "Would you like something to drink?"

"Yeah. I'll have a small glass of milk. Do you want anything to drink?" Raheem asked as he turned to face Crystal.

"Just water, please and thank you."

"Can you make that two glasses of water?" Raheem directed his request to Jennifer.

"Sure! Anything else?"

"Naw, I think we're good for now," Raheem replied with a smile.

"Okay. So that will be a Grand Slam breakfast, half sausage, half bacon, both turkey. Eggs scrambled, no cheese, a small glass of milk and *two* glasses of water?"

"You got it! And please don't forget the extra plate and another set of utensils," Raheem politely reminded the server.

"Uh... of course sir," Jennifer replied. "I'll be back with your beverages and silverware shortly." The server smiled nervously before scurrying to the rear of the restaurant.

"Why is everybody in this restaurant acting so strange?" Raheem sighed.

"Who knows?" Crystal shrugged. "You know half the damn population is completely throwed off!"

The young coupled laughed in unison at Crystal's comment.

"You ain't never lied," Raheem agreed. "That's kinda why I need a break from reality. I'm just glad I ran into somebody who is on the same type time as me!"

"You and me both, Raheem," Crystal replied with a smile, batting her eyelashes at her new male companion.

"So, what's your situation, ma?"

"My situation, huh? I knew that question was coming sooner or later," Crystal grinned.

"Well, I mean, you said you came from out of town to visit somebody, but they left you hanging," Raheem began. "You were coming to visit a dude?"

"Yeah, I was," Crystal replied shyly. "We have been talking for a few months and he told me he wanted to meet me in person. We made plans for me to visit him. I got here this morning, and all of a sudden, he's acting like he doesn't want to meet up anymore. He said he doesn't need any more confusion or drama in his life. So, now I'm mad. Like, first of all... how you gonna tell me that after I came all the way out here? Plus, I felt like he was saying *I* was gonna cause confusion and drama in his life! Why would I do that? I don't need that shit either! That was insulting. He wasted my time!"

"Plus wasted money too, right? I mean, now you gotta stay in a hotel until you can catch a flight home. That's drawing," Raheem sighed as he shook his head in disappointment. "Where are you from?"

"Let's just say I'm from an obscure, far-away place you've probably never heard of," Crystal replied with a seductive smirk.

"Oh... a mysterious woman, huh?" Raheem chuckled. "You don't want to tell me where you're from? It's all good. Maybe you'll feel more comfortable opening up after we get to know each other a little better."

"That sounds like a possibility," Crystal smiled. "So, what's your situation, Raheem?"

"My situation," Raheem began, stroking his chin hairs. "Well, I'm married, but I'm recently separated. We have a newborn daughter."

"Aw shit," Crystal sighed as she rested her forehead in the palm of her hand.

"I know how it sounds, but it's not even like that," Raheem continued. "I got married young, then she got pregnant. She pressured me to move in with my parents to save money while she was still pregnant. Shit went downhill from there. That house has been filled with daily beef ever since we moved in. Things went too far yesterday. I'm done with my wife and my parents. Now I'm just trying to figure out where I'm gonna live. I'm basically homeless right now. That's why I was going to the hotel."

"Damn, Raheem," Crystal replied sympathetically as she reached across the table and caressed Raheem's hand. "I'm sorry you're dealing with all that! So, you said this happened yesterday? Where did you stay last night? Did you have to sleep in your truck?"

"My truck? Oh, naw… I haven't even slept yet. Last night was a wild one. I haven't slept since I woke up to get ready for work yesterday morning."

"Really? Wow, that's ironic. What do you do for work?"

"Ironic? What makes you say that?" Raheem's asked, initially ignoring Crystal's question about his employment. His interest was visibly piqued.

"Because I haven't slept yet either. I was traveling here all night. I actually just made it here about an hour before you and I met," Crystal explained. "I contacted dude when I got here and he played me. I've never been to Philly before and I only came to visit him, so I really have no idea what I'm going to do. That's why I said I was lost in the sauce."

"I feel you," Raheem compassionately replied. "That was out of pocket. I would never leave a woman hanging like that. Especially one who looks as good and seems as cool as you!"

"Aw, shit," Crystal giggled bashfully. "You spitting game Raheem?"

"I'm just spitting facts," Raheem smoothly replied. The young man threw both hands in the air in mock surrender.

The young couple laughed together but regained their composure when they noticed the server approaching their table carrying a tray resting in her palm above her shoulder.

"Here's your milk, your waters and your extra plate and set of silverware," Jennifer stated cheerfully with a smile, her voice trembling. "I'll bring your food as soon as it's ready. Do you need anything else in the meantime?"

"No, we're good for now. Thank you, Jennifer," Raheem smiled as he discreetly glanced at Crystal.

Jennifer, the server, nodded and quickly walked away. Raheem observed as Jennifer stopped across the room and whispered to the hostess, who looked in Raheem's direction. Raheem and the hostess locked eyes momentarily before she quickly looked away and whispered to the server. Both women then quickly scurried away in opposite directions.

"You're right," Crystal began. "These people are weird."

"I know, right?"

"Why do you think they're acting like that?"

"Who knows?" Raheem shrugged. "Working in food service is stressful. Maybe they're having a rough morning. You know what Jay-Z said back in the day, 'never eat at Denny's and party like Little Penny!'"

"'Who You Wit?' Yaaaaas! That was my shit!" Crystal grinned widely and clapped her hands before reaching across the table to shake Raheem's hand.

"What you know about that, girl?" Raheem grinned and nodded his head. "Let me find out!"

"Yeah, I prefer 90s Jay-Z," Crystal explained. "Everything after that Kingdom Come album has been 'so-so' compared to the old Hov!"

"I definitely prefer, '*cough up a lung, where I'm from, Marcy son,*' Jigga over, '*show me what you got lil' mama,*' Roc Nation Hov," Raheem added, chuckling. "You really have good taste in hip-hop, huh, Crystal? Let me find out I ran into a woman who's just my type, the day after me and my wife break up!"

"Hey, you never know…" Crystal shrugged bashfully as she smiled and batted her eyelashes. "Everything happens for a reason. The Universe provides…"

"I know we just met, but you seem so dope to me," Raheem confessed, gazing at Crystal longingly. "What do you do for a living?"

"Me? You never told me what you do!" Crystal smiled, once again reaching across the table and caressing Raheem's hand. "But me… I'm a spiritual advisor."

"Word?" Raheem excitedly exclaimed. "That's what's up! I need somebody like you in my life right now! That's crazy!"

"Like I said… the Universe always provides," Crystal softly replied as she caressed both of Raheem's hands from the opposite side of the table. "What do you do for a living?"

"Oh, uh," Raheem stuttered. "I'm kinda in transition right now, but I'm an unloader at UPS. I take packages off the back of the big tractor-trailers all day."

"That explains why you're in such good shape," Crystal seductively replied as she gripped Raheem's hands extended across the table in her direction.

Raheem's body shivered as the young couple locked eyes. He was not only captivated by the woman's appearance, he was impressed by her energy. He assumed she would judge his employment status harshly like many women do, especially considering the fact that she was a professional and an entrepreneur herself. Instead, she used the opportunity to compliment him.

"Kim could use some lessons from Crystal on how to speak power into a man," Raheem thought to himself.

"But if you don't mind me asking," Crystal continued, "how do you afford an Escalade on a UPS salary? Do you have another job, or a side-hustle?"

"Yeah. I mean… I used to," Raheem stuttered. "That's what I meant when I said I'm in transition."

"I understand. Sorry. I'm not trying to be all in your business," Crystal apologized. "I mean, it's a really nice truck, that's all."

"Yeah, it is. Thanks…"

The conversation was abruptly cut short when the server approached with Raheem's breakfast plates.

"So, here's your food. Syrup is right there and you already have your utensils. Do you need anything else, sir?"

Raheem looked inquiringly in Crystal's direction. She nodded her head, "no." Raheem then turned to address the sever, who was impatiently waiting for his response.

"No, we're good for now. Thanks Jennifer."

"Right," Jennifer nodded nervously, forcing a smile. "Well, you be sure to let *us* know if you need anything else, sir. You can pay at the front counter whenever you're ready. Enjoy your meal and the rest of your weekend."

Raheem was somewhat startled when the young woman abruptly slammed a pad containing the charges for the meal on the table and quickly walked away.

"The fuck is wrong with these people?" Raheem huffed, removing his fork and knife from the napkin wrapped around them. "You wanna just split the whole meal in half?"

"Oh, no. Thanks Raheem," Crystal politely declined. "I'm really not hungry at all. I'm good with the water for now. Maybe if you don't finish I'll have your leftovers."

"You sure? You should eat *something*."

"Yeah, I'm good. I'll eat later if I get hungry."

"If you say so," Raheem replied, shrugging his shoulders before embarking on the task of cutting his pancakes into small squares for easier consumption. "Let me know if you change your mind before I fuck this whole thing up on some greedy shit!"

Crystal chuckled as she watched Raheem drench his pancakes in syrup.

"You want some pancakes with your syrup, King?" Crystal teased Raheem with an enchanting smile.

"You got jokes, huh?" Raheem chuckled with a mouth full of half-chewed pancakes. He chewed rapidly and sipped his milk before continuing. "Don't judge me! You gave up the right to comment on my pancake-to-syrup ratio when you said you weren't hungry!"

"What? Whatever! I'm just messing with you anyway," Crystal erupted in laughter. "But for real, though… what are you going to do after we leave here? I was thinking, maybe we could hang out until we both figure some things out. I think we definitely met for a reason. Maybe we can help each other."

Raheem paused and slowly put his fork down. The young man chewed and swallowed his food as he gazed intently into the young woman's hypnotic eyes.

"Yeah," Raheem replied, nodding his head in agreement. "I'm definitely with it."

Chapter 7

Raheem and Crystal got better acquainted as he slowly forced himself to finish his large breakfast. After shoving the last forkful of pancakes in his mouth, he dropped his silverware and gulped down the last of his glass of milk.

"Damn, I'm stuffed," Raheem exclaimed as he exhaled deeply and rubbed his enlarged belly. "I really wished you would have helped me finish that!"

"You're a big boy," Crystal smiled. "You killed that! You were obviously hungry!"

"Yeah, I guess you're right," Raheem acknowledged. "You ready to get up outta here?"

"I'm ready when you are, love."

"We out, then," Raheem nodded as he rose from his seat, picked up the bill, reviewed the charges and retrieved his wallet from his pocket. Raheem led the way as the two made their way to the front counter where the hostess was stationed.

"How was your meal?" the hostess quietly asked Raheem without making eye-contact.

"It was good, thanks," Raheem replied with a smile. "I'm stuffed! It would have been nice if my lady-friend had helped me out, but it's all good." Raheem chuckled as he turned to look at Crystal. "She was acting all shy, had me looking like some type of selfish jerk who wouldn't order my date anything but water!"

"Hey… to each his own," the hostess chuckled nervously as Raheem handed her a twenty-dollar bill. The woman stared down at her station intently as she punched several buttons on the cash register, counted out Raheem's change, handed it back to him and slammed the register drawer. "Thanks for coming in today. Enjoy the rest of your weekend. Be safe."

"Thanks. You too," Raheem hesitated as he placed the money into his wallet and looked at the hostess awkwardly. The woman continued to look down at the cash register, aimlessly shuffling the contents of a small plastic bin next to the register.

Raheem looked at Crystal, rolled his eyes and shook his head in disappointment. The young man led the way out of the restaurant, holding the door open for Crystal as she exited before him.

"These motherfuckers are some weirdos," Raheem exclaimed as the young couple walked away from the restaurant entrance. "I felt like we were in the Twilight Zone in there!"

"I can't argue with that," Crystal sighed as she shook her head and rolled her eyes. "What? Are there not a lot of Black people around here?"

"That's the crazy part," Raheem huffed. "There actually are plenty of Black people around here! Southwest Philly, Chester and a few other mostly Black hoods are around here. There's a casino down the street, the airport is five minutes away and there are plenty of cheap motels around here. I really don't know why those ladies were acting so strange."

"Yeah, well, at least that's over with," Crystal chuckled. "Remind me not to eat there again."

"Again? You actually didn't eat there today," Raheem teased.

"Hey, you do have a point, there," Crystal giggled. "So, what's our next move?"

"Well, it's a quarter after twelve now," Raheem acknowledged after glancing at his watch. "I guess we should walk back over to the hotel and check in."

The new acquaintances walked up the driveway and approached the hotel where they had initially met less than an hour beforehand. As they walked past the shiny Cadillac truck Raheem had arrived in, the young man paused and admired the vehicle. When they reached the front door of the hotel, Raheem gripped the handle, pulled the door open and held it as he gestured for Crystal to enter.

"Thanks Raheem! You're such a gentleman! I feel like you're too good to be true," Crystal smiled as she caressed Raheem's cheek as she walked past him.

"Oh yeah? Naw, this is the real me. I ain't perfect, but I know how to treat a woman!"

Raheem and Crystal approached the front counter and waited for the clerk to acknowledge them. She seemed to be oblivious to their existence as she gazed intently at a half-finished crossword puzzle and sipped a cup of coffee. After waiting for approximately one minute, Raheem cleared his throat loudly in an attempt to alert the clerk of their presence.

"Yes?" The middle-aged woman slammed her pencil on the counter, slowly looked over her bifocals and cut her eyes at the young man.

"Look, lady... I don't want any issues with you," Raheem began. "We just need a room."

"Queen-sized bed or two full-sized beds?" the woman asked impatiently.

"Oh, um," Raheem stuttered as he turned to Crystal inquiringly. "You want to get two beds in the room?"

"It's up to you, love," Crystal bashfully replied. "You're doing me a favor right now letting me chill with you until I figure out what I'm doing. Whatever you want to get is fine with me."

"Yeah, um, we'll get the Queen sized jawn," Raheem replied to the hotel clerk who was staring at him with an irritated expression plastered across her wrinkled face.

"Smoking or non-smoking *jawn*?" the woman asked sarcastically.

Raheem observed the woman's puzzled look and condescending tone. He paused before responding. The brown-skinned man glared at the pale-faced woman for a while. His stomach grew uneasy when he noticed how damaged the skin on her face appeared to be. Her makeup was smeared across the wrinkles, bumps, craters and moles on the woman's drooping skin stretched across her pointy cheekbones. Time and gravity had not been kind to the pasty woman.

Her attempts to use excessive amounts of makeup to hide her age and the physical toll her past had taken on her looks had been in vain. Her wretched appearance paled in comparison to the negative, ugly spirit she exuded. Raheem's assessment of the woman was disappointing and humorous to him. The internal satisfaction he received from the realization that the woman was so nasty because she was so miserable made him refrain from reciprocating her negativity.

"Smoking *jawn*, please," Raheem grinned slyly as his skin tingled when a sudden euphoric feeling resurged throughout his being.

"Fill this out," the miserable woman sluggishly commanded as she slid a pad and pen under the window. "I need your driver's license. It's ninety-five dollars per night. Cash or credit?"

"Cash. I'll pay for two nights up-front."

Raheem pulled out his wallet, counted one-hundred and ninety dollars and slid it through the opening between the counter and the plexiglass window. He quickly completed the personal information form, but had to stop when he reached the section designated for the hotel guests' vehicle information.

"Um, I don't even know the truck's license plate off the top of my head."

"Don't worry about it," the disgruntled woman barked. "Just write the year, make and model."

Raheem nodded as he wrote the make, "Cadillac," and model, "Escalade," on the form. He neglected to list the year of the vehicle. Raheem was not sure exactly which year the truck had been manufactured. He slid the form back to the clerk and chuckled to himself. Raheem thought it was ironic that this bitter woman was probably infuriated to see a young Black man with such an expensive, luxury vehicle. Little did she know he didn't even own it!

Raheem's amusement quickly subsided when he considered the fact that he still had not been able to recall the events of the morning before he began his journey to the hotel.

"Is it cool if I leave the truck parked there?"

"Yeah. Your room is on this side of that building," the woman nodded her head to the side as she slid the room key and receipt across the counter to Raheem. The irritable hag quickly resumed her cross-word puzzle without another word.

Raheem shook his head, chuckled, turned to Crystal and smiled.

"We're good to go, ma."

Chapter 8

Raheem and Crystal exited the motel lobby, walked across the parking lot and along the side of the neighboring building until they found their room. Raheem inserted the room key into the door and pushed it open for Crystal to enter. He followed her in and closed the door behind them.

"Oh, this is cute," Crystal exclaimed as she looked around the apartment-style motel room.

"Yeah, it's not bad for the price," Raheem acknowledged. "That's why I came here. I've stayed here a few times before."

"Oh, yeah?" Crystal replied curiously with a sly grin. "So, is that what you do? You come to the hotel and look for random, lost women to befriend, then take them out to eat and offer to let them stay in the room with you for the weekend?"

"Ah… you're funny," Raheem chuckled. "Naw, I usually come here when me and my peoples are going through it."

"Your 'peoples?'"

"Yeah," Raheem hesitated. "My wife and parents. I'm married with a newborn daughter, remember? We moved in with my parents shortly before the baby was born and it's been nothing but drama ever since. We broke up for good yesterday. I'm trying to figure out my next move, so I came here to clear my head."

"Oh, right… I'm really sorry to hear you're going through that."

"Thanks, but I wouldn't have met you if it hadn't happened," Raheem replied nonchalantly as he sat on the large bed centered in the middle of the room. "I believe everything happens for a reason. The Universe is working. I just need to figure out what I need to do to work with it."

"Yeah, I feel you," Crystal acknowledged. "I'm the same way. I definitely agree we were supposed to meet. Everybody we meet plays a role in our lives. But are you okay, though? I mean, for real? I *am* a spiritual advisor. Maybe I can give you a reading later."

"Yeah, I'll be good. I might take you up on that reading after I figure out what I'm gonna do. Thanks ma."

"You're welcome, Raheem. I've never been married and I don't have any kids, but I imagine breaking up with your spouse when you have a newborn is extremely difficult," the attractive young woman replied empathetically.

"Yeah, it's drawing, but it is what it is," Raheem sighed. "The things that happen to us aren't as important as how we react to them."

"Well, I agree. That's a good attitude to have," Crystal replied as she walked across the room and sat on the bed next to Raheem. "Um... So, you said y'all separated yesterday?"

"Yeah. It's been a long time coming, though," Raheem explained "Basically, me and my mother got into a real bad argument when I got home from work. My soon-to-be ex-wife took my mother's side. By the time my father got involved, the whole situation was out of control, so I just left."

"So, if you left home yesterday, why didn't you come get a room yesterday?" Crystal innocently inquired.

"Because, um..."

Raheem hesitated before continuing. He quickly decided not to reveal any more details about his situation until he knew he could trust Crystal. She seemed cool, but so did Sarah. Raheem could not remember what had transpired after they took the molly together and had sex, but he was preoccupied with an ominous feeling that whatever had happened had not ended well.

"I was chilling with my homey."

"Oh, okay. Well, I hope spending time with your homey helped you feel a little better," Crystal smiled and rubbed Raheem's shoulder.

"Yeah... thanks," Raheem sighed. "So, what do you like to do for fun?"

"Well, to be honest, I'm kind of a free-spirit. I like to go with the flow. I'm pretty easy-going."

"That's what's up," Raheem exclaimed. "It will be nice to spend time with a laid-back woman for a change!"

"I guess I should take that as a compliment," Crystal giggled. "So, what do you like to do for fun?"

Raheem sighed and paused as he glanced around the room. He suddenly realized that the molly-high he felt after snorting the drug before he and Crystal met had vanished. He attributed the loss of his high to the passing of time coupled with Crystal's most recent line of questioning. Raheem's mood was rapidly declining and he was prepared to do whatever was necessary to prevent himself from spiraling into depression – especially while Crystal was in his presence.

"You ever done molly before?" Raheem reluctantly asked.

"Yeah, I've done it a few times. Only when I was with other people who had it, though," Crystal confessed. "It's been a while since I did it. Honestly, I can't really remember whether I liked it or not! It kind of messes with my memory."

"Yeah, it does that sometimes," Raheem chuckled as he reached into his pocket and retrieved the bag of molly. "You fucking with it?"

"That's molly right there? Is that the high-quality shit, though? I'm not trying to be rolling around butt-naked," Crystal laughed and her eyes lit up as she eyed the clear, zipper-bag half-full of the crystalline powder.

"Yes ma'am," Raheem chuckled. "It's the best of the best! What's wrong with rolling around butt-naked though?"

"Boy! You're crazy! Ain't nothing wrong with rolling around butt-naked under the right circumstances." Crystal smiled as she gazed at Raheem seductively. "You know what I mean, though. I've seen too many videos online of people taking bad molly and running around the streets with their clothes off. I'm not trying to go viral!"

"Aw, hell no! This is high-quality shit! Don't worry ma. I only want you to get naked if you want to," Raheem grinned slyly. "I value my privacy so I'm not trying to go viral either!"

"Okay Raheem. I'll take your word for it…"

"So… are you fucking with it?" Raheem asked again as he dangled the clear bag in front of Crystal's face.

"I'm down to do whatever you want to do while I'm with you, Raheem," Crystal stated resolutely as she looked intently into her male companion's eyes.

"Oh, shit," Raheem chuckled. "You better make sure you really mean that because I'ma hold you to that!"

Raheem and Crystal locked eyes. Raheem felt his manhood swell as a vision of rolling in the sheets naked with the attractive young woman flashed through his head. Everything about her intrigued Raheem. He had never met an albino woman he was so attracted to. Raheem thought it was interesting how Crystal's skin was actually lighter than the pasty, miserable motel clerk's, but she wore it so much better. Crystal's skin was smooth, hydrated and flawless. She was a beautiful Black woman although her hair and eyes lacked the pigment typically associated with "Black girl magic." Her personality was also extremely warm and inviting.

"I'll be right back." Raheem quickly rose from the bed, walked into the bathroom and stared in the mirror. The newly single young man took note of his thought process and realized that he was quickly growing infatuated with the young woman. "I gotta chill. I can't keep catching feelings for these hoes on some rebound shit just because me and Kim broke up."

Raheem shook his head as he stared at himself a few seconds longer. He then walked over to the toilet, urinated, flushed the toilet and washed his hands. He retrieved a fresh roll of toilet paper and exited the bathroom.

"So, you ready to get it popping?" Raheem asked excitedly as he approached Crystal, toilet paper in hand and sat on the bed next to her.

"Yeah, I'm ready to have some fun," the young woman cheerfully replied.

"Oh, wait a second. We need water. We gotta make sure we stay hydrated while we're on this. I'm gonna run to the gas station down the street and grab a case of water. Do you want to ride with me?"

"Are you gonna be gone long? I would kinda rather stay here and freshen up while you're gone," Crystal replied.

"Shit... I need to hop my ass in the shower too," Raheem exclaimed. "That reminds me – I need to grab some soap and deodorant and shit. There's a Wal-Mart not too far from here, so I'm gonna go there instead. You need anything?"

"No, I think I'm good for now, thanks," Crystal declined. "I'll be ready when you get back."

"Say less."

Chapter 9

Raheem parked the Cadillac in front of the door of his motel room when he returned from the store. When he entered the room, he was greeted by the sound of R&B music emanating from a small Bluetooth speaker. He closed the door behind him and placed the bottled water, along with a few small bottles of liquor he purchased on his way back to the motel, in the small refrigerator in the corner of the room. Raheem then walked to the bathroom door while carrying a plastic bag containing the toiletries he had purchased during his short trip to the store.

"Yo, ma! You good?" Raheem called out after knocking on the bathroom door.

"Yeah. Come in!"

Raheem followed the young woman's instructions and entered the bathroom. He was overwhelmed when he saw Crystal. The attractive young lady was immersed in bubbly bath water. The copious white suds in the water did little to disguise her voluptuous figure, however. Crystal's perky breasts seemed to float on the surface of the froth. Her large, erect nipples seemed to beckon Raheem as soon as he entered the bathroom.

"Aw snap," Raheem exclaimed. "You weren't playing when you said you would be ready when I got back, huh?"

"Yes, daddy," Crystal smiled. "I figured I'd hook up my phone to my Bluetooth speaker, listen to Pandora and soak in the bath while I waited for you to get back. Now I'm ready for whatever."

"That's what the fuck I'm talking about! I grabbed a bottle of Henny too. I'm about to make these parachutes so we can take some of this molly."

"Oh, okay," Crystal hesitated.

"Is something wrong?" Raheem asked, sensing the apprehension in Crystal's voice.

"No. Nothing's wrong," Crystal passively replied. "It's just that – doesn't that shit work better if you snort it? I figure it we're gonna do it, we might as well do it *for real*."

"Say no more," Raheem blurted out as he returned the fresh roll of toilet paper to the corner of the vanity where he initially found it. "I didn't want to put any pressure on you, but yeah, it definitely works better when you snort it."

"I appreciate that, but I already told you… I'm a free spirit. I go with the flow. I don't feel any pressure from you, Raheem. I'm here to do whatever you want to do. We met for a reason, so let's make sure we have as much fun as possible during our time together. Okay?"

"Sounds like a plan," Raheem agreed, bearing a large grin which revealed his growing excitement.

"So, strip and hop your ass in," the attractive young woman commanded with a smile as she looked up at her male companion.

Without another word, Raheem removed his clothes and carefully stepped into the relatively large tub. As he did so, Crystal adjusted her position to allow Raheem room to get comfortable. Once Raheem sat down, leaned back and settled in, Crystal placed her legs on either side of his and slid forward, closer to the man.

"Where's that molly at, King?" Crystal asked as she reached under the bubbles, gently grabbed Raheem's manhood and began to caress it. "Oh, that's not it!"

"Naw, you definitely can't snort that," Raheem laughed quietly before he let out a long sigh of satisfaction. "You gotta swallow that!"

"Oh, my fault," Crystal smirked, offering a mock apology as she abruptly withdrew her hand.

"I didn't want you to stop, though," Raheem chuckled as he reached over the side of the tub and retrieved his knife and the bag of molly from his pants pocket. He unfolded his knife, unzipped the bag and inserted the blade into the bag's contents. When he removed the knife, a small mound of molly was resting on the tip of the blade.

Crystal leaned forward, her nose pointed slightly upward. Raheem carefully held his knife near Crystal's face, at which point she placed a finger on one of her nostrils, quickly snorted the crystalline substance and jerked her head away, revealing a clean, powderless blade.

"Wooh," Crystal exclaimed as she tilted her head back, rubbed her nose and rapidly blinked her eyes, which had begun tearing. Raheem smiled as he repeated the process himself.

Raheem reached over the side of the tub to return the molly and knife to the inside of his pants pocket on the bathroom floor. As soon as Raheem returned to his relaxed position, Crystal resumed caressing his member under the warm, soapy bath water. At that very moment, the previous song ended and an old, R&B song entitled, "Knockin' Da Boots," by a group named H-Town blared through the speakers.

"Oooooh, yeah, yeah," Raheem bellowed along with the lead singer of the group as the song echoed off the bathroom tiles. "This is that work!"

"Yeah it is," Crystal agreed with a seductive smile as she continued to manually stimulate the man she had met less than two hours prior. "I guess that's my cue, then."

Crystal released Raheem's private parts and took hold of one of his hands with both of hers. She then submerged his hand beneath the water and guided his index and middle fingers in between her legs until they were inside her.

Raheem, whose manhood was already fully erect, felt a powerful surge of pleasurable sensations in his crotch as he observed Crystal's obvious pleasure. The woman opposite him in the tub moaned sensually as her eyes fluttered and her light skin grew flush. She reached her hands back across the tub, underneath the water and began to firmly stroke Raheem's throbbing penis with both of her hands. The two new acquaintances increased the pace with which they manually stimulated each other until they were engaging in rapid mutual masturbation.

Within several minutes, Crystal released Raheem's private parts, gently moved his hand away from her vagina and stood up.

101

"You good, sexy?" Raheem growled as he gazed up at Crystal. His raspy voice sounded even deeper than usual due to his spiked testosterone levels. "Why did you get up?"

"Because I want that dick," Crystal growled sensually as she looked down at Raheem before squatting on his lap and guiding his thickness into her warm, extremely wet canal. "Oh my God, Raheem!"

The two moaned simultaneously as Crystal rested her perfectly shaped rear end on Raheem's thighs when he entered her.

"Fuck!" Raheem moaned aloud. "Goddamn, girl!"

Crystal passionately shoved her tongue into Raheem's mouth as she gyrated her hips back and forth, sliding his manhood along the inside of her slick vaginal walls. Suds and bath water splashed and spilled onto the bathroom floor as the duo lost themselves in the act of submitting to the power of their passion which had been heightened by the effects of the illicit substance they had both inhaled.

The H-Town song concluded, followed by several more equally sexually explicit, classic, 1990s R&B songs. The playlist on Crystal's phone seemed to be comprised of extremely provocative, "baby-making music" whose lyrics were ironically appropriate for the occasion. "Sex Me," by R. Kelly, "Red Light Special," by TLC, "Freak'n You," by Jodeci and "I Like," by Kut Klose all played to completion; but even the most explicit lyrics did not match the sexual energy and aggression exuding from the young couple's bodies. Raheem and Crystal were still deeply engrossed in the act of passionately kissing, biting and sucking each other's upper bodies while simultaneously slamming their pelvises together to increase their sexual pleasure.

When a song entitled, "The Softest Place on Earth," by a female group named Xscape began to play, Crystal once again stood up without a word. She turned around and sat back down on Raheem's lap, once again guiding his manhood directly between her pulsating lower lips. The soaking wet, voluptuous woman grabbed both of Raheem's hands and placed them on her breasts as she squeezed them under Raheem' grip, encouraging her lover to caress her hardened nipples. The increasingly voracious woman rocked back and forth on Raheem's lap at a medium pace, riding his manhood as she faced away from him. Raheem smiled as his eyes rolled back into his head which felt like it was spinning in ecstasy. He stroked Crystal's breast, licked her neck, gently bit her shoulders and enjoyed his favorite sexual position while he silently marveled at Crystal's sexual prowess.

As the Xscape song reached its conclusion, Raheem felt his body grow warmer. Before he realized it was coming, he erupted inside of Crystal, whose body responded in kind. The young woman trembled uncontrollably as the skin covering her body transitioned from a milky color to a light pink color resembling a smooth strawberry milkshake.

As Raheem's manhood jerked inside Crystal, she firmly gripped Raheem's legs and dug her nails into his thighs as she turned her head slightly to tongue kiss him. Raheem momentarily winced in pain as the two interlocked tongues, but the pain he felt from Crystal's nails paled in comparison to the overwhelming satisfaction he felt from her warm, moist vaginal lips which enclosed his hardened, pulsating manhood.

Crystal moaned directly into Raheem's mouth, further exciting him and increasing the intensity of his orgasm, which in turn heightened Crystal's pleasure. Crystal continued to grind against Raheem until she reached the peak of her stimulation. She discontinued kissing Raheem in order to catch her breath. Crystal immediately released a series of loud moans and shrieks as her naked, glistening body convulsed on top of the man. She tried to brace herself with her feet, but they slipped along the slick floor of the bathtub. Crystal grabbed and pulled Raheem's long chin hairs with one hand as she continued to dig her nails in his thigh with the other. This continued for roughly thirty second before she abruptly lowered her legs, released her grip on Raheem and laid back against his chest. Crystal gently caressed Raheem's leg as he held her around her waist and softly kissed her back.

"Damn, baby!" Crystal exclaimed in sheer delight.

"'Damn' is right!" Raheem sighed, his voice even lower than it had been the last time he spoke. "Talk about the softest place on Earth! Shit! Your box is the truth!"

Chapter 10

After the young couple reached their climax, Crystal relaxed on Raheem's lap for several minutes before she stood up. The shapely young woman braced herself by grasping the edges of the tub and slowly rose, soap suds and water dripping from her voluptuous frame. Raheem watched her longingly as she carefully tip-toed across the bathroom, retrieved a towel and wrapped herself in it. He felt as if he was watching an exotic, seductive actress in a scene from an erotic movie. The only difference was, this time, he played the leading male co-star.

"You feel like smoking some tree?" Raheem proposed.

"Yeah, I'm down."

"You mind rolling up while I take a shower?" Raheem asked reluctantly. "I'll go grab the tree and the roll-up out of my bag. You can grab that Henny too if you wanna drink while you wait for me."

"That sounds good to me. I actually need to take a shower too," Crystal replied with a smile as she looked at Raheem's reflection from behind her in the large bathroom mirror which covered the entire top half of the wall.

Raheem stood up and scurried out of the bathroom, into the bedroom portion of their motel room. He quickly retrieved a quarter-ounce of marijuana, a grinder and a wrap and zipped his bag closed. As he turned around, Crystal approached him from behind and he handed her the instruments so she could prepare the marijuana for their consumption.

"You want to take a shot with me before you hop in the shower?" Crystal asked cheerily. "The bottle is in the fridge, right?"

"Yeah. Good looking, ma. You want to take your shower first?"

"Naw, you go ahead, daddy. I can wait," Crystal softly replied as she poured a small amount of the brown liquor into two plastic cups and handed one to Raheem. "To new beginnings, the Universe bringing us together and the best sex I've ever had! Cheers!"

"I co-sign that toast," Raheem chuckled. "Cheers!"

The two touched glasses before quickly swallowing their bitter-sweet beverages.

"Ugh," Raheem grunted to alleviate the burning sensation the liquor sent coursing through his insides. "You sure you don't want to take a shower first?"

"Thanks Raheem, but no, love. You can go ahead. Wash that manly sex-funk off your ball-sack," Crystal chuckled.

"Alright sexy. I'ma take a quick shower. I'll be out in a minute."

Raheem smiled and pecked Crystal on the lips before grabbing his cell phone, walking into the bathroom and closing the door behind him. He turned the shower water on, adjusted the temperature and sat down on the toilet with his phone in hand.

Raheem thought for a moment about how considerate Crystal seemed to be. She was the polar opposite of his wife. He had initially retrieved his phone so he could listen to music while he showered, but the thought of his wife motivated him to check for any missed calls or text message notifications from Kim or his parents.

"Still nothing? Word?" Raheem huffed to himself. "See… they really don't give a fuck about me! They probably planned the whole shit. It's whatever, though. Fuck 'em!"

The disgruntled young man opened a music streaming app on his phone, picked a playlist and hopped in the shower. As soon as the warm water touched Raheem's face, the calloused, emotionless, nonchalant role he was attempting to play dissipated. Tears streamed from his eyes and mixed with the shower water. The emotional pain Raheem felt from his parents and his wife turning their backs on him and not even attempting to reach out to him almost a full day later was too much for him to bear at the moment. The physically strong, young, Black man grew emotionally weak and sobbed for several minutes as he allowed the water to roll down his face.

"Alright nigga! Time to stop bitching," Raheem commanded himself under his breath. "You have this super-bad jawn waiting on you, rolling up in the other room wearing nothing but a towel and a smile. Fuck Kim and fuck your parents. They don't care, so neither should you!"

Raheem gained control of his emotions and lathered his washcloth full of soapy water. He began to scrub his body and sing along with the old Total and Notorious B.I.G. song which reverberated off the bathroom walls.

"Hey Raheem! Can I come in?" Crystal's soft voice called out after she tapped lightly on the bathroom door.

"Yeah, come on in. You good?"

Crystal strutted into the bathroom, slightly opened the shower curtain and peered in.

"Yeah, I'm good," Crystal assured her male companion. "I could be better though. Did you scrub your sack yet?"

"Yeah… but why are you so preoccupied with my balls, ma?" Raheem asked as he erupted in laughter.

"Isn't it obvious?" Crystal replied with a sly grin as she dropped her towel and carefully stepped into the shower, joining Raheem. She faced Raheem, standing close to him and began to kiss and lick his chest as she slowly stroked his manhood. Raheem's shaft quickly grew fully erect and Crystal proceeded to squat down in the shower. The young woman carefully placed Raheem's entire manhood in her mouth and slowly began to bob her head back and forth as she salivated and gently caressed his testicles.

Raheem groaned as he placed his hands on either side of Crystal's head and held her hair away from her face. He looked down at Crystal and marveled at her ability to continually administer fellatio under the constant flow of shower water running down her scalp and face without pausing to take a breath. Raheem let out a long sigh, bent his legs slightly and leaned back against the tiles as he enjoyed the sensation of Crystal's warm mouth coupled with the warm water streaming from the showerhead. The intoxicated young man went into a trance, his body overcome by testosterone, molly and passion. The soulful music echoed through the hotel bathroom and filled the couple's ears, further heightening their sensuality.

After what seemed like an eternity, Crystal abruptly unwrapped her lips from around Raheem's penis. By the time the young man realized Crystal had stopped performing oral sex on him, he opened his eyes to see her facing away from him, bending over with her hands resting on the opposite side of the tub. Her beautiful face was pointed downward towards the floor, while her perfectly shaped rear-end was pointed upward in his direction. Her vaginal lips protruded slightly, inviting Raheem to enter as the shower water splashed against her flesh and streamed down her shapely frame.

Raheem's fully erect penis pulsated along with the rest of his body. He was filled with carnal passion. The young man firmly gripped each of Crystal's rear cheeks, inserted his private parts into hers and began to rapidly pump his manhood back and forth inside of her.

"Go slower, love," Crystal moaned as she reached her arm back and gently rested her hand on Raheem's thigh. Raheem immediately complied and slightly decreased the pace of his strokes. "Slower baby. Concentrate. Feel how my pussy is responding to your dick. This will be the best nut of our lives if you can slow down and catch the perfect rhythm. Ooooh! Yeah…"

Raheem braced himself, his feet planted as firmly as possible on the slippery floor of the tub while his hands firmly grasped Crystal's derriere. Raheem heeded Crystal's advice and began to focus his attention on the pulsations emanating from her vaginal canal as her lips rhythmically gripped and released his rod. Raheem began to rock back and forth, slowly, but deliberately as he matched the pace of the vibrations he felt from Crystal's pleasure center. Within less than a minute, he had perfectly synced his movements with the rhythm of her insides.

"Oh God… yes!"

Crystal moaned sensually as she gripped Raheem's leg with the hand she had previously rested on his thigh.

"Raheem… Oh shit, Raheem! Uhhhhhmmm…."

The sound of Crystal's ecstasy added to the sexual soundtrack and caused Raheem to feel sensations throughout his body which he had never before experienced. Raheem grew ever more sexually excited but concentrated on maintaining the same pace so as not to disturb their rhythm. Crystal's shrieks and moans grew increasingly sexier, louder and more frequent as Raheem kept up the pace. He focused all his energy into the act of responding to the communication between his and Crystal's enmeshed sexual organs. After several minutes, their movements were so in sync it was as if Crystal's lips were pulling Raheem's pole inside her without direction or intervention from either of them.

Raheem gazed down at Crystal's wet, naked body as it gracefully rocked forward and back again. Crystal's back was arched downward toward the floor of the tub while her round buttocks seductively jiggled as Raheem continued to penetrate her. He opened his mouth in an attempt to talk dirty to her, but Raheem's motor functions had to surrendered all their resources to his sexual pleasure. He attempted to speak but could do nothing but groan like an animal in the act of primal copulation.

The wet, synchronized sex continued for several more minutes before the couple reached mutual climax. The echoes of their ecstasy resonated throughout the motel bathroom so loudly they drowned out the sounds of bass, drums and vocal harmony originating from Raheem's phone.

Crystal slid away from Raheem, turned over and slowly dropped to the floor of the tub, laying on her back. She gazed up at Raheem sensually as the shower water bounced off their hot bodies before closing her eyes.

"You good?" Raheem asked as he stared down at his beautiful female companion.

"Good? Naw, King... I'm great! I just need to chill here for a minute. What you about to do?"

"I think I'ma have another drink and smoke. You want some more liquor?"

"Not right now, thanks, baby," Crystal declined. "I'll wait until I come back out. I just need to relax and enjoy this feeling for a while."

"I feel you," Raheem nodded with a smile as he turned off the shower and carefully stepped out of the tub. "I'll be in the bed waiting on you."

""Can you run the bath please, love?"

"No doubt."

Raheem closed the drain and turned the water back on, adjusting the temperature until Crystal nodded in approval. He retrieved his phone, exited the bathroom and closed the door behind him.

Chapter 11

Crystal and Raheem spent the remainder of the afternoon repeating the cycle of snorting molly, drinking alcohol, smoking weed and having tantric sex. After more than a dozen sessions of passionate, drug and alcohol fueled love-making, the couple drifted into sleep together in the queen-sized bed.

Less than two hours later, Raheem abruptly woke up from his sleep, panting rapidly and heavily. The young man was soaked in sweat. At the same time, his body was shivering as if he were freezing cold. He quickly sat up in the bed and looked frantically around the room, searching for a clue as to where he was. The blinds were drawn shut and the motel room was immersed in pure darkness. Raheem sat motionless in the bed, frozen by an irrational fear he could not understand.

"You okay, baby?" Crystal asked as she stirred in the large bed next to Raheem.

"Oh. Yeah, I'm cool," Raheem reassured his concerned lover. The sound of her voice had quickly brought him back to reality and reminded him of where he was. "I just had a bad dream, that's all."

"Poor baby," Crystal replied empathetically in the darkness as she sat up and rubbed Raheem's shoulder. "Oh my god, love! You're soaking wet! That must have been some dream!"

"Yeah, it was…"

"What was it about?" the young woman inquired curiously. Crystal used her hand to search the darkness and locate the switch for the lamp which sat on the nightstand located on her side of the bed. Once she found it, she turned the knob, illuminating the motel room. "You wanna talk about it?"

"I mean," Raheem hesitated. "I don't remember everything. This molly is really fucking with my memory. All I remember is before I woke up my parents' house got shot up and everybody was killed."

"Oh wow," Crystal gasped. "That's terrible! Good thing it was just a dream."

"I know, right?" Raheem concurred. "I need to take a shower. I feel nasty!"

"Okay, love. I'm gonna lay here and relax until you come out, then I'm gonna take a shower my damn self."

"Alright, bet. You hungry? We haven't eaten anything since this morning."

"Yeah, I guess eating dick and pussy doesn't count," Crystal chuckled. "But I'm still not very hungry, though. Maybe I'll be ready to eat by the time we finish taking showers. Are you hungry?"

"Honestly, not really," Raheem confessed. "The molly is probably suppressing our appetites. I think we should try to eat something before it gets too late, though."

"Yeah, it's dark as hell," the woman exclaimed. "What time is it?"

"It's almost nine-thirty," Raheem informed his companion as he looked at his phone. "I'ma hurry up and hop under this water so you can take a shower and we can figure out what we're gonna eat. We can go to a restaurant or order take-out. Try to figure out what you're in the mood to eat and I'll figure out where we should go."

"That works for me," Crystal replied as she located the television remote control, turned the television on and began surfing the channels. "You can use my speaker while you're in the shower if you want."

"Good looking. You're too thoughtful Crystal."

"I like you, Raheem. You seem to be a good guy and you're showing me love by letting me stay with you," Crystal explained. "I would be stranded in a strange city if it weren't for you. I'm just trying to return the favor and make sure you enjoy your time with me and don't regret letting me keep you company this weekend."

"I appreciate you, ma. I have no idea how I could ever regret spending time with you," Raheem replied matter-of-factly as he looked Crystal square in her mesmerizing, almost transparent eyes. "I already feel like running into you was the best thing that could have happened to me this weekend."

"I'm glad you feel that way, daddy! The feeling is mutual." Crystal smiled as she sat up, closed her eyes and pursed her lips, inviting a kiss from her male companion. Raheem complied, bent over the bed and pecked Crystal on her lips repeatedly before she gently gripped his long chin hairs and tongue-kissed him. As they kissed, several beads of sweat dripped from Raheem's saturated forehead and landed on Crystal's exposed breasts.

"My fault, shorty," Raheem exclaimed as he abruptly pulled away from the attractive young woman. "I'm sweating all over you! Let me hop in the shower."

"It's all good," Crystal laughed. "A little sweat ain't never hurt anybody! I've had your bodily fluids inside me… I'm not worried about it. But go ahead and freshen up, handsome."

"You're something else Crystal. I'm not used to a woman like you."

Raheem paused and looked down at Crystal, revealing a large grin of satisfaction. He bent over and gently kissed her on her forehead before turning and walking into the bathroom.

"That girl is amazing," Raheem said aloud to himself as he stood over the toilet and relieved himself. He lowered the lid and flushed the toilet before reaching into the shower and turning on the water. "I've never met anybody like her in my life!"

Raheem picked up his cell phone, enabled the Bluetooth feature and wirelessly connected his phone to the speaker. He sighed in frustration when he realized he still had not received any phone calls or text messages from his family.

"Family ain't shit, yo," Raheem huffed to himself as he opened his music streaming app, selected a playlist and slowly entered the shower as the music began to play.

Raheem had finished showering, drying and putting lotion on his body by the time three full songs had played in their entirety. He disconnected his phone from the speaker and exited the bathroom wearing nothing but boxer-briefs.

"Sexy, sexy!" Crystal chuckled as she cat-called Raheem when he exited the bathroom.

"You're a funny girl," Raheem laughed.

"And you're a sexy, chocolate man," Crystal retorted with a grin. "Let me hop my ass in the shower before I molest you again!"

"Don't start no shit, won't be no shit," Raheem smirked. "Did you figure out what you want to eat?"

"You mean, besides your meat?" Crystal asked slyly. "Naw, I hadn't really thought about it. I got preoccupied watching the news while you were in the shower. Philly is crazy! All these shootings and murders... They said there was a double-homicide in some neighborhood called Upper Darby. A man and a woman around my age were found dead in their apartment this afternoon. The man was beat to death and the woman was shot in the head. Isn't that horrible?"

"Oh shit! Yeah, that's fucked up," Raheem huffed as he shook his head. "Upper Darby actually isn't a neighborhood in Philly, though. It's a large suburb right outside the city. That's where I live. I mean, that's where I lived until yesterday. I'm basically homeless now..."

"I know you're stressed about that right now, Raheem," Crystal replied compassionately as she rose from the bed and gently embraced the man. "Try not to worry too much about that right now, though. I'm sure everything will work itself out. Besides, just think about it this way – you said that happened in your neighborhood? At least it wasn't you or anybody you know. Imagine how stressed you would be if somebody you know had just been murdered."

"True," Raheem reluctantly acknowledged. "Well, maybe you can try to figure out what you have a taste for while you're in the shower."

"I'll do my best, love. If not, we can just eat wherever you want to."

"That'll work," Raheem replied. "But I'm gonna need you to stop being so perfect or else I'm not gonna be able to trust you!"

"Yeah, whatever, nigga," Crystal laughed before pecking Raheem on his cheek. She grabbed her purse and scurried into the bathroom.

Raheem turned the television off and sat in silence for several minutes until he heard Crystal turn the shower on, followed by music from her Bluetooth speaker. He reached for his phone and searched the internet for details of the double-homicide in Upper Darby.

After searching for a few short seconds, Raheem found several articles on the local news sites about the murder. He read the articles in full, searching for details to help him figure out the identity of the victims. All three articles stated that the victim's identities had not yet been released. However, the location of the incident deeply troubled Raheem. The murders had occurred in the same apartment complex where Sarah and her boyfriend lived.

Raheem shook his head in frustration. The nagging feeling that his failing memory was preventing him from remembering whether he had committed a heinous act of violence worried him greatly. The young man sat motionless on the edge of the bed as he racked his brain in attempts to remember what occurred between him and Sarah after their first session of intercourse the previous night. He became so engrossed in his thoughts he didn't realize how quickly the time had passed until Crystal exited the bedroom.

"You okay, daddy?" Crystal asked when she saw Raheem still sitting in his underwear on the foot of the bed twenty minutes after she had entered the bathroom.

"Uh, yeah," Raheem lied. "I just got a lot on my mind."

"I'm sure. I'm sorry you're going through it, baby," Crystal softly responded as she strutted towards him wearing only a bra and panties. The seductive, young woman sat on Raheem's lap, wrapped her arms around the back of his neck and kissed him on his lips. "I promise to do everything in my power to make you feel better when we get back. I was thinking – can we get cheesesteaks since this is my first time in Philly?"

"Good idea! When in Rome, right?"

"Exactly," Crystal agreed as she stood up and retrieved a shirt and pants from her duffle bag. "Let's hurry up and go so we you can fuck my brains out when we get back!"

"Say no more!"

Raheem quickly rose from his seated position and rifled through his own duffle bag, pulling out a t-shirt and basketball shorts. He dressed quickly and sat back down on the bed as he watched Crystal slowly maneuver her way into her skin-tight jeans.

"You wanna do some more molly before we leave?" Raheem asked.

"Yessir," Crystal chuckled. "We might as well take a shot too. That is, unless you are already too tipsy. I don't want to get into an accident and crash that beautiful truck of yours."

"Yeah," Raheem hesitated. "I'll be good. I'm not worried about banging out."

Raheem reached into his duffle bag and retrieved the bag of molly as Crystal walked over to the refrigerator to grab the bottle of Hennessey.

"Oh shit," Raheem exclaimed as he examined the contents of the almost empty zipper-bag. "We mangled this shit!"

"I'm not really familiar with your Philly slang," Crystal chuckled. "But if by 'mangled' you mean we took almost all of it, then we 'mangled' the Henny too!"

The albino woman displayed the almost empty bottle as she approached Raheem. His eyes grew large in shock at the sight of the nearly empty bottle Crystal gripped.

"I guess time isn't the only thing that flies when you're having fun," Crystal joked. "Can you get some more molly? I'll pay for it."

"Yeah… uh, about that," Raheem started. "I kinda came up on this on the hum-bug. I only know of one nigga who sells quality molly and we're not really cool enough for me to ask him to sell me some…"

"Oh well, we might as well finish what we have and figure it out while we're out and about," Crystal suggested.

"Sounds like a plan," Raheem concurred.

Crystal poured the remainder of the brown liquor into the two plastic cups and handed one to Raheem. At the same time, he poured the remainder of the Crystalline powder onto the nightstand and separated the small mound into two equally proportioned lines. He gestured to Crystal indicating that she should snort her line first. Once she had done so, Raheem proceeded to bend over and inhale the second line into his nostril. Once the molly had made the short trip from the nightstand into the couple's bloodstreams, they raised their cups before quickly guzzling the small amounts of alcohol.

"You ready?" Raheem asked as he grunted and cleared his throat.

"Yes sir!"

"We out then. I don't know if you have ever heard of any cheesesteak places before, but I'm telling you… most of the places people hear about in other states ain't even that good. I know plenty of papi stores and local pizza places who make way better cheesesteaks than the famous spots people in other cities always hear about."

"We can go anywhere you want to go, love. I defer to your expertise," Crystal replied with a beautiful smile, revealing her perfectly aligned white teeth and healthy pink gums.

The couple exited the motel room, entered the Cadillac truck and pulled away from the building. The two listened to music and engaged in casual conversation as Raheem drove the approximately thirty-minute commute from the motel to his Delaware County neighborhood. He had the phone number for his favorite suburban pizza spot located on Baltimore Pike saved in his phone contacts, so he called and ordered their food while he drove.

Once they arrived, Raheem parked the truck on the main street, exited the vehicle and walked into the establishment to pick up their order. Within a few minutes, he returned to the Escalade and pulled away from the curb to return to the motel.

"Did you figure out where we can get some more molly?" Crystal inquired as Raheem approached Church Lane and began to make a right turn, heading towards Southwest Philadelphia.

"Naw, I was actually just trying to figure that out," Raheem confessed.

"Oh, okay," Crystal passively replied. "No pressure. I just figured I'd remind you before we got back to the hotel."

"It's all good," the young man replied. "You might not be trying to pressure me, but I definitely want some more asap!"

"We'll figure it out, love. Don't stress yourself about it."

"Oh shit! The law is behind me," Raheem exclaimed in a panic.

"Don't worry about it, baby. It's the weekend, so they probably don't have anything better to do than to try to catch people driving drunk. You'll be good, though. You don't seem drunk or anything."

"Yeah, but I'm riding dirty, though," Raheem nervously exclaimed. He pulled the vehicle to the side of the road and stared in the rearview mirror as the police officer exited his vehicle and cautiously approached the Escalade.

"Dirty?" a confused Crystal repeated. "Dirty, how?"

"Don't worry about it," Raheem abruptly instructed as he rolled down the driver's side window. "I'll handle it."

"License, registration and insurance," the officer commanded when he reached the open driver's side window of the truck.

"Can I ask why you pulled us over, officer?" Raheem asked timidly.

"License, registration and insurance," the officer repeated, a blank expression plastered across his face. His ghostly white complexion contrasted his slicked back hair which was dyed jet-black.

"Uh, officer," Raheem stuttered. "I have my license, but I can't find my registration and insurance card," Raheem lied.

"That's a pretty big bag of food. You must be hungry! Are you okay, son?" the officer questioned the young man as he shone his ultra-bright flashlight into the cabin of the vehicle. "You seem nervous... you're sweating bullets!"

"Yeah, I'm good," Raheem replied unconvincingly as he attempted to regain his composure. "It's just been a rough weekend so far. I had a bad argument with my family yesterday and I had to abruptly move out my house. Me and my girlfriend just came out to get something to eat. We're on our way back to our hotel room now."

"Oh... is that so?" the officer asked suspiciously as he unbuttoned the strap on his holster. "Step out the car please, sir."

"For what?" Raheem asked nervously, his raspy voice trembling.

"So I can conduct my investigation. Step out the vehicle please, sir."

"But, why? We didn't do anything wrong. We're minding our own business. We're just trying to get back to our hotel room so we can eat and chill, officer," Raheem protested.

"Step out of the vehicle immediately, sir, or I'll be forced to remove you," the officer barked as he unholstered his weapon, grasped the door handle with his other hand and opened the driver's side door of the large truck. "I'm not going to ask you again..."

Chapter 12

"Oh shit, Raheem!" Crystal shrieked as the Escalade sped away from the scene of the traffic-stop. "So, that's how y'all get down in Philly?"

"We're not even back in Philly yet," Raheem corrected his female companion. The irritation in his voice was apparent.

"Philly, Upper Darby, whatever!" Crystal snapped as she turned in her seat and stared out the large rear-window of the truck. She continued to look back at the flashing lights atop the police vehicle as the sight of the squad car and the police officer's lifeless body grew smaller until they were no longer visible from her perspective. "Okay... so, that's how y'all get down in *Pennsylvania*?"

"I guess they call it 'Pistolvania' for a reason," Raheem laughed nervously as he tried to focus on the road ahead.

"I'm a rider all day, Raheem," Crystal continued. "But that shit was crazy! I'm not upset with you, but I gotta be honest... I've never been that close to anybody getting shot before, let alone a cop!"

"Yeah... there's a first time for everything," Raheem replied nonchalantly.

"I didn't realize you had such a morbid sense of humor, Raheem," Crystal sharply replied. "But for real, I need some answers, love. What was he talking about when he said the truck came back as stolen when he ran the plates?"

"Okay," Raheem let out a heavy sigh before continuing. "Remember when I told you I came up on that molly on some random shit and that the only molly dealer I know personally is somebody I'm not cool with? Well, basically, he's my next-door neighbor's daughter's boyfriend. That was his molly and this is his truck. I ran into her after I left home last night. She was upset because she caught him cheating. We chilled and did molly, but I don't remember what happened after that."

"Oh, shit!" Crystal gasped in astonishment. "The molly really fucks your memory up pretty bad, huh?"

"That seems to be an understatement! I can't remember shit that happened after I took molly with her last night. That was actually my first time doing the shit."

"Wow... for real?" Crystal asked incredulously. "So... let me get this straight... you did molly for the first time with your neighbor's daughter and now you have her boyfriend's car, but you don't remember anything else?"

"Yeah. Pretty much," Raheem confirmed as he tapped the vehicle's brakes to fall in line with the speed limit when he crossed over Cobbs Creek Parkway and entered the Philadelphia city limits.

"Shit! That's crazy!"

"Another understatement," Raheem replied nonchalantly as he drove through Southwest Philadelphia.

"You seem really calm about this whole situation, Raheem," Crystal observed aloud.

"Do I? I must be a good actor, because I'm actually trying really hard not to lose it!"

"Aw, don't lose it, baby," Crystal attempted to comfort her partner as she gently rubbed his arm. "Everything will be okay. We'll get through it together. I got your back."

"Word? You really mean that?" Raheem's deep voice cracked as he turned and made eye-contact with Crystal when he stopped at the red light located at the intersection of 70th Street and Woodland Avenue. "You're probably just trying to spin me until you can get your phone and call the law to turn me in!"

"Now, if I wanted to call the cops I could have done that already," Crystal corrected her companion as she raised her cell phone in the air. "Why would I do that? You've looked out for me since we met this morning. I know we haven't even known each other a full twenty-four hours, but I feel like we've bonded. I have no idea what I would have done today if you hadn't approached me. I don't want to be without you now. Besides, I'm kind of an accomplice to the shit now…"

"I'm *so* sorry, Crystal," Raheem apologized as he suddenly burst into tears. "I don't know what the fuck is going on! I swear I didn't mean to get you caught up in this shit."

"Aw baby… don't feel bad," Crystal consoled Raheem as she gently rubbed his shoulder. "It will be okay. I guess we're the Black Bonnie and Clyde now!"

The young woman joked to diffuse the tension. Raheem regained his composure by the time the traffic light transitioned to green and he resumed driving.

"I gotta get rid of this truck!"

"Yeah, that would probably be smart," Crystal agreed. "But how are we gonna get around?"

"We need to get another car," Raheem stated grimly as he quickly darted his eyes at Crystal.

"Get another car?" Crystal asked, her interest piqued. "What do you plan on doing, love?"

"I don't want to do it, but we have to steal a different car…"

"You're gonna jack somebody, Raheem?" Crystal gasped.

"Does it really even make a difference now?" Raheem posed the question in an unintentionally sarcastic manner. "I just shot a fucking cop in the face!"

"Yeah, I guess you're right," Crystal agreed, ignoring the man's condescending tone. She knew he was under an immense amount of pressure and felt no need to add to it by addressing how he was speaking to her at the moment. "This shit is crazy. I can't believe this. Do you still have the gun? I didn't even know you had a gun!"

"Uh, yeah," Raheem hesitated as he revealed the firearm. "This is the molly dealer's ratchet. It was in the truck. I found it when I got to the hotel right before I saw you. I gotta get rid of it, but I damn-sure wasn't gonna leave it at the scene with my finger prints all over it!"

"That's smart," Crystal acknowledged. "But what are we gonna do if you get rid of the gun? It's probably not a good idea to be without one since you did just kill a cop."

"I thought about that too," Raheem admitted as he reached down and retrieved a police-department issued nine-millimeter handgun. "I grabbed the cop's burner before I hopped back in the wheel."

"Hmmmm," Crystal sighed as she nodded her head in approval. "You're smart, Raheem! I would have never guessed you were a criminal master-mind!"

"You got a lot of jokes! You better be glad you're so sexy," Raheem chuckled apprehensively.

"Don't forget loyal," Crystal replied confidently. "Oh, wait a second, Raheem! Slow down."

Raheem quickly complied with his crime-partner's demand and pumped the brakes as she frantically tapped his arm and pointed out the passenger's side window of the truck.

"What's up, sexy?"

"You see that dude double-parked in that alley, carrying bags from his trunk?" Crystal whispered. There was no real reason for the young woman to speak quietly since nobody else was in the truck with them and the windows were sealed closed. "Why don't we jack him and take his car?"

"Talk about a criminal master-mind," Raheem replied with a devious smile as he slowly turned the corner to ride around the block and enter the opposite side of the alley. "You're getting with the program pretty fast, huh, sexy? I guess you're not as innocent as you look!"

"Yeah, well… I guess that makes two of us," Crystal winked at her male companion in the darkness. "I'm just trying to survive out here like you are. Shit just got real back there! We gotta help each other even more now."

"You ain't never lied," Raheem acknowledged as he turned off his headlights when he approached the entrance of the alley. The young cop-killer's heart raced and he began perspiring heavily when he saw the target vehicle parked with its hazard lights blinking at the opposite end of the alley. He carefully handed the pistol he had used to shoot the police officer to Crystal and retrieved the firearm he had stolen from his victim. "You ready?"

"Yes sir," Crystal replied confidently. She gripped the forty-five-caliber firmly and cocked it back before placing it in her purse. She left her purse unzipped and positioned the firearm with the barrel pointed downward so the handle was partially exposed. "Stop here. I have an idea. Wait here for a second."

Crystal quickly opened the door and exited the vehicle without uttering another word. Raheem watched nervously as Crystal quickly walked about twenty feet down the alley until she approached the target. The middle-aged Black man had just returned from the inside of his house and was bent over his trunk retrieving more bags. Crystal approached cautiously as the man turned around with several plastic bags in each hand. The man began to trudge towards the back door of his house, seemingly oblivious to the sudden appearance of the unfamiliar light-skinned woman.

"Excuse me sir. I'm not from around here and I'm stranded. Can I use your phone real quick please?"

"What? Who's there?" the man paused, quickly turned around and squinted as he tried to locate the source of the voice in the darkness.

"Sorry to bother you, sir," the stranger continued. "I'm stranded and I was wondering if I could use your phone to call for help."

"What's that?" the older gentleman asked abrasively as he strained his eyes to see in the dark alley. "Who's there?"

"Fuck this," Raheem huffed as he jumped out of the Escalade, his gun in hand. Raheem quickly jogged down the alley, approaching Crystal and their middle-aged target. "Don't move," Raheem barked. The older gentleman's eyes grew large with fear when he heard the younger man's command and saw him rapidly approaching, his eyes glazed like a wild animal, a large pistol pointed in his direction. Crystal's innocent, helpless demeanor quickly vanished as she retrieved her weapon from her purse and pointed it at the couple's target.

"Oh shit!" the older man exclaimed. "What the hell are you doing, young-boy?"

"I'm taking your wheel," Raheem barked. "Drop the bags and get on the fucking ground! Face down!"

"Ain't this some bullshit?" the older man huffed as he slowly raised his arms, his bags in hand, bent his knees and slowly knelt to the ground.

"I said drop the fucking bags old-head!" Raheem commanded as he walked closer and leveled his gun at the older man's face from a distance of approximately five feet. "I'm not fucking playing with you. You really tryna get shot over a car? I know you got insurance on that pretty motherfucker!"

"Look young-boy," the man snapped. "I got insurance on that bitch, but not on these goddamn groceries! Don't make me ruin my food too! I have two-dozen eggs in one of these bags. I'm not even gonna be able to drive to the store to replace them and my wife needs this shit for her catering business. I'm dealing with enough bullshit with you... don't add to the drama, young-blood!"

Raheem chuckled as he quickly glanced at Crystal. She smiled at Raheem and shrugged her shoulders.

"You got it, O.G.," Raheem sighed. "I'm not trying to do you dirty, bro. Just give me your car keys so we can get the fuck outta here."

"Uh, okay," the man wearily replied as he finished laying face-down on the gravel. "The keys are in the back door of my house. Just take them."

"Alright. Don't fucking move bro," Raheem commanded as he slowly walked backwards towards the back door of his victim's home. He kept his gun pointed in the older man's direction.

"Alright man... alright! Just do what you came to do and leave me the fuck alone!"

Raheem cautiously approached the rear entrance of the man's residence and removed the keys from the lock. He ran back to the rear of the vehicle and slammed the trunk shut. The young larcenist nodded in his female companion's direction and opened the driver's side door of the older man's luxury vehicle.

"Come on, ma! We gotta dip! Sorry old-head. I wish I didn't have to do this to you, but you know how shit goes!"

Raheem quickly jumped into the vehicle, slammed the door and started the engine as he waited for Crystal to finish entering the passenger's side.

"Fuck you! Crazy, young punk!" the older man called out in the darkness as the two young criminals sped away in his prized Lexus. "I just bought that shit!"

Chapter 13

The powerful six-cylinder engine of the late model Lexus GS 350 roared as Raheem sped down Island Avenue in Southwest Philly. He hurriedly made his way to the ramp to I-95 South in an attempt to return to the safety of their motel room before their victim alerted the authorities of the car-jacking and the police started searching for the stolen vehicle.

"This jawn gets up," Raheem excitedly exclaimed as he gradually placed increased pressure on the gas pedal and cruised down the highway. "It rides smooth as shit too!"

"Yeah it does," Crystal agreed with a smirk as she reached over, unbuckled Raheem's belt, unzipped his pants and began to caress his penis. "But I'm worried about getting this *jawn* up so I can ride it smooth when we get back to the hotel!"

"Damn, babe," Raheem replied with a grin as he shifted his position slightly to make it easier for Crystal to stroke his private parts. "Let me find out you're a nympho!"

"Only for you, love," Crystal replied. "I know it sounds bad, but seeing you get all aggressive and take control of that situation was such a turn-on!"

"Oh, I see… you got a low-key gangster fetish, huh?" Raheem chuckled.

"Guilty!"

"Hey… whatever's clever, ma," Raheem smiled.

Crystal unbuckled her seat belt, leaned over in Raheem's direction, placed her wet lips around Raheem's penis and slowly bobbed her head up and down as he drove.

"Oh shit," Raheem exclaimed quietly as he slightly lifted his foot from the gas pedal. "Be careful, sexy. I'm not tryna bang out! We're almost at the exit for the hotel."

"Don't bang out then, baby," Crystal whispered as she momentarily removed her mouth from Raheem's manhood before she resumed administering fellatio.

Raheem attempted to concentrate on the road ahead as he simultaneously enjoyed the road-head and pondered how much he enjoyed spending time with Crystal. She seemed perfect for him. She was definitely a "rider" – she was down for whatever, extremely supportive and she didn't switch up on him when things didn't go as planned. He only wished they had met before – even a week prior. Raheem concluded that if they had met sooner, it was very likely that he wouldn't be on the run, facing a laundry-list of charges that would surely result in a life-sentence or the death penalty if the police ever caught up with him.

"We're around the corner from the telly," Raheem grunted as he exited the highway and turned onto the road leading to their motel.

"That's great," Crystal replied as she quickly discontinued performing oral sex on the man and sat back in the soft, leather passenger's seat. "That means we can do the damn-thing for real!"

Raheem carefully navigated the pot-hole-ridden driveway leading to the motel and parked the stolen luxury vehicle in front of the door of their room. The couple quickly exited the vehicle and rushed into the motel room. Crystal aggressively pushed Raheem onto the queen-sized bed and removed his pants as she crouched over him.

"Oh snap! We forgot the food in the car," Raheem exclaimed, perturbed.

"It's all good. We can worry about that later. I wanna eat *this* meat first," Crystal replied with a seductive smile before lowering her face into Raheem's crotch and lubricating his manhood with the saliva inside her mouth.

"Say no more," Raheem acquiesced as his words turned into unintelligible moans when Crystal rapidly began sucking his penis.

A few short minutes later, Crystal's oral prowess brought Raheem to his climax. She walked to the bathroom and quickly returned with a warm, wet washcloth. The attractive, young woman handed the rag to Raheem and returned to the restroom while Raheem wiped down his private parts and pulled his pants back up. He grabbed the keys to the stolen Lexus, walked outside and opened the rear driver's side door.

The young man retrieved the bag containing the cheesesteaks from the back seat and closed the door. He paused in mid-stride and decided to search the car before returning to his room.

Raheem walked around the vehicle, opened the passenger's side door and sat down. He bent over, opened the glove compartment door and rifled through its contents. He removed the registration, insurance card, owner's manual and other random contents, revealing a shiny, chrome forty-caliber handgun.

"Oh shit," Raheem exclaimed as he removed the handgun and examined it in the dim light provided by a lamp affixed to the side of the motel near his room door. "Shit could have gotten ugly if we ran up on old-head at the wrong time!"

Raheem returned the paperwork and other miscellaneous items to the glove compartment and shut the door before exiting the vehicle. He pressed a button on the electronic car key, causing the trunk-latch to release. The young fugitive opened the trunk, leaned in and searched inside. The trunk appeared to be empty and Raheem assumed the vehicle's previous owner had vacated the contents of the trunk before he had approached and demanded the keys.

Raheem closed the trunk, but then paused again and pressed the remote to open it and search once more. After doing so, he lifted the panel which concealed the spare tire.

"Good shit," Raheem exclaimed upon noticing a zipper-bag containing a green, leafy substance. He carefully removed the bag from inside the spare tire, held it up to the light and marveled when he realized the bag was filled to capacity. The young smoker's cheeks salivated when he unzipped the bag and smelled its contents. He quickly closed the trunk and jogged several steps until he had entered the relative safety of his motel room.

"Hey, daddy. What you got there?"

"Old-head was getting it," Raheem exclaimed as he tossed the bag of marijuana onto the bed and carefully placed the handgun on the nightstand.

"This has to be over a pound of loud right here!"

"Oh shit! That's lit," Crystal exclaimed. Her face beamed in excitement as she clapped excitedly. "You wanna smoke some now before we eat?"

"Sounds like a plan," Raheem nodded as he reached inside his duffle bag and retrieved a blunt and his grinder. "But I don't want to smoke too much of this shit. We can make a good amount of money if I sell this shit. Then we can use the money to get the fuck out the state before the cops catch up with us."

"That's an excellent idea," Crystal nodded. "But who are you gonna sell it to? We gotta be extra careful now, babe."

"You already know I'm on it, ma," Raheem replied resolutely as he placed several buds of the potent marijuana in his grinder and began to twist the top. "I'ma holla at my cousin out West Philly. He's a street nigga and most of his niggas smoke and hustle."

"Oh, okay. Cool," Crystal replied apprehensively. "I'm sure that shit we did to the cop has been on the news by now. You know how people act when a cop gets killed. People act like cops' lives are worth more than everybody else's and they shut everything down to try to find who did it. I'm not from Philly, but I feel like that 'blue lives matter' shit is universal! What if your cousin saw you on the news and knows the cops are looking for you? Do you trust him like that? You're not worried about him ratting you out when you come around?"

"Hell naw!" Raheem firmly replied. "Taj is sturdy as fuck! He's not just my cousin – he's my brother! Taj would never switch up on me!"

"Oh, okay. That's good. I would like to meet him one of these days since you speak so highly of him. Maybe you can see if he knows anybody with some molly. Hopefully he can help."

"Oh, shit! I almost forgot we took the last of that shit before we left earlier," Raheem exclaimed. "We definitely need more of that! We might be able to make that happen if I don't get locked up first," Raheem laughed nervously.

"Aw, baby… please don't think like that," Crystal protested. "Everything will be okay. I got your back!"

"You know what's crazy," Raheem replied as he finished licking the blunt, sealing it shut. "I really believe you. I appreciate you for that, ma. I've only known you a day and you've already shown me more loyalty than my own parents and my nut-ass wife!"

"Hey… what can I say? I'm a real one," Crystal smiled as she watched Raheem light the cigar full of marijuana, inhale and let out a harsh cough. "Damn, baby! You cool?"

"Ha-ha," Raheem laughed mockingly as he attempted to catch his breath. "Stop tryna play me! This is some good-ass weed! Let's see how you handle it. Here…"

Crystal extended her hand and Raheem passed her the lit blunt. She put it to her mouth and closed her lips around it suggestively as she glanced at her lover out of the corners of her eyes. The pale-skinned seductress dramatically sealed her eyelids as she inhaled deeply. Crystal held her breath for a half-a-minute and stifled the urge to cough as she slowly exhaled the pungent marijuana smoke through her nostrils. The young woman gradually opened her gem-like eyes as tears enveloped her pupils before she passed the blunt back to Raheem.

"Daaaaaaaamn! I'm impressed!" Raheem nodded his head approvingly before taking another long drag of the marijuana. "You really are a G!"

"Aw, come on, daddy! Don't tell me you already forgot how good I am at holding my breath," the young woman teased.

"Never that! Your head-game is unforgettable," Raheem replied with a devilish grin. "Smoking is a little different, though. I've been blowing since I was a young-boy and I can't even toke like that! Did you grow up in Cali or something?"

"No, but I spent a decent amount of time there. California really does have the best weed I've ever smoked!"

"I just thought about something." Raheem paused and took another drag of marijuana before handing the blunt back to Crystal. "We've been

130

doing all this wild shit together, fucking each other's brains out all weekend and I don't even know your last name or where you grew up!"

"I move around a lot," Crystal timidly confessed as she exhaled more smoke. "I'm kinda like a Black gypsy! I can't ever remember staying in more than one place for too long. It doesn't matter though. I'm here with you now. I'll stay with you for as long as you want or need me to."

Crystal stared at Raheem intently as she slowly handed him the half-smoked marijuana cigar. They locked eyes for a moment before Raheem placed the blunt in a make-shift ashtray located on the nightstand next to the bed. He immediately pounced on the woman, kissing her passionately. Crystal responded with equal passion and the couple interlocked tongues as Crystal hurriedly ripped her own pants off, followed by Raheem's.

The aroused young woman firmly clutched Raheem's lower back and pulled his pelvis into hers. She moaned loudly as his manhood penetrated her already soaked vagina, causing its walls to spasm and produce even more natural lubrication. Raheem pumped his hips as Crystal aggressively removed his shirt. She placed the palms of her hands against her lover's bare chest and applied gradual, steady pressure. He followed her direction and leaned back, until he was laid on his back. The beautiful, bottomless young woman straddled him and began to rock back and forth slowly.

"Fuck!" Raheem grunted as he gripped the woman's hips while she rode his manhood.

"Oh, Raheem! Oh baby... I love this dick!"

Crystal planted her palms against Raheem's chest and continued to slowly gyrate her pelvis as sweat trickled down her forehead, streamed down her chest, over her erect nipples and dripped onto Raheem's chiseled abdomen. The two aroused fugitives grunted and moaned for nearly twenty minutes as they enjoyed their sexual connection.

Suddenly, Crystal's body began to jerk and she shrieked in ecstasy as oxytocin hormones flooded every square inch of her body, inside and out. Her lashes fluttered rapidly as her light eyes rolled back into her head when her vaginal walls began to contract around Raheem's penis. The young man groaned deeply as his body and spirit reacted to Crystal's and joined her in sexual climax.

The remnants of the last dose of molly they had ingested earlier left their bodies along with the fluids which drained from their private parts and mixed on their flesh, flowing onto the linen.

"Oh… oh… shit, baby! Oh my god," Crystal panted as she brushed her hair from her eyes and fanned herself with her hand while she continued to straddle her sweaty companion. "Are you hungry, baby? Do you want me to heat up the cheesesteaks in the microwave so we can eat?"

"Naw, fuck those jawns," Raheem chuckled. "I'm not even hungry anymore. I'm about to pass the fuck out."

Sunday . . .

September 13, 2015

Chapter 14

Raheem slowly rolled over in bed and pulled the sheets over his head as the sun shone through the cracks in the vinyl blinds which hung from the motel window. He groaned in agony as his brain pulsated violently. The suddenly sober young man felt like his brain was trying to slowly expand until it cracked his skull and broke free from the inside of his cranium. Without opening his eyes, Raheem reached over to put his arm around Crystal but the only thing remaining on her side of the bed were two pillows.

"Crystal," Raheem called out faintly when he realized Crystal was not in bed with him. "Crystal... where you at, ma?"

Raheem slowly rose from the bed and stretched. The light intensified his headache, so he only opened his eyes partially as he stumbled to the bathroom and knocked on the door.

"Crystal," Raheem whimpered. "You in there?"

The groggy young man pushed the bathroom door open and walked in. He made his way to the toilet and urinated. Raheem's body swayed as he attempted to regain his balance.

"I wonder where she went. I don't even have her phone number to call and ask her what's up. I guess she changed her mind and decided to bounce on me. So much for all that talk about being a 'rider'," Raheem sighed and shook his head in disappointment after he flushed the toilet and washed his hands. He squinted as he stared at himself in the mirror while he rinsed the soap from his hands. "Damn... I look rough!"

Raheem slowly exited the bathroom, stumbled across the motel room and flopped down onto the soft, queen-sized mattress; rubbing his temples with his forefingers in an attempt to alleviate his intense headache. He slowly reached across the bed and retrieved his cell phone from the nightstand without opening his eyes, then squinted and entered the security code to unlock the screen.

"Oh shit! It's almost one in the afternoon," Raheem exclaimed. "I don't think I've ever slept that long in my whole life! I gotta stop bullshitting and get myself together!"

The tired young man opened his contact list, scrolled through it until he found his cousin's name and dialed the number.

"Yizzo," a cheerful voice answered after the phone rang several times. "What's good cuzzo?"

"Shit, my nig," Raheem faintly replied. "I gotta holla at you."
"Word? What's the deal?" Taj asked his older cousin. "You good, man?"

"Yeah," Raheem hesitated. "Shit has been kinda wild since you dropped me off on Friday."

"Aw shit," Taj chuckled. "Let me guess... family shit?"

"You already know, cuz," Raheem sighed. "You at the crib?"

"Yessir! You about to slide?"

"Alright, bet. I'm about to hop under this water and come get with you," Raheem informed his trusted first-cousin. "Can you meet me at the Walgreen's on Market Street? Oh, and please don't tell your moms you're linking up with me. I don't know if she has spoken to my pop and I don't need any extra drama or to pull you into the nut shit."

"She's at work now anyway, but say less I'll see you in a minute. Be safe cuzzo."

"Alright, cool. I'll be there in about an hour. See you soon."

Raheem disconnected the call and slowly rose from the bed. He stumbled over to his duffle bag and almost fell when he bent over to select the clothes he would wear after showering.

"Goddamn," Raheem exclaimed to himself as he stepped into the shower and the warm water cascaded down his sore frame. "I need to man up! I feel like garbage! I wonder if that molly shit can cause withdrawal symptoms if you stop taking it abruptly."

After showering, Raheem dressed and removed the remainder of his clothes from his duffle bag, replacing them with the stolen marijuana and firearm he found in the Lexus. He made up the bed, placed the "Do Not Disturb" sign on the outside of the door handle, entered the shiny, stolen vehicle and began his journey to West Philadelphia.

Raheem drove carefully, making sure to pay attention to his surroundings. He strictly adhered to the various speed limits on the different roads he navigated during his commute. The man grew nervous every time he passed a police squad car, but he made it to the assigned meeting place without being pulled over. The young fugitive spotted his cousin's Buick when he entered the Walgreen's parking lot.

"Okay cuz! I see you!" Taj excitedly greeted his cousin as he exited the Buick upon Raheem's arrival. "That shit is cleaner than a mug!"

"Oh, thanks," Raheem replied disingenuously as he exited the stolen Lexus and shook his cousin's hand. "What's good with you?"

"Ain't shit, cuz," Taj answered with a smile. "What the fuck is up with you? You said you had a rough weekend?"

"Shit, my nigga… you don't know the half," Raheem sighed as he shook his head.

"If I didn't know you I wouldn't be able to tell," Taj exclaimed. "I fuck with the new wheel! The shit is hard as fuck. You're looking stressed, though, cuz. What's going on?"

"Let's go somewhere to talk in private," Raheem nervously suggested.

"That works," Taj agreed. "You wanna give me a ride in your new wheel?"

"Um," Raheem hesitated. "We should probably take your car, if you don't mind. Let's find a back-block where we can park up so I can let you know what's up."

"Say less. We out!"

The two young men entered the older Buick and Taj drove away from the parking lot. He drove a few minutes until they found an area with very little traffic where Raheem felt comfortable talking.

"So, what's the deal cuz?" Taj asked. "I don't remember ever seeing you look this stressed. You tryna blow a Dutch?"

"Yeah, but I got some new shit I want you to try. That's part of the reason I needed to link with you. I came up on about a pound of loud and I'm tryna off it asap! I figured you might know a nigga who is tryna cop it for the low."

Raheem opened his duffle bag, pulled out the zipper-bag of exotic marijuana and handed it to his cousin. Taj unsealed the bag and smelled its contents.

"Aw shit," Taj exclaimed as the strong cannabis aroma consumed his nostrils. "Yeah, I'm tryna smoke this shit right the fuck now! Look at this bud! Where the fuck did you get this shit?"

"Yeah... that's not even important right now, cuz," Raheem hesitated. "I just need to off it asap..."

"Damn, nigga," Taj glanced at his older cousin inquisitively. "You acting like you robbed a nigga for this shit! Hold up... did you rob a nigga for this shit? Wasn't I just telling you to stay away from the street shit the other day? You went from zero to one-hundred real quick, cuz!"

"Yeah, but you don't even dig it, bro," Raheem explained as he placed several small marijuana buds in his grinder and twisted it while he spoke. "I've had the wildest weekend ever! I got into a crazy argument with my people after you dropped me off on Friday. My pop kicked me out and Kim's disloyal, nut-ass didn't say not one word to defend me! She was just standing there looking stupid! All them motherfuckers ain't shit! Everything I've done for my family and they turn around and do me like that over some nut-ass religion? That's that bullshit!"

"Stop playing," Taj exclaimed, surprised. "Uncle Has kicked you out? This happened on Friday?"

"Yeah, man," Raheem shook his head as he emptied the contents of the weed grinder into a wrap. "Please don't tell me this is the first time you're hearing about this!"

"Nigga! I already told you they don't tell me or my mom shit anymore," Taj sighed.

"That's fucked up, yo," Raheem exclaimed after lighting the rolled blunt, taking a few puffs and passing it to his cousin. "They've been acting real nutty since they converted."

"You ain't never lied," Taj concurred as he exhaled a hearty amount of marijuana smoke and passed the drug back to his cousin. "White Jesus really has niggas' souls on lockdown! Niggas' brainwashed like shit! Imagine all the shit we could accomplish if we had that same type of mind-control over just a couple people! Niggas could run the world! I'm about to convert from Islam and start my own damn religion!"

"Let me know how that works out," Raheem chuckled as he puffed on the pungent greenery. "It's corny as shit! I haven't heard from none of these motherfuckers since I left the crib Friday night."

Oh, word? Yeah, that's dirty," Taj sympathized with his cousin. "But on some real shit, I'm kinda pissed at you right now! I mean, you obviously been handling shit by the looks of that brand-new Lex you pulled up in! I'm your cousin, though, my nigga! You should have called me! I just told you that you could stay with us if shit went south with your people. Where you been staying?"

"I've been staying at one of the hotels near the airport," Raheem reluctantly confessed. "I met this bad, Black albino jawn too! She stayed with me the past couple days."

"Aw shit, nigga! That's why I haven't heard from you," Taj laughed heartily as Raheem passed the lit blunt back to him. "You finally got some new pussy, huh? What about that bad jawn we met at the beer store before I dropped you off at the crib on Friday? Why didn't you link up with her?"

"Yeah, man… I'm not even really trying to talk about bitches right now, though," Raheem quickly changed the subject. "Do you know of anybody who would want to buy the whole pound? I need bread to get a crib, like yesterday!"

"No doubt," Taj replied confidently as he coughed and choked on the weed smoke. "This shit is fire! I would buy it myself if I had the bread! How much you want for it?"

"I'll let the whole thing go for fifteen-hundred. You know anybody who would be able to cop it today… like now?"

"Yeah," Taj replied as he stroked his chin. "I was locked up with these niggas from Chester who get it the fuck popping. I was cool with these two niggas who were booked for a body, but they beat that jawn. The witness didn't show up to court, if you know what I mean. They actually got out a month before I made bail. I just talked to the one nigga yesterday. I'll holla at him now."

"Alright, bet. One more thing, though," Raheem hesitated as his cousin pulled out his cell phone and searched his call log for his associate's phone number. "You know anybody who has molly on deck? Good shit, though. No bullshit."

"Molly? What you know about that shit, cuz?"

"I know a little something," Raheem replied nonchalantly.

"Since when?" Taj asked incredulously. "You know that molly shit is a whole different game. How you gonna off some molly if you don't even have any clientele for this bomb-ass tree? You know that shit costs a grip, right?"

"I linked up with some people who fuck with it," Raheem replied, only partly telling the truth. "I'm not gonna buy a lot at first – maybe a half-ounce just until I see how it moves."

"You sure you wanna get down like that, cuz?" a concerned Taj asked his older cousin. "I know you're going through it with the fam right now, but I really think you should just wait and see what happens. If your money is fucked up you should check out of that nut-ass hotel and come stay with me and my mom until you save some bread up. That way, you can get a crib even if you and Kim don't get back together. I just don't want you to end up like me... getting booked and shit. You know once you're in the system the white man does everything to make sure you stay in the system!"

"I feel you, cuz. I appreciate your advice and your offer but I gotta handle my business. I'm pushing thirty, my nigga – What would I look like sleeping on my cousin's couch in my aunt's basement!"

"You would look like a nigga who has family who fucks with you even if your wife and parents don't," Taj answered assertively. "Look, cuz... I understand you're a grown man and you're gonna do what you feel like you need to do, but I just feel like the streets ain't your twist. I'm not trying to insult you at all. I know you ain't no bitch, I'm just saying, aren't you a little too old to be trying to get into the street-life now?"

"It ain't even a choice at this point, Taj," Raheem confessed. "I know you've always been the street-nigga of the family, but I'm still your older cousin! Don't sleep on a nigga! I'll be good."

"Ha! Okay, my fault, cuz. Let me hit this nigga up and see what's good."

Taj dialed his associate's number and placed the phone on speaker while it rang.

"Yo, Philly! What's up, boy?" a loud, deep, slurred voice echoed through the speaker of Taj's phone.

"Yo, Man-Man," Taj replied. "You're on speaker. You sound like you're already on one, my nigga!"

"Come on, bro… you know how I rock," Man-Man replied as he let out a hearty laugh. "So, what's the move?"

"I got my cousin with me and he has some work for the super-low. You want to link to see if you're tryna grab?"

"That'll work. Come through."

"You want us to come to the spot?" Taj asked.

"You already know," the intoxicated, young killer replied.

"Oh, hold up," Taj interjected. "You or anybody you know have any E-pills or molly on deck?"

"It's around. We'll talk when you get here," Man-Man concisely replied.

"Say less. We're on our way," Taj replied before disconnecting the call and turning to address his cousin. "It's on. You ready?"

"I'm waiting on you, cuz. That nigga's name is 'Man-Man?' That's a young-boy nickname! How old is that nigga?" Raheem asked in a condescending tone.

"He's your age," Taj chuckled. "Don't say shit to him, though. That nigga is shot the fuck out. I guess when you're a known shooter you can be grown and still let niggas call you 'Man-Man' because ain't nobody gonna talk shit! He's cool, though."

"If you say so," Raheem sighed. "That's why I stay the fuck outta Chester. The niggas *and* the bitches crazy out there!"

"Well, you're gonna have to get over that shit because we'll be there in twenty minutes," Taj informed his cousin as he drove away from the curb. "And please don't start with that shit-talking about Chester. I dealt with so much bullshit while I was in the County. There was all this Philly-Chester beef in there and Philly niggas were mad at me for being cool with Chester niggas. I had to run down on a few niggas in there behind that bullshit!"

"Word? My fault. I didn't even know it was like that," Raheem replied in shock.

"Yeah, nigga, neither did I! That's why I'm tryna tell you – this street shit comes with a lot of bullshit niggas don't know nothing about until they're knee-deep in it!"

"I feel you, cuz. I appreciate the advice."

Taj increased the volume of his stereo while Raheem rolled another blunt full of marijuana. The cousins smoked and enjoyed the sound of rapper, Troy Ave's "Major Without a Deal" mixtape as the Buick floated through traffic on their way to the city of Chester.

Chapter 15

"Who is it?" a gruff voice aggressively called out from behind the closed door of the dilapidated rowhome.

"It's me, nigga! You already know!"

"Philly? My nigga!" the tall, stocky, dark-skinned man greeted Taj with a smile after unlocking and opening the door. Man-Man reached behind his back and placed his gun in his pants where it had been concealed before he unlocked the door. He extended his right arm and shook Taj's hand. "This is your peoples you was telling me about?"

"Yeah," Taj confirmed. "Man-Man, this is Heem. Heem, Man-Man."

"What's up bro?" Raheem greeted the large, heavily-tattooed young man as they exchanged handshakes.

"What's the deal, fam?"

Man-Man stepped outside, allowing Raheem and Taj to enter the house. In his usual fashion when conducting illegal business from the residence, he quickly looked around outside, surveying the block and searching for any unfamiliar faces or vehicles. After perusing to his satisfaction, he reentered the house. He did not possess the deed to the home, but he and all the other residents of the neighborhood knew Man-Man "owned" the entire block.

"Come on, y'all."

Man-Man walked through the vestibule, past Taj and Raheem and led the way to the living room where two of his associates waited. The young men were seated on the sofa. The dark-skinned man was seated upright, rolling marijuana into a natural-leaf cigar while the light-skinned man was sprawled out on the sofa with the television remote in hand, scrolling through the channels. Both men were heavily tattooed – ninety percent of their exposed flesh was covered in body ink.

"Yo, Black! Gunz! This is my nigga, Philly, I was telling y'all about," Man-Man loudly informed his associates.

"What up?" Black, the dark-skinned man casually greeted the two guests.

"Yizzo," Gunz replied without looking away from the television.

"I met you before, Black" Taj informed Black as he approached him, his arm extended to shake the man's hand.

"Oh, my fault, my nigga," Black replied as his eyes lit up. He quickly jumped up from the sofa, brushed the marijuana crumbs from his pants and shook Taj's hand. "I be high as shit, dog. You was locked up with my cousin, right?"

"You already know," Taj chuckled. "I met you when I got out."

"Yo, Gunz," Black excitedly continued as he turned to address his light-skinned friend. "This nigga, Philly, held my cousin down in the Hill while we were holding him down in the streets! Wasn't he, Man-Man?"

"Yeah, my nigga! Philly's thorough as shit," Man-Man confirmed. "He was the only Philly nigga on the block in the Hill who wasn't on no nut shit. And there was mostly Philly niggas and the ops from the other side of the hood in there! This nigga held it the fuck down for a nigga!"

"That's what's up," Gunz replied as he abruptly discontinued channel surfing, dropped the remote and rose from the sofa to shake Taj's hand.

"That wasn't about nothing," Taj humbly replied, shrugging his shoulders. "Man-Man was my cellie and he seemed like a cool nigga, so when I heard niggas plotting I let him know what was up. Niggas got it popping before they could get the drop on him."

"That's why I fucks with this nigga, Philly," Man-Man exclaimed as he patted Taj on his shoulder. "So, you said you tryna handle some business?"

"Yeah," Raheem quickly interjected. "My cousin said y'all got that molly on deck..."

"Hold up," Man-Man interrupted before Raheem could continue. "I thought Philly said you're selling some work for the low!"

"Yeah, I am," Raheem impatiently replied. "But I'm only offing this shit for the low so I can grab the molly. I'm really trying to do a trade, so if you don't have any, then it's not even worth it."

"It's around," Gunz casually replied as he huffed and looked Raheem up and down, sizing the man up. "But I know you ain't come up in my man's crib to cop work with no bread, assuming niggas want to trade. This ain't Africa, motherfucker! You want to grab some work, you better bring that bread next time, nigga. I don't know how niggas get down in your hood, but this is Chester, nigga!"

"Slow down, Heem," Taj calmly instructed his older cousin. "Show them the work, cuz."

"Chill, Gunz," Man-Man interjected. "It ain't that deep. Let my man's cousin show us the work before you start talking about how you don't wanna trade! Besides, don't you trade that molly shit for percs with your cousin all the time anyway?"

"Yeah, but that's my cousin and that ain't none of these niggas' business! That ain't got shit to do with what's going on now," Gunz sharply replied before turning to address Raheem. "Where's the tree?"

"Check this shit out," Raheem discreetly rolled his eyes as he feigned enthusiasm to conduct business with the aggressive young man known as "Gunz." He unzipped his duffle bag and retrieved the sandwich bag full of marijuana before bypassing Gunz and handing it directly to Man-Man. "That's a whole P of Grade-A loud, straight from Cali."

"Oh shit," Man-Man exclaimed as he placed his face near the open zipper-bag and the strong aroma filled his nostrils. "Yeah, we need to smoke some of this shit! How much you want for the whole jawn?"

"I'm selling the whole pound for fifteen-hundred," Raheem replied. "So, you can just give me an ounce of molly for it."

"Smell this shit, fam," Man-Man instructed as he passed the bag of marijuana to his cousin, Black. "What you think?"

144

"Ooh-wee! Yeah, I'm tryna roll an L of this shit asap," Black excitedly replied as he held the open bag up to Gunz's nose. "This shit smells good as fuck, right, my nigga?"

"Yeah, it's alright," Gunz replied nonchalantly. "That don't mean shit, though! How does it smoke?"

"There's only one way to find out," Man-Man loudly interjected. "Let's roll up. Then you can see if you're tryna trade with this nigga!"

"Hold up, though," Raheem irritably replied as he observed Man-Man pull a blunt wrap from the pocket of his cargo shorts. "That's cool... y'all can smoke my shit and all that. But shouldn't you let me test the molly too, though?"

"This nigga," Gunz huffed as he dramatically threw his arms in the air.

"Chill, Gunz," Man-Man interrupted his friend's mild temper-tantrum. "He's right, though! It's only fair. Let him get some of the powder."

"You right," Gunz sighed as he cut his eyes at Raheem before slowly turning and walking to the rear of the house. Raheem glared at the light-skinned man.

"Don't mind my nigga, Gunz," Black addressed Raheem when he noticed his guest's perturbed expression. "He's been snapping the past couple days. That nigga pops mad Perc 30s and he ain't had none all weekend, so he's in his bag. He needs to smoke some of this good shit you brought so he can chill the fuck out!"

"Yeah... it's cool," Raheem nonchalantly replied as he nodded his head and shrugged his shoulders.

"Fuck that nigga," Raheem thought to himself. "This tatted face, dumb nigga probably thinks he's tough because his dickhead homies call him 'Gunz!' The fuck kinda name is that? This nigga doesn't know me! I'll fuck around and bust his bitch-ass with his own '*gunz*' if he doesn't chill with all that tough shit!"

"Here," Gunz abruptly addressed Raheem when he reentered the living room. He walked past the other young men and placed a zipper-bag containing a quarter-pound of crystalline molly powder onto the living room table. The slim, muscular young man begrudgingly opened the bag and retrieved a switch-blade from his pocket before scooping a small mound of the molly onto the glass-top table. "Do your thing, nigga."

"Y'all might as well go ahead and smoke," Raheem nervously suggested. "Didn't you already roll up?"

"Man, fuck that bullshit Black was about to spark," Man-Man's voice boomed. "I'm tryna smoke some of this shit right here!"

"You got it."

"Say no more," Man-Man chuckled as he picked several large marijuana buds from the bag and crushed them between his fat fingers. He sprinkled the sticky green dust into the open natural-leaf wrap until it was filled to capacity before rolling and sealing the cigar. He lit the large blunt and inhaled deeply before coughing hoarsely and quickly passing the marijuana to Gunz. "This shit right here, nigga! This shit, right here!"

The three men laughed at Man-Man's appropriately timed comedic reference to a popular classic Katt Williams stand-up routine. Across the room, Raheem hesitated as he noticed Taj watching him. He took his own knife from his pocket and used it to scoop a small amount of the molly onto the tip of the blade. Raheem was apprehensive when he remembered his cousin did not know he had taken molly before. Snorting the powder now would directly contradict the story he had told Taj about why he wanted to obtain the illicit substance in the first place.

"Fuck it! I guess I gotta test it, right," Raheem nervously asked, shrugging his shoulders as he barely made eye-contact with his younger cousin.

"Yeah… I guess so," Taj shrugged as he shook his head, turned and approached the other men to fall in line with the blunt rotation.

As soon as Taj had engaged in conversation with Man-Man, Black and Gunz; Raheem quickly snorted the mound of molly from the tip of his blade. He rapidly scooped another small mound onto his blade and snorted it before repeating the process two more times in rapid succession.

"Shit," Raheem sighed quietly as he sat down in the chair next to the dining room table when his head began to spin. He instantly felt a surge of energy as his body responded when the drug rapidly infiltrated his bloodstream and took over his senses.

"Yo, nigga… you said you tryna trade this whole jawn for an ounce of that molly?" Gunz turned and asked Raheem as he exhaled the pungent marijuana smoke through his nostrils.

"Yessir," Raheem excitedly replied as he began to sweat profusely and quickly tapped his foot on the hardwood floor. "You fucking with it, huh," Raheem beamed.

"Yeah, it's cool," Gunz gruffly replied. "I'll break the ounce down and bag it up for you in a minute."

"Alright, alright! Bet, my nigga! Good shit," Raheem smiled as sweat trickled down his forehead.

"You cool?" Gunz hesitated as he stared at Raheem suspiciously. "You look like you're tweaking, nigga!"

"Yeah, I'm good," Raheem quickly answered as he jumped up from the chair. "Yo, Man-Man! Can I get some water?"

"Yeah, it's gonna be Chester City tap water, though! Unless you wanna run to the papi store and get a bottle…"

"Can I use your bathroom?" Raheem interrupted.

"Yeah," Man-Man slowly replied. He was irritated by Raheem's abruptness, but he figured he'd let the disrespect slide since Raheem was "Philly's" cousin. "Down the hall to the left."

"Good look," Raheem nodded as he briskly walked past the group of young men and disappeared down the narrow hallway. He walked to the end of the hallway and opened a door which led into the master bedroom.

"Wrong room, fam," Man-Man called out when he heard the jingle of the bell he had affixed to the back of his bedroom door. "It's the door to the left of that one."

"Oh, my fault," Raheem nervously called out as he partly closed the bedroom door. "I got it."

Raheem quickly entered the bathroom and closed the door behind him. He ran the cold water from the sink's faucet, bent over and drank directly from the spicket for several minutes before splashing the cold water onto his perspiring face. He then stood upright and stared at himself in the mirror. He relished the surge of energy he received from the drug as his body grew warm. Raheem leaned in closer to the mirror and rubbed his wet face when he noticed his pupils growing large. The young man felt as if his brain was bouncing around loose within his skull and as if his veins and internal organs were dancing along to the rhythm of his rapidly increasing heartbeat.

"Yo, Philly. What's up with your cousin, yo," Man-Man quietly chuckled as Taj passed him the marijuana. "Is he cool?"

"Yeah… he's cool," Taj hesitated. "He's just going through it right now."

"Breaking News: It's been a bloody weekend in Upper Darby with the fatal shooting of a veteran police officer last night on Baltimore Pike shortly following the discovery of a gruesome double-homicide in an apartment complex on Marshall Road. Authorities believe the incidents may be related. More details along with the identities of the victims – after the commercial break."

"Damn, Upper Darby niggas tryna get it popping like how we do out here, huh?" Black chuckled. "Don't those niggas know we're the hardest in The County?"

"Yo!" Gunz suddenly exclaimed, startling the other men. He let out a large groan as he pointed to the television. "That's my fucking cousin!"

"Who? That goofy nigga on the car commercial?" Black asked with a puzzled facial expression as he turned around to face the television and noticed an advertisement for a local dealership.

"No, dickhead!" Gunz huffed as he marched over to the sofa and retrieved the remote. He pushed the "rewind" button as he used the DVR to backtrack the live television broadcast until the picture of a middle-aged, white police officer and the images of a young, Black man and woman were plastered across the high-resolution screen. "That's my cousin, Marcus and his babe, Sarah! Yo! What the fuck, dog! My cuz got murdered!"

148

"Oh shit! That *is* Marcus!" Black and Man-Man stated in unison.

"Damn, Gunz," Man-Man sighed as he approached his friend and patted him on his shoulder. "That's fucked up. Marcus was a cool nigga. Probably some hating-ass, pussy nigga. We'll find out who did it and bust they ass."

"Yo, Gunz. I'm sorry for your loss, man," Taj sympathetically began. "That's crazy, yo. I just remembered I saw that shit on the news earlier. I didn't know them, but the girl is my cousin, Heem's neighbor."

"Small city, huh?" Black sighed and shook his head. "I'm sorry Gunz. We're gonna get the nigga who did that shit. You already know."

"Y'all knew my cousin?" Gunz abruptly asked Taj, ignoring Black's condolences.

"Uh… I'm not sure if he knows your cousin," Taj hesitated. "I don't know either of them but I just met her at the store around the corner from Heem's crib the other day. He told me she was his next-door neighbor's daughter."

"Oh, for real?" Gunz asked suspiciously. "And where did he say he got the tree from?"

"He didn't say. You gotta talk to him about that," Taj sternly replied as his relaxed demeanor transitioned and he intuitively activated his internal defense system. "I just made the phone call."

"And you came out here with him too," Gunz continued aggressively. "My mans knows you and all that, but I don't know you like that! Now I find out my cousin got killed and some random Upper Darby niggas from out his way pop up with a pound of loud for the low. What type time you on, my nigga?"

"First off," Taj abruptly replied. "We ain't no Upper Darby niggas! We're both from West Philly. My cousin moved out the County last year, even though that ain't got shit to do with what the fuck you're talking about. I'm sorry for your loss, but that shit has nothing to do with what we came up here for."

"Yo, Gunz. Chill, my nigga," Man-Man interjected. "You're getting hyped with the wrong nigga, bro. Save that energy for the niggas who did that shit to Marcus and his babe!"

"How the fuck am I supposed to know these ain't the niggas who did that shit to Marcus and Sarah?" Gunz snapped as he walked over to the sofa, reached down and retrieved a pistol.

"Chill nigga," Man-Man excitedly commanded his enraged light-skinned associate. "I can't vouch for his cousin but Philly is good-money. I vouch for my nigga and I put that on my momma! Put the fucking ratchet down!"

"Fuck that!" Gunz protested. "Where the fuck is your goofy-ass cousin? The fuck is taking him so long in the goddamn bathroom?"

"Yo, nigga," Man-Man loudly called out as he marched down the hallway to the bathroom and aggressively knocked on the door before opening it. Raheem was startled by Man-Man's abrupt entry and jumped and hit his mouth on the faucet, busting his lip. "Come on, nigga. My nigga, Gunz, wants to holla at you."

Raheem quickly complied and followed Man-Man back to the living room. His mouth was sore, but he was so elated from the effects of the molly, the pain didn't negatively impact his mood. Raheem cheerily strutted into the living room behind Man-Man, oblivious to the confrontation which had ensued moments beforehand. Raheem's smile quickly disappeared when he entered the living room and noticed the tense expressions on the men's faces. The fact that Gunz was firmly gripping a firearm and pacing the room in a frenzy also caused him great alarm.

"What's good?" Raheem asked timidly as he entered the living room and walked until he was standing next to his cousin, Taj.

"My paranoid-ass homey just found out his cousin got killed yesterday and he wants to ask you if you know anything about it," Man-Man informed Raheem matter-of-factly.

"Niggas love calling a nigga paranoid just 'cause a nigga pops percs! Fuck all that 'paranoid' shit!" Gunz barked as saliva flew from his lips. "Your cousin said you knew my cousin and his bitch!"

Gunz pointed his gun towards the paused television, directing Raheem's attention to the large images of Marcus and Sarah which were still plastered across the screen.

"Oh, shit," Raheem attempted to act surprised when he saw the images on the screen. He was, in fact, truly surprised to learn that Gunz was related to his first victim. He was startled to see their images on the news, along with the heading, "Bloody Weekend in Upper Darby."

"The fuck is the deal, yo?" Gunz continued. "Where did you get that work from and why you selling it so cheap?"

"Look, man," Raheem replied cautiously. "I'm sorry for your loss, but if you think I robbed your cousin for this tree, you're dead wrong."

"So, you didn't know my cousin?" Gunz asked incredulously.

"Naw, I never met him," Raheem lied. "I barely knew Sarah. Her parents are my parents' next-door neighbors, so I only met her about a dozen times."

"So, you didn't know my cousin had molly on deck?" Gunz continued his line of questioning.

"Think about it, my nigga," Raheem replied. "Why would I risk coming all the way out here if I knew a nigga around the corner had it?"

"Philly's cousin does have a valid point," Man-Man added. "Just chill out, and let's smoke and pour some liquor, bro. We'll figure out who did that shit and go get them niggas after Philly and his cousin dip."

"Alright... I guess so," Gunz hesitated.

"I got that bottle of Henny Black I've been saving. Let's go grab it from the kitchen," Man-Man suggested. "We can pop that jawn in Marcus' memory."

"Alright, bet," Gunz reluctantly agreed as he and the other men followed Man-Man into the kitchen.

Raheem hesitated as he eyed the quarter-pound of molly sitting alone on the dining room table. He remained alone in the living room as the bag enticed him. The open zipper mechanism resembled an open mouth to the intoxicated young man and he swore he could hear the bag whispering – beckoning him to place it inside his pocket.

"Heem! Psssst! Yo, nigga! Just grab me and put me in the tuck real quick. These dumb niggas won't even notice until you and Taj are halfway back to West Philly!"

Raheem quickly walked over to the table and zipped the bag closed before stuffing it in his pants pocket.

"Heem," Taj quietly began as he reentered the living room, startling his cousin. "The fuck, yo?"

"The fuck are you doing, you shiesty-ass nigga?" Gunz barked as he quickly reentered the living room behind Taj, a half-filled cup of liquor in his hand. "I knew I shouldn't trust y'all Philly niggas!"

"Huh? Um, naw," Raheem stuttered once he realized he had been caught stealing the agitated young shooter's molly. "I was just…"

"Fuck what you talking about!" Gunz barked before gulping some of his drink while simultaneously retrieving his pistol from his belt.

"The fuck is going on?" Man-Man asked as he approached from behind Gunz.

"I just caught this bitch-ass, molly-fiend tryna steal my work," Gunz growled.

"Now, hold up," Taj interjected anxiously. "My cousin ain't no fiend and he ain't no thief. Let him explain…"

"Fuck talking," Gunz barked as he cocked back his firearm and leveled it in Raheem's direction. "I don't wanna hear anything either one of y'all lying-ass Philly niggas gotta say!"

"You don't want to do that, my nigga," Taj aggressively retorted as he slowly reached for his gun.

"Move again and I'ma bust you," Gunz threatened as he pointed his gun at Taj.

"Yo, Man-Man… get your people," Taj calmly addressed his former cellmate as he slowly continued to reach for his gun. "It doesn't even have to go down like this…"

"Nigga, didn't I tell you to stop reaching?"

Gunz fired his weapon before Man-Man had the opportunity to completely exit the kitchen to intervene. Raheem watched in horror as a large chunk of his cousin's flesh detached from his head upon the impact from the slug from Gunz's large revolver. The loud thud from Taj's lifeless body hitting the hardwood floor seemed to echo in Raheem's ears as he watched the horrific scene unfold in what seemed to be slow motion.

Raheem's reflexes seemed to be heightened by the molly he had taken shortly beforehand, and he quickly pulled the gun from his own waist and returned fire. Raheem pointed his firearm in Gunz's direction and fired at the doorway leading from the living room to the kitchen. Bullets whizzed above Taj's dead body, striking Gunz in his chest and shoulder, spinning him around as he fell back onto Man-Man. Raheem continued to shoot, emptying the guns magazine into the front of the interior of the house. He rushed over to Taj's body, bent over and rifled through his pockets to retrieve the keys to his cousin's Buick.

Raheem quickly rose and ran through the gun smoke. Tears filled the young man's eyes as he exited the rowhome into the daylight; gun in hand, molly in his pocket and jumped into the driver's side of his dead cousin's car. Raheem started the car and quickly fled the scene, leaving yet another violent incident of death and destruction in his wake.

Recklessness, violence and murder were quickly becoming the pattern directly resulting from Raheem's new addiction.

Chapter 16

"Hey baby! You're back," Crystal greeted Raheem with a smile as she muted the television.

"Oh shit," a startled Raheem jumped as he closed the motel room door and whipped around to face Crystal. "I thought you left!"

"Come on, now! I wouldn't leave you, baby," Crystal smiled warmly. "I just walked to the store to get some lady products!"

"I feel you, but if you're really riding for me, you just can't leave like that without letting me know," Raheem sternly instructed. "Shit is dangerous for me out here. We gotta communicate and stay on point – *together*!"

"Okay," Crystal nodded compliantly, her concern evident in her face. "What's wrong, daddy? Did something happen?"

"My cousin, Taj…" Raheem's voice trailed off as he leaned his back against the wall, buried his face in his palms and burst into tears.

"Oh, baby… what happened?" Crystal quickly rose from the bed and rushed over to embrace Raheem. "What's wrong love? Tell me what happened."

"We went to Chester to trade the weed for molly with some niggas Taj knew from jail," Raheem began as he paused to catch his breath. "One of them niggas was this shot-the-fuck-out perc-fiend. The shit about the cop and my neighbors' murders came on the news and this nigga started snapping, talking about that was his cousin and accused me of doing it. He pulled out and shot Taj. Taj got killed defending me!"

"Oh, baby… I'm so sorry!"

"This is that bullshit," Raheem groaned. "What the fuck is happening?"

154

"I know, baby… shit is crazy," Crystal sympathized. "I'm so sorry that happened to your cousin. You're right though… we gotta stick together even more now. Those situations with the cop and your neighbors being on the news is no good. It was bound to happen sooner or later, though. We should just turn off our phones and lay low until we figure out what we're gonna do."

"You're right," Raheem sniffled as he retrieved the zipper-bag of powder from his pocket. "Thanks for the pep-talk, sexy. I didn't get any money, but at least I got all this molly."

Crystal's mouth salivated and her eyes grew large with anticipation when she caught sight of the large amount of molly.

"So…" Crystal grinned as she leaned over and pecked Raheem on the lips. "What do you want to do?"

"On some real shit, I want to go back in time and undo these murders from this weekend – especially my cousin," Raheem groaned.

"Well, I can't do anything like that," Crystal pouted, "But I can do my best to help take your mind off it for a while. How does that sound, love?"

"You can try," Raheem shrugged as he looked to the ceiling and tears streamed down either side of his face.

"Okay, cool! Just lay back and relax."

Crystal turned off the television, placed her cell phone on "airplane mode" and cheerily hopped up from the bed. She pranced to the bathroom, returned with a roll of toilet paper, connected her phone to the wireless speaker and began playing an older Musiq Soulchild song entitled "So Beautiful" from the playlist of music downloaded on her cell phone. The attractive, young woman sang along to the neo-soul melody as she constructed several molly parachutes for the young couple's consumption.

An emotionally devastated Raheem glanced up at his companion and couldn't help but smile at the sight of her singing and bobbing her head as she twisted the toilet paper around the crystalline powder. She was going out of her way to make him feel better and he appreciated her for that. She was the polar opposite of his wife, Kim. Raheem thought to himself that she would be perfect "wife-material" if she weren't so ready-and-willing to engage in reckless behavior with him. He couldn't have children with a woman like that. He had to acknowledge that she was absolutely perfect for the role she currently played in his life.

"What you thinking about, daddy?" Crystal asked innocently when she looked up and met eyes with Raheem. "You want me to stop singing?"

"Naw, ma," Raheem chuckled. "Keep singing. You're cheering me up."

"For real?" Crystal giggled as she bashfully placed her hand in front of her mouth. "My voice is horrible! I just love to sing anyway!"

"No, it's not," Raheem objected with a smile. "I've definitely heard worse! Besides… it's your spirit, your energy. I fuck with you heavy. Thanks for rocking with me, ma."

"Aw! My pleasure Raheem! Thank you for letting me spend time with you," Crystal smiled from ear to ear. "I got more than I bargained for with you but I wouldn't change it. I feel like it was meant to be!"

"Word? You really mean that?"

"Yes, Raheem," Crystal stated resolutely as she looked into Raheem's eyes. "I truly mean that. I know we just met, but I feel like we are twin-flames or something. Like, I think maybe we are soul-mates…"

"Hmmm…," Raheem paused before continuing. "That's crazy. I've been kinda feeling the same way. I didn't want to say anything and sound like a bitch!"

"Well, I guess it's good I said it then!"

The two laughed heartily as Crystal gently wiped the tears from Raheem's face, gripped his chin hairs and kissed him passionately.

"You ready to pop this molly and this pussy?" Crystal asked seductively.

"Come on, now! What kind of question is that? Does Donald Trump love to 'grab 'em by the pussy?'" Raheem chuckled. "You already know!"

"Let's do it, then, daddy," Crystal excitedly giggled as she handed Raheem a bottle of water along with a molly parachute.

The young couple swallowed their molly in unison and drank an entire bottle of water each before pouncing on each other sexually. Their passion was heightened not only by the drug, but also by the circumstances. They were both under an extreme amount of emotional stress and were on the run from the authorities for multiple homicides. They had essentially just confessed their love for each other, although it would have been better described as infatuation – maybe even trauma-bonding. The conditions under which they met and grew close had caused them to grow abnormally attached to each other in an unusually short period of time.

Raheem and Crystal were so aroused they almost physically fought to administer oral sex on the other until they realized they would be better off engaging in the "69" position. Once they had both reached their climax from the sixty-nine, they rested for a short while, ingested more molly and had sex again. This pattern continued several times throughout the afternoon, into the early evening. The young couple engaged in carnal, molly-fueled sex in multiple positions until their private parts were aching.

"Shit! Damn, Crystal," Raheem gasped as he collapsed on the bed next to his naked, sweaty, voluptuous female companion.

"What's up, love?" Crystal panted. "What did I do?"

"The damn thing!"

"Ha! That's what's up," Crystal smiled. "I'm glad you love having sex with me as much as I love having sex with you!"

"I think I love *you*, though…"

"Do you *think* you love me, Raheem? Or do you *know* you love me?" Crystal asked as a serious expression slowly appeared on her flawless face.

"I love you Crystal," Raheem blurted out. His brain was flooded with hormones from the several doses of molly he had taken that day alone and from experiencing multiple orgasms that afternoon. "I love you."

"Aw baby! I'm so happy to hear that," Crystal squealed in excitement. She placed her palms against Raheem's hairy cheeks and pushed her tongue inside his mouth, kissing him for several minutes. "I love you too! I was sent here to love you and for you to love me. The Universe told me so."

"You're so cute," Raheem chuckled. "That's part of what I love about you. I'm tired as shit all of a sudden, though, baby. This molly wearing off and busting all those nuts has me ready to pass out! I'ma take a quick nap, then we can order something to eat and get back to our marathon sex session since we gotta lay low for a minute. Is that cool with you?"

"Yes, love," Crystal agreed. "I'm not really tired, so I'll just watch T.V. until you wake up."

"That's crazy… you're the only woman I ever met who sleeps less than I do!"

Raheem laid back and closed his eyes as he cradled Crystal in his arms. As she retrieved the television remote and began channel-surfing, Raheem thought about how much he enjoyed Crystal's company and how he genuinely *loved* having sex with her. He knew the quality of the sex had influenced how strongly he felt about her, but she was such a sweet girl. And her sexual prowess was so impressive – he could not imagine ever growing tired of having her as a sexual partner.

Raheem contemplated whether he truly loved Crystal or not. He thought about how he probably should not have told her so before giving the matter more thought. They had only known each other for the weekend and they were grown – they weren't teenagers. Still, some women take those words more seriously than others and will overreact if the relationship does not go as anticipated.

"Oh well," Raheem thought to himself. "I'ma try my best to survive this shit. Realistically, though – I'm probably going to have to fall back from her before I get her killed. I doubt I'll make it through the end of the week."

Raheem's racing thoughts gradually slowed as he drifted off into sleep.

Chapter 17

"Damn, yo! My head is whamming! What time is it?"

Raheem opened his eyes in the darkness and rubbed his head, which felt as if his brain was violently pulsating against the insides of his skull. The young fugitive waited momentarily for a response from his female companion before realizing that she was no longer in the bed next to him.

Raheem observed that the television was still on with the volume turned low before he glanced at the clock on the nightstand and noticed the time – 10:08 in the evening.

"Crystal," Raheem called out as he grabbed the television remote from the bed and surfed the channels before stopping on a channel which was playing a local news program.

"Upper Darby Police say their investigation into the murder of a veteran officer is leading them closer to naming and apprehending a suspect. The Chief of Police was quoted as saying 'justice for the family of the fallen hero and for the department seems imminent.' More details after the commercial break."

"Fuck that shit," Raheem growled as he walked over to the television and unplugged it from the wall. "You in the bathroom Crystal?"

Upon receiving no response, Raheem rose from the Queen-sized bed and made the short trip to the bathroom before knocking on the closed door.

"Crystal. Crystal!"

The perturbed young man slowly opened the interior door and saw that the bathroom was empty – no Crystal.

"Where the fuck did this disappearing-ass girl run off to now?" Raheem growled under his breath.

The absconder from American justice walked to the front door of the motel room, cautiously opened it and peeked out to scour the parking lot for his new love interest. He still saw no sign of the young, Black albino woman.

"That's that bullshit," Raheem huffed as he firmly closed the door, careful not to slam it for fear of drawing attention from neighboring motel guests.

The young man unlocked his cell phone and realized he had never turned it off like Crystal had suggested earlier. He had missed a call from his wife less than five minutes beforehand. He came to the realization that his phone ringing had initially startled him out of his slumber.

"Shit," Raheem sighed to himself. "She finally decided to call and see what's up with a nigga, huh?"

Raheem sat in silence and stared at his phone for several minutes before dialing Kim.

"Raheem?"

"Ain't that what you have my number saved as? Or did you change it to 'nigga I don't really give a fuck about?'" Raheem sneered.

"Come on, baby," Kim's voice trembled. "We haven't seen or spoken to each other in days and that's the first thing you say to me? I've been worried about you."

"Then why is this the first time I'm hearing from you?" Raheem snapped.

"I'm sorry baby," Kim whimpered. "Everything has been so crazy over here since you left. Can you come by so we can talk?"

"'Baby?' 'Talk?' Now you want to talk?" Raheem growled. "The fuck you wanna talk about now after you let my parents do me dirty without saying shit to defend me? I'm your husband and the father of your only child and you left me hanging, Kim! That was dirty as fuck!"

"I'm sorry baby, but we really need to talk. Can you please come and see me and the baby tonight?" Kim pleaded.

"Alright," Raheem begrudgingly agreed. "I'll slide through for a minute, but *only* because I miss my daughter. I ain't really got shit to say to you. Let me get myself together. I'll be there in an hour or so."

"Really? Thanks, Heem!"

"It's whatever," Raheem coldly replied. "Like I said, I'm really only coming to see the baby, but you can say whatever you need to say while I'm there. Just make sure my parents don't start any problems while I'm there because I'm definitely not in the mood for the bullshit tonight!"

"I'll do my best, Heem," Kim sheepishly agreed. "I miss you and I love you. I can't wait to see you, baby!"

"Yeah, alright," Raheem replied coolly before abruptly disconnecting the call.

-Click-

"I guess Kim is back on my dick for some reason," the grumpy, young man chuckled to himself cynically. "But where the fuck is Crystal, though?"

Raheem shook his head in disappointment as he slipped his basketball shorts on, placed his wallet in his pocket and shoved his feet into his sneakers. He exited the motel room and walked across the parking lot, towards the motel office.

"Great! *This* bitch," Raheem huffed as he approached the office door and noticed the same unpleasant, middle-aged, female motel clerk he encountered when he initially checked in. "This miserable, ugly, old hag must never get a day off!"

"What do you need?" the wrinkled white woman asked without looking up from the newspaper she pretended to be engrossed in reading.

"I need two more nights in room 112," Raheem stated matter-of-factly as he slid two-hundred dollars under the window.

"That's fine," the woman reached over and retrieved Raheem's payment, seemingly without looking away from her newspaper. "Your new check-out date is Wednesday at noon."

The woman slid the ten-dollar bill constituting Raheem's change across the counter to her guest and continued to read her newspaper and smack her gum as if she was all alone in the motel lobby.

The young man felt himself grow irritated at first. Raheem almost reprimanded the older woman for her gross lack of customer service skills. Then he thought about the fact that her demeanor and the fact that she barely ever looked at or acknowledged him was perfect considering the fact that he was hiding from the police. Raheem decided to return to his room immediately. The fewer people who were able to identify him, the better things were likely to go for him and Crystal.

Wait a minute – could that be where Crystal had disappeared to? Had Crystal gotten cold-feet and decided to turn Raheem in to the police? Was she afraid of getting caught with him and being charged as an accessory to the crimes he had committed over the weekend? Had Crystal decided to save herself instead of being the "ride-or-die chick" she claimed and was pretending to be? Was all that talk about making him feel better and being soul-mates just the sales-pitch she used to "rock him to sleep" and make him comfortable enough to relax while she plotted against him? Paranoia overtook Raheem's entire being as the terrifying questions flashed through his head while he walked across the parking lot back to his motel room.

Beads of sweat trickled down the brown skin of Raheem's forehead. Anxiety overwhelmed the man. The anxious felon entered his motel room, slammed the door behind him and rushed to the nightstand where the bag of molly waited for him. Raheem hurriedly dumped a mound of the substance onto the slick surface of the nightstand, his hands trembling from anxiety, and recklessly snorted an abnormally large amount of molly at once.

The frantic young man rested on the floor next to the bed. Raheem concentrated on breathing slowly in order to prevent himself from hyperventilating. In under a minute he noticed his heart rate slowing and a calming sensation overtaking his mind and body.

Raheem sat in silence for several minutes, enjoying his newfound calm. The young molly-fiend allowed his paranoid thoughts of Crystal setting him up to dissipate and replaced them with flashbacks of their most recent sexual encounters of the day. As the illicit substance flooded his blood stream, he continued to fantasize about making love to Crystal and unconsciously began to rub his own manhood. Raheem closed his eyes as he drifted deeper into his fantasy and grew increasingly higher on the molly until he was officially "rolling."

Several minutes passed and Raheem decided to get up, take a shower and get ready to visit Kim and their daughter before too much time passed. It was already almost eleven-o'clock at night and he did not want to drive at all; let alone at a time of night when it would be more likely for him to be pulled over in a random traffic stop or sobriety checkpoint.

"Oh shit!"

Raheem exited the bathroom after taking a quick shower and was startled to see Crystal sprawled across the bed, nonchalantly surfing the channels on the television set.

"What's wrong baby?" Crystal asked innocently as she looked up at Raheem. "Did I scare you?"

"Where the fuck you been?"

"Whoa, Raheem! What's with the attitude, love?"

"For real, Crystal?" Raheem shot back. "You keep disappearing and shit! Didn't you *just* say we need to lay low for a while?"

"Um… yeah…"

"So, where the fuck do you keep running off to?" Raheem interrogated the young woman. "You do realize how serious this shit is, right? You can't be dipping off without communicating with a nigga! I mean, unless you're gonna leave and not come back. This in-and-out, back-and-forth shit has gotta stop, Crystal! Come on, ma… I know you know better."

"Okay," Crystal whined. "I'm sorry Raheem, but you don't have to be so mean about it! You're right, but I had to go get some more feminine products from the gas station. You were asleep so I didn't want to wake you just to tell you that. I figured you'd still be asleep by the time I got back but you must have woken up right after I left."

"Yeah, well… I'm not trying to stop you from getting whatever you need to take care of your box," Raheem hesitated. "I'm just saying… you really need to stop disappearing without letting me know something. A nigga was worried. It's dangerous out here for both of us right now. If we're going to get through this alive and without getting booked, our communication has to be on point and we have to stick together!"

"I understand," Crystal conceded.

"Do you, for real, though?" Raheem snapped. "I'm just making sure because this wasn't the first time you did that shit!"

"Oh, okay! I can tell somebody is extra tense right now," Crystal rolled her eyes and sighed. "Look, Raheem, I'm sorry I upset you and had you worried, baby. It won't happen again. I promise."

"I hope not," a still perturbed Raheem abruptly replied as he dried himself off, rubbed lotion onto his skin and moisturized his thick beard as Crystal gazed up at him.

"What do you think about having a threesome?" Crystal suddenly blurted out. "Like, tonight?"

The young man stopped mid-stride on his way to retrieve his underwear from the opposite side of the motel room.

"With who?" Raheem asked incredulously.

"We can look for a girl online who will come to us," Crystal suggested. "I'll pay for it. You're under a lot of stress and I know I upset you, so I really wanna make it up to you. I figure this would be something nice to switch it up for you…"

"Hmmm… That's love! I'm with it," Raheem enthusiastically replied. "That sounds right on time!"

"Come on, love," Crystal smiled as she patted the bed next to her. "Lay next to me and let's search for a girlfriend for us for the night!"

"Cool, but we're gonna have to do that later, ma. I gotta go handle something. We can do that as soon as I get back."

"I'll come with you," Crystal replied as she quickly rose from the bed.

"Naw, sorry… that would not be a good look," Raheem hesitated. "I gotta go to my parents' crib."

"Your parents? You mean you're going to see *your wife*?"

"Yeah, well, she called me while you were M-I-A and begged me to come talk about some shit," Raheem admitted. "I'm just going to see my baby-girl, though. I don't give a fuck what Kim is talking about."

"Then why can't I go?"

"Come on Crystal," Raheem scoffed. "That doesn't even make sense. We're dealing with enough drama already. Why add to it by bringing my new girlfriend to my parents' crib two days after me and my wife break up? That doesn't even sound right!"

"Well, you just snapped on me about communication and sticking together and now you're going back out to where all your problems started? Now, *that* doesn't make sense to me!"

"It doesn't have to," Raheem retorted as he rapidly dressed himself. "My family. My daughter. My decision."

"Wow… I didn't realize it was like that," Crystal scoffed as she shook her head in disappointment. "Well, I don't think you should go. Remember your dream? I don't want you to go Raheem…"

"Look, that was just a bad dream. It's late as shit already," Raheem impatiently replied. "We already spent too much time talking about this. It's not up for debate. I'm going, so let's not waste any more time or energy arguing about it."

"But Raheem," Crystal began before stifling herself and letting out a loud sigh of frustration.

The young man leaned over the bed to kiss his female companion before he departed. She leaned back to avoid his kiss, at which point Raheem contorted his face in sheer disappointment.

"You know every time one of us leave this motel room, we risk not coming back," Raheem reminded the young woman. "You're mad, so you don't want to kiss me? The reason why you're mad I'm leaving is the same reason why you should kiss me goodbye – just in case."

Crystal looked up at her male companion; her transparent, blue-gray eyes glistening as tears welled up in them. She pursed her luscious lips, leaned forward and gave Raheem a kiss.

"I'm sorry, baby… I just don't like it," Crystal confessed. "You going to see her at this time of night makes me nervous. Please don't make love to her!"

"For real, Crystal?" Raheem's voice cracked due to his surprise at the woman's comment. "I'm on the run for multiple bodies and you're worried about me fucking my wife? That's the last thing you should be worried about!"

"Please just promise me you're not going to fuck her!"

"Wow," Raheem sighed. "If you're really worried about that shit, then yeah. I promise."

Raheem exited the motel room, the keys to his cousin's Buick in hand. He entered and started the vehicle, then sat in silence for several minutes, contemplating the events of the weekend.

"Damn, man! These fucking women!"

Raheem shook his head and laughed out loud to himself before driving away.

Chapter 18

"Hey love," Kim answered her phone softly after it had rung only once. Raheem's newly estranged wife had been sitting up in their bed, her phone in hand, anxiously anticipating her husband's arrival.

"I'm here."

Raheem quickly disconnected the call and exited Taj's Buick. He had used extreme caution while driving the half-hour from the motel near the airport to his parents' home in Upper Darby. Once he arrived, he parked down the street from the house and called Kim to let her know he was outside.

Raheem hastily exited and locked the Buick before trudging down the block to the walkway leading up to his parents' home. As he approached and walked up the steps, Kim hurriedly exited the front door, closing it behind her. Raheem noticed his wife had her cell phone in hand and that it was initially lit up as if she had just ended a call or sent a text message before she came outside.

"So, what's up? Who were you on the phone with?"

"The phone? What are you talking about?" Kim stuttered.

"Yeah, your jawn was still lit up a second ago. Why you being all secretive?" Raheem questioned his wife.

"Here you go with that paranoid shit," Kim huffed.

"Bye Kim," Raheem sighed as he turned to walk away. "I already told you I don't have time for the bullshit. That includes you too."

"Raheem, wait! Please don't go," Kim pleaded as she placed her hand on her husband's shoulder. "We need to talk."

"What you tryna talk about," Raheem impatiently asked as he turned around begrudgingly and sat on the patio furniture strategically placed on his parents' partially enclosed porch.

"Why haven't you called me all weekend?"

"I've been busy," Raheem replied nonchalantly. "Plus, the phone works both ways."

"Yeah, well, you're here because *I* called *you*!"

"Look, Kim. Are you tryna argue or you tryna talk?" Raheem asked coldly.

"Sorry. I just feel like things were crazy when you left and I was trying to give you your space at first."

"I still need space," Raheem sneered. "Like I said before… I really just agreed to come so I could see my baby-girl. I'm trying to go in and see her."

"Well, um," Kim stuttered. "She fell asleep before you got here. I don't want to wake her up now."

"The fuck difference does that make?" Raheem snapped. "I can hold her while she's asleep. I do it all the time. I'm the one who gets up with her at night most of the time any goddamn way, so I'm about to go in and see my daughter."

"Your parents told me not to let you in," Kim nervously replied.

"Of course they did! Fuck both of them and fuck you for cosigning their bullshit!" Raheem growled as he retrieved his keys from his pocket and searched for the key to the front door of his parents' house. "Excuse me, Kim. Excuse me!"

The emotional young woman stepped aside so her husband could access the doorway. He inserted his key into the lock and attempted to turn it several times without success. He grew visibly frustrated when the door did not unlock.

"What the fuck is going on?"

"Your father changed the locks yesterday morning," Kim timidly informed Raheem.

"See, that's the bullshit I've been talking about," Raheem roared in the darkness. "I know this is their house, but they're acting like I'm not even their son... like *my wife* and *my daughter* still don't live here! Let me in the fucking house so I can see Chanel!"

Kim grew frantic as Raheem began to pound his fist against the front door and yell for his parents to open it.

"They're not home baby," Kim timidly informed her husband. "They're on their way back from the Walker's thirty-fifth anniversary party."

"Oh, so, *that's* who you were talking to before you came outside..."

"Um, yeah," Kim admitted. "Your father asked me to call and let him know if you were really coming and to tell him when you got here. They're on their way back, so if you want to come in, you're going to have to wait for him to get back and let you in."

"Shit! You know I don't even want to talk to them right now. I'm barely tryna have to deal with you!"

"Don't be an asshole, Raheem," Kim huffed. "It is what it is at this point. You can stay and talk to me until they get here and try to see if they'll let you come in, or you can keep cussing me out, or you can just leave because I'm getting tired of trying to reconcile with you!"

"That's funny as shit, Kim," Raheem bellowed. "You're tired of me? I'm tired of y'all and your disloyal bullshit!"

"Disloyal?" Kim asked incredulously. "How you figure? I've never cheated on you or even *talked* to another nigga since we first started dating!"

Raheem was at a loss for words. It was true – he believed Kim had never cheated on him with another sexual partner. At the same time, however, his mind raced with thoughts about how he could not understand why Kim did not comprehend how remaining silent when his father kicked him out was an act of disloyalty from his point of view. He remained silent, however, because he was consumed with guilt over the fact that he

169

had sex with two separate women in the same number of days since he had left home. Not to mention the fact that he had murdered one of them, had argued with another, even promising Crystal he would not to have sex with his own wife. They had also made plans to order an escort in order to have a threesome when he returned to the motel room he was sharing with the strange, attractive woman. Raheem's guilt resulted in his unwillingness to argue over Kim's statement.

"Yeah, alright," Raheem acquiesced. "You got it. You don't even know, Kim. You just weren't ready for me, yo. You got a young-girl's mentality. Remember the wedding vows – 'for richer or for poorer?' You should not have married me if you weren't ready to live on your own as an adult and deal with not always having extra money to blow on getting your hair and nails done and going out to eat every week!"

"Why are you out here making all this noise in the middle of the night, boy?" Hassan, Raheem's father, asked aggressively as he abruptly exited the front door of his home and closed it behind him.

"I thought you and Mommy weren't home," a startled Raheem noted.

"Yeah, we just got back. We parked in the alley," Hassan replied matter-of-factly. "Not that I have to answer to you! Anyway… what have you been up to the past couple of days, Raheem?"

"Minding my business. How about you?"

"Watch your mouth, boy," Hassan antagonistically instructed his son. "Just because you don't live here anymore doesn't mean I won't kick your behind up and down this street!"

"Yeah, alright," Raheem huffed.

"Where's your cousin, Taj?" Mr. Brown asked suspiciously. "Me and your mother saw his car parked around the corner when we pulled up."

"I'm not his keeper, Pop," Raheem casually replied. "I don't know. He's a grown man. Maybe he has a girlfriend around here or something."

"Yeah, alright," Hassan replied, unconvinced.

"So, anyway… since this was obviously a set-up, why did y'all want me to come through?"

"Have you spoken to the Tonen's daughter?" Hassan asked quietly, albeit sternly.

"Who, Sarah?" Raheem asked nervously, his voice trembling. "Naw! You know I barely know her!"

"I asked if you spoke with her," Hassan asked skeptically.

"And I told you I didn't," Raheem growled through clenched teeth.

"Well, her and her boyfriend were murdered sometime Friday night after you left home acting like a rabid animal," Raheem's father informed him. "The police found their bodies Saturday morning."

"Damn," Raheem feigned surprise. "That's messed up. Do they know who did it?"

"Not yet," Hassan hesitated.

Raheem observed the cynical tone in his father's voice and glanced over at his wife who was staring at the ground with her arms folded across her chest in her usual fashion.

"Hold up! Now, I *know* y'all didn't call me over here to interrogate me about Sarah's death like I had something to do with it!" Raheem roared as he quickly rose from his seated position.

"Lower your voice, boy," Hassan instructed. "You want her parents to hear you?"

"What the fuck difference does it make?" Raheem loudly objected. "I'm sure y'all shady motherfuckers already told them your crazy son probably did that shit!"

Hassan marched several steps across the porch until he was standing toe-to-toe with his grown son.

"Boy, I'll break all the teeth out your head if you don't quit using that foul language when you're talking to me!"

"Whatever, yo," Raheem sighed, defeated, as he sat back down.

"What's all this noise out here?" Mrs. Brown shrieked as she rushed out the front door of the residence. "What did he say? Did he do it?"

"What?" Raheem roared. "Oh, fuck all y'all! Y'all shady as fuck! Y'all swear I'm the bad guy but don't ever stop to think about how dirty y'all act even though y'all supposed to be Christians. Doesn't that mean you're supposed to do what Jesus would do? I don't think he would treat his son like this, even if his son wasn't a Christian!"

"Are you gonna let this boy talk to us like that?" Mrs. Brown shrilly addressed her husband.

"That's the problem," Raheem screamed. "Y'all still treat me like a little goddamn boy, but I'm a grown-ass man with a whole wife and my own family."

"The only man I see standing on this porch is my husband – *your father*," Mrs. Brown callously replied. "You're not *acting* like a man – living with us. How do you have a job, but y'all don't contribute any real money for rent, don't have a car, don't go to church, don't pay tithes and you're still broke?"

"I don't live here anymore, remember," Raheem snapped.

"Come one y'all," Kim interjected. "Please stop fighting. Y'all are gonna wake up the baby, let alone the rest of the neighborhood."

"Fuck this nut-ass neighborhood..."

Braaaaaaaaaaaaaat! Braaaaaaaaaat Braaaaaaat! Braaaaat! Braaaaaaaaaaaaat!

The shots from the automatic weapons seemed to erupt from nowhere. Bullets whizzed past Raheem's head where he was seated on his parents' porch and struck the walls of the exterior of the house, penetrating the brick façade. Raheem immediately ducked down and watched in sheer terror as dozens of hot, metal projectiles tore through his family within seconds.

Kim was hit several times in her torso at first. Dark blood flowed from Kim's body, soaking her pajamas as she slowly fell to the ground. Hassan turned and attempted to shield his own wife from the barrage of bullets which showered the patio, but he was too late. Mrs. Brown had already been shot in her head, the meat exploding upon the impact from multiple bullets. Mr. Brown groaned in both physical and emotional pain as bullets ripped through his back and exited his chest.

Raheem had been very cautious when driving to his parents' house. He had observed the speed limit and all the traffic signals, being careful not to draw any attention from the police he noticed during his commute. He stayed on the lookout for hidden squad cars, speed-traps and unmarked police vehicles.

What Raheem had missed, however, was the dark-tinted Nissan Maxima that started following him as he navigated McDade Boulevard. He had no way of knowing Man-Man and several of his associates from Chester had been driving around, looking for him since the shooting had occurred at Man-Man's house. The young thug happened to notice Taj's vehicle and instructed his driver to follow the Buick.

Raheem was also unaware that Man-Man had instructed his driver to park down the block from where Raheem had parked Taj's vehicle. Man-Man patiently waited while Raheem and Kim spoke on the porch.

The young, heavily tattooed drug-dealer wanted to make sure Raheem did not have any reinforcements nearby or anybody else watching his back. When he saw Raheem's mother exit the home, he figured it would be the opportune time to unload the extended magazine of his AK-47 in the direction of the Brown's family residence. Man-Man intentionally wanted to kill as many of Raheem's innocent loved ones as possible as repayment for the murder of his associate, Gunz, less than twenty-four hours beforehand.

When the shooting finally stopped, Raheem quickly rose from his position, crouched down on the porch, and stood erect with his gun in hand. He gave chase on foot and fired several shots at the tinted, late-model Nissan Maxima. His retaliation was too little, too late, however. The car had already started to speed away.

"Oh shit!" Raheem wailed in agony as he ran back onto the porch and viewed the bullet-riddled bodies of his dead mother and wife. He knelt over their carcasses as the tears flowed from his face, dropping to the ground and mixing with the blood which stained the porch. He heard his father gasping for air and carefully turned him onto his back. "Pop! I'm so

173

sorry! Keep breathing! Don't close your eyes! I'm gonna make sure someone helps you!"

Raheem immediately stood up, tucked the hot firearm into his pants and ran to his parents' next-door neighbor's house. He frantically banged on the door repeatedly until the man of the house, Mr. Tonen, answered the door. Raheem awkwardly stepped away from the door when he saw the man's fatigued countenance. Evidently, the older gentleman had not slept much since his daughter's murder, and from his expression, Raheem seemed to be the last person Sarah's father wanted to see.

"Hey, uh, Mr. Tonen," Raheem panted. "I'm sorry, but can you call the law please? My family just got shot! I gotta go, but my father is still alive."

"What? Wait. Slow down, son. I thought those were fireworks! Those were gun shots?"

"Sir, I'm sorry to hear about your daughter," Raheem continued in a panic. "But they can still save my father. Please call 9-1-1!"

Mr. Tonen observed Raheem's blood-stained shirt and shook his head with tears in his eyes.

"Lord, Jesus. I'll call them now."

"T-t-t-thank you, sir," Raheem hyperventilated. "I'm so, *so* sorry."

Raheem quickly ran down the front steps of the Tonen's porch, sprinted to Taj's Buick and sped away.

"Damn, yo," Raheem sobbed as he drove. He wiped his eyes constantly to clear his vision. "What the fuck? I'm a widower and about to be a twenty-five-year-old orphan now? Mommy's dead! My father got hit up bad... I can't stand none of them 'cause they been on some nut shit. I never wanted them to die though. That shit was just like my dream, but worse! It should have been me instead of them..."

Monday . . .
September 14, 2015

Chapter 19

Copious volumes of tears and mucus streamed down Raheem's face as he drove back to the motel. The rush of adrenaline, fear, anger, sorrow and the draining of so much of his bodily fluid caused the high from the molly to quickly vanish before the man had even left Upper Darby and reached the Philadelphia city limits.

Raheem arrived at the motel shortly after midnight, parked Taj's Buick and rushed into the motel room to tell Crystal the horrific news.

"Crystal! Crystal!" Raheem sobbed as he stomped around the empty motel room and bathroom in search of his girlfriend. "Where you at, ma?"

To Raheem's dismay, Crystal was once again nowhere to be found.

"What the fuck, yo? She's gone again? I really hope she comes back soon," Raheem groaned. He broke down, falling to the floor and burst into tears once again. "Oh Allah! My family, though? Why, merciful Allah? Why?"

The devastated young man sat on the floor, his head in his hands, sobbing heavily for close to fifteen minutes.

"Shit," Raheem sniffled as he regained his composure to a degree. He gradually stood up, slowly walked to the bathroom and washed his face. He stared at his reflection, observing his beet-red, bloodshot eyes and let out a loud sigh before drying his face with a towel. "You know what time it is, nigga!"

Raheem exited the bathroom, grabbed the bag of molly and dumped several grams onto the nightstand. The young molly addict sat on the bed next to the nightstand, leaned over and snorted the entire mound of molly – in a similar fashion to how Tony Montana binged on powder cocaine in the final scenes of the classic "Scarface" movie.

The molly had a similar effect on Raheem's mood as cocaine had on Tony Montana's mood. One major difference, however, was that the molly initially had a calming effect on Raheem, especially when he was already feeling paranoid. It made everything seem right in the world – at first. Raheem's main issue with taking the drug was that he consumed too much at once.

The young man had never been one to do hard drugs. Before his initial rendezvous with Sarah, he had never ingested any illicit substance other than marijuana, which he rationalized since it is a plant he felt should never have been made illegal in the first place. He had researched the history of how the timber and cotton industries had launched a marijuana smear campaign in the early-1900s and he had even watched the old "Reefer Madness" movie from the 1930s during his personal research. As somebody who considered himself socially conscious, he refused to comply with laws he knew were based in political corruption and greed, so he discreetly maintained his sporadic marijuana-smoking habit without feeling any remorse for breaking the law. Its effects were calming and he had never experienced any truly negative side-effects other than literally "burning" the money he spent on purchasing the green, leafy substance and the occasional lack of motivation he experienced when he smoked too much.

MDMA or "Molly" affected Raheem on a much deeper level, however. He had only first taken the drug slightly more than forty-eight hours beforehand and he was already clearly addicted.

Raheem was also known by those close to him as being naturally paranoid. Of course, he did not agree with this assessment of his character, although most people who spent enough time around him observed Raheem's hyper-vigilance in most scenarios. When called on it, Raheem would rationalize his thought process, speech and behavior by stating, "I just pay attention to details more than the average person. I don't miss anything and I don't forget a thing. I don't understand why people get upset and want to call me 'paranoid' just because I stay on point! That's corny!"

Nonetheless, if questioned by a trusted associate, even Raheem would have admitted that the molly caused him to be truly paranoid when he was high, or "rolling." In addition, even though Raheem spent approximately two-hundred dollars on his marijuana habit each month – much more than he should have considering his living situation – he was not addicted to marijuana. He simply enjoyed smoking, had been doing so since his early teens and used it as a temporary escape from his reality and for stress relief since he did not really spend money buying himself clothes or indulging in expensive recreation.

Raheem had become addicted to MDMA the first time he tried it though. He had never smoked or even sold crack-cocaine, but from what he heard, the molly seemed to have had a similar effect on Raheem as crack did on addicts. A quick calculation would have revealed that if he had actually paid for it, Raheem would have spent more money on molly in the last forty-eight hours than he had spent on marijuana in the entire calendar year.

Not to mention the fact that the molly was causing Raheem to black out. Out of all the negative media coverage the drug had received, Raheem had only heard about people taking bad batches which caused them to strip out of their clothes and run around the city naked and hallucinating. During all his black-outs, Raheem never came out of them naked unless he had done so intentionally because of having sex with either Sarah or Crystal. He was confident he had not suffered from any visual or auditory hallucinations either. Raheem was sure he would remember the horrifying trauma and emotional disturbance he would have felt from seeing or hearing things that weren't truly there.

There was no denying the damage his new molly habit had caused Raheem and those close to him, however. He had murdered Sarah and her boyfriend and did not even remember how or why. The next night he robbed an innocent man at gunpoint and murdered a police officer. His actions were also responsible for the deaths of his cousin, Taj, his mother, his wife and possibly his father. Raheem had never been involved in any real illegal activity before this weekend – definitely not to this extent. Now he was on the run for multiple murders and was responsible for the deaths of those closest to him. What about his daughter? Chanel's mother and grandmother were both dead, her father was on the run from the police, likely facing multiple life sentences in prison or even the death penalty if he was apprehended by the law and her grandfather was barely clinging to life the last time Raheem saw him.

Raheem tried to clear his mind of all the negativity, death and destruction he and his molly habit caused. As the excessive amount of molly-powder he snorted circulated through his bloodstream and overtook his system, his mind wandered back to Crystal.

"I really need her to come back and make me feel better," he sighed to himself as he visualized her naked body straddling him and gyrating on his penis. Raheem grew increasingly aroused as clips from his many sexual encounters with Crystal flashed through his consciousness. He unconsciously began to caress his own private parts before he realized what he was doing. "Aw, hell no! I'm not gonna play myself by playing with myself when I know Crystal's fine-ass will be probably be back soon!"

The horny young fugitive turned his cell phone on, logged onto a website known for procuring sex workers and started his search for a prostitute. He scoured the site for a woman he thought would be physically appealing to both himself and Crystal for their agreed upon threesome. He stopped and clicked on a particular listing when he saw a picture of a light-skinned young woman who favored Crystal. She was obviously Black, but she was very fair-skinned, her hair was dyed blonde and she appeared to have hazel eyes.

"Crystal might feel a way about that, though," Raheem thought aloud. "This chick is bad as fuck, but she looks a little too much like Crystal. Shorty might catch feelings, thinking I'm trying to replace her!"

Raheem decided against calling the young woman for her services. He kept scrolling the site until the profile picture of a beautiful, voluptuous dark-skinned woman caught his eye. He clicked on her profile and read the description she had posted.

"Chocolate Goddess – South Philly – 23 years old - 5'4"- 115lbs athletic and thick!!! — I look good, I smell good, I'm clean and get tested regularly. I can make your day or night. I'll make your dreams come true while you're wide awake! In-Calls - $150/hour – Out-Calls - $200/hour. Call me."

"Oh yeah! She's the one," Raheem exclaimed excitedly. He quickly dialed the number in the listing and impatiently waited for the escort to answer.

"Hello?"

"Hey… um, is this Chocolate Goddess?" Raheem reluctantly asked.

"Yes, baby," the young woman seductively replied. "What's your name, love?"

"Who, me?" Raheem stuttered. "My name is, um, Ricky."

"Oh, okay Ricky," the young woman's smile was apparent in her tone of voice. She could tell the caller had lied about his name and it always amused her when clients did so. "What can I do for you, *Ricky?*"

"I want a date with you," Raheem nervously answered. "Are you available tonight?"

"Yes, I'm available," Chocolate Goddess affirmed. "In-call or out-call?"

"Um," Raheem hesitated. "I need an in-call. Can you come to my hotel?"

"Of course I can, but that would be an out-call, love," Chocolate Goddess replied. "I need you to text me your address."

"Can you just write it down now, please?" Raheem nervously requested. "I'm not really trying to send my location over text message right now. I'm trying to be as discreet as possible."

"Being discreet is the most important part of my business! It's all good as long as you're not in your Jack the Ripper bag," the young prostitute laughed. "Give me a minute to find a pen. Sounds like this is your first time doing this. What, are you married or something?"

"Yeah, um, something like that," Raheem reluctantly replied as his voice cracked. He thought about his dead wife and grew emotional for a moment before regaining his composure. "We're trying to have a ménage. I've never done this before."

"Oh okay. Well, the price is gonna be higher since there's two of y'all. We'll talk about it in person though. What's the address?"

Raheem opened the nightstand drawer, located the motel address on a pad of stationary and provided the address to the "Chocolate Goddess."

"Okay cool. I'll be there in less than an hour."

Raheem and "Chocolate Goddess" disconnected the phone call and Raheem sat in silence for a moment, contemplating the path his life was taking. The molly high had taken the edge off of his deepening depression, which he was thankful for.

"Let me hop under this water before she gets here," Raheem thought to himself. "I hope Crystal gets back before the hooker gets here. If not, then I guess I'm gonna have to bust the Chocolate Goddess' ass my damn self!"

Raheem entered the shower and allowed the water to cascade over his head, down his body as it mixed with the remainder of the tears he purged from his body as he contemplated the sudden, violent deaths of his family members. After he finished crying, Raheem lathered himself in soap and cleaned himself in preparation for his first threesome.

"Raheem! You almost finished baby?"

Crystal's soft voice reverberated against the walls of the small motel room when she called out to her boyfriend.

"Yeah, I'll be out in a minute," Raheem called out excitedly upon hearing his girlfriend's voice.

"Hmmmm! Now I know you're gonna let me have some of that D since you came out here letting it hang like that," Crystal greeted Raheem with a warm smile when he exited the bathroom in the nude a few minutes later.

"You already know," Raheem chuckled. "I ordered the escort for the threesome while you were gone, so I figured I'd wash my ass!"

"I'm not mad at ya," Crystal laughed. "Sorry I left again. I had to go handle something…"

"Shit, I ain't even worried about it right now," Raheem sighed as he rubbed lotion into his skin. "It's probably better you weren't here when I got back anyway."

"Are you okay, daddy?" Crystal asked, concerned when she noticed Raheem's distressed facial expression. "Your eyes are blood-red! Are you high or are you upset?"

"Both!"

"Aw… come here, love," Crystal extended her arms, beckoning Raheem as she sat upright on the sofa. "Tell me what's wrong."

Raheem slipped on his boxers, slowly walked over to the bed and plopped himself down next to his female companion who began to rub his shoulders.

"Oh my god, Crystal," Raheem began. "Where do I begin? My family is dead!"

"I'm sorry baby. I know you're upset about your cousin…"

"Yeah, but I'm not talking about Taj," Raheem interjected. "I guess them niggas from Chester followed me to Upper Darby. I was on the porch talking to my daughter's mother and we started arguing. A few minutes later, my parents came outside. Shit got even more heated and then all of a sudden…"

"All of a sudden, what?"

"Just… so many gun shots! They sprayed the porch! I don't know why I'm still alive," Raheem began to sob. "They blew my mother's head off Crystal! They shot my father all in his back when he tried to shield my mother. And Kim – my daughter's mother is dead too! I got my whole family killed! I don't even deserve to be alive!"

"Oh my god, Raheem! Are you serious? That's the same thing that happened in your dream! I'm so, so sorry baby," Crystal compassionately responded to a hysterical Raheem as she held him in her arms and rocked back and forth in an attempt to calm him down. "That's horrible."

"H-h-h-horrible ain't even the word," Raheem gasped. "The shit is evil. I deserve to die! I got my whole family killed!"

"Don't talk like that baby," Crystal protested. "I'm glad you're still here with me. We got through all this other shit together. We'll get through this too."

"Fuck that," Raheem snapped. "I don't even know if I want to get through this bullshit anymore. Maybe I should just turn myself in or let the law shoot me to death before I get you killed too."

"Stop it, Raheem," Crystal softly commanded her boyfriend. "Please don't talk like that! We'll help each other make it through all of this. One day we'll look back and wonder how we did it, but we'll do it! We're all we got now!"

"What about my baby-girl? Who does she have now that her grandparents got shot up, her father is on the run and her mother is dead? I got my wife killed! Oh my fucking god!"

"Wait a minute," Crystal paused as she pulled away from Raheem, her body language growing more distant by the second. "Are you still in love with her?"

"*In love* with her?" Raheem sobbed angrily. "How the fuck can I be in love with a corpse? I swear you be worried about the wrong shit!"

"I'm just saying… you seem awfully upset about the death of a woman you told me treated you like shit," Crystal snapped as she folded her arms and leaned back against the headboard.

"That shit ain't got nothing to do with the fact that she's dead now and my daughter doesn't have a mother! How can you be so self-centered? My fucking wife is dead!"

"I'm just getting tired of hearing you calling her your wife," Crystal retorted matter-of-factly. "I'm sorry your family got hurt, but I'm here with you. I've been really supportive this whole time, but I'm not perfect. Vent about anything you want, but I really don't want to hear about your wife anymore if you don't mind!"

"For real, Crystal?" Raheem sniffled angrily. "How are you gonna expect me to not talk about her at all? She was my wife and the mother of my only child!"

"There you go again with that 'W' word! I'm so tired of hearing you call her that! She's dead and she obviously didn't love you anyway! You just told me you love me and now you're crying over that bitch! Maybe that was her karma for fucking you over!"

"Hold up! What the fuck did you just say," Raheem roared as he quickly rose from his seated position on the bed next to Crystal.

Knock-knock-knock!

The young couple immediately discontinued their argument upon hearing the wrapping on the motel room door.

"Who the fuck is that?" Raheem asked warily.

"That's probably your hooker friend," Crystal sneered.

"Oh shit! I totally forgot about her that fast!" Raheem retrieved the gun from where he had placed it on the nightstand when he initially returned to the hotel room and carried it to the door. He peered through the peep-hole and saw the beautiful, young prostitute patiently waiting on the other side of the door. "Yeah, it's her."

"I'm not in the mood anymore Raheem," Crystal sighed. "Tell her we changed our mind. Make her leave."

"She's gonna charge me anyway, so you might as well take some molly and fix your attitude so we can get it popping with this girl," Raheem coldly suggested as he carefully hid the gun under the mattress before walking back over to the door.

"Why are you being such an ass, Raheem?" Crystal snapped as she stood up. "You were so sweet when we met, now you're being a jerk! You changed!"

"Shit, well I guess that's something else we have in common," Raheem jeered as he unlocked the motel room door.

"Whatever! Fuck you Raheem!" Crystal screamed as she stormed into the bathroom and slammed the door behind her.

"Chocolate Goddess? Hey, I'm Rah – Ricky," Raheem timidly greeted the attractive escort and extended his hand to shake hers.

"Hi *Rah-Ricky*," the beautiful, young prostitute giggled as she shook Raheem's hand. Her smile revealed two rows of perfectly straight, pearly-white teeth. Raheem took a moment to observe the woman's beauty. He wondered why a young woman who was so attractive had decided to sell her body for a living at such a young age. "You can call me Neveah. Chocolate Goddess is just my nickname for work."

"Come on in, Neveah," Raheem instructed his guest. "That's a unique name!"

"Thanks," Neveah smiled. "It's not that unique though. It's just 'heaven' spelled backwards!"

"Oh snap! I would have never known!"

"Oh, you would have figured it out after you got a piece of this pussy," Neveah stated quite seriously. "This pussy will make you feel like you're in heaven – especially when you hit from the back!"

"Oh shit," Raheem grinned slyly. "I can't wait!"

"So, you said you ordered me for a threesome? Is it another guy or another girl?"

"Another guy? Fuck no!" Raheem roared. "I don't rock like that!"

"Hey…you never know," Neveah shrugged. "Different strokes for different folks. It's an extra seventy-five dollars per hour for the threesome. So, where's your wife?"

"My wife? Um, naw. My *girlfriend* is in the bathroom, getting her attitude together," Raheem whispered.

"Is she mad you pushed this on her?" Neveah asked as she placed her purse on the desk next to the television stand. "If she's not with it then it's not a good idea."

"Naw, it's not even like that," Raheem objected. "This whole thing was her idea!"

"She got cold feet when I showed up, huh?" Neveah grinned. "Don't worry. It happens all the time. I know how to make her feel more comfortable."

"It's just been a rough weekend," Raheem continued as he sighed and buried his face in his hands.

"Are you okay, sweetheart?" Neveah asked as she began to lightly massage Raheem's shoulders. "You seem stressed out."

"You don't even know the half, ma!"

"I mean," Neveah began, "I can leave if this isn't a good time. I'll just charge you seventy-five dollars for my commute and my time. Or I can give you a few minutes to figure out what you and your boo want to do…"

"Yeah, let me go holla at her real quick. I'll be right back."

The horny young man scurried into the bathroom and quickly closed the door behind him. A perturbed Crystal, who was sitting on the edge of the bathtub, looked up at her boyfriend with tears in her eyes.

"I want her gone, Raheem!"

"What? Why? This was your idea," Raheem objected. "Why you switching up now?"

"Well, I guess your '*girlfriend*' hasn't gotten her attitude together yet!"

"Oh shit… you heard me say that?"

"Of course I did, Raheem," Crystal sobbed. "You just told me you love me yesterday! How dare you talk shit about me to some hooker you just met!"

"I wasn't talking shit," Raheem replied innocently. He decided not to address the irony of her last statement, considering the circumstances. "I wasn't trying to hurt your feelings, Crystal. I'm sorry, but if I tell her to leave I still have to pay her seventy-five dollars just for coming out here."

"Well, then, pay her and let her leave. Or don't pay her and tell her to kick rocks. I really don't care either way. I just want her to leave!"

"For real, though?" Raheem shook his head in disappointment. "You got me all hyped for this shit and now you're changing your mind? That's corny as fuck!"

"Look, Raheem," Crystal began. "You know I'll suck and fuck you until you're empty, but you can't really expect me to open up to some random bitch you were just out there talking crazy about me to after we had our first real argument. Please make her leave. I don't care what you tell her or how you do it."

"Shit, Crystal!"

"Look, daddy... I'll do *anything* for you," Crystal pled her case. "I truly believe we are soul-mates. I've been riding with you regardless. But if you choose this pussy-selling heifer over me, then I might as well leave and you can have her! See if she'll ride out for you like I have been!"

"Alright ma. I'll handle it."

The frustrated young man slowly exited the bathroom, his head hung low in disappointment.

"Is everything okay now, honey?" Neveah inquired as she concluded reapplying her makeup when Raheem reentered the room.

"Naw, I'm sorry," Raheem hesitated. "I'm going to have to ask you to leave. She changed her mind."

"Oh, shit," Neveah sighed. "You want me to talk to her? Maybe I can make her feel more comfortable."

"Thanks, but it's not even about that," Raheem informed the prostitute. "Ain't no talking to her right now."

"Damn... well, that sucks," Neveah shook her head. "That was a waste of my time and your money! I'll just need my seventy-five-dollar fee and I'll be on my way. On to the next one!"

"Um," Raheem hesitated. "I was thinking maybe we can work something out."

"We can work out you putting seventy-five dollars in my hand," Neveah laughed while simultaneously extending her hand to receive the payment.

"I know you're about your bread and all that," Raheem continued, "but do you think maybe we can reschedule? We're about to move out of town this week and I definitely want to get with you before we leave. Can you put the charge on my tab?"

"My nigga," Neveah's demeanor drastically changed from a kind, understanding sweetheart to a cold, calculating business woman. "You don't even have a tab! I just met you five minutes ago! I don't do tabs anyway. Not to be a bitch, but have you ever heard the expression, 'fuck you... pay me?' Well, if I fuck you, you pay me. If I come out and y'all decide not to fuck me – you still gotta pay me. Pussy ain't free and my gas and my time ain't free either!"

"I feel you, but…"

"Ain't no 'buts' except for this soft-ass you're passing up the chance to get inside," Neveah callously interrupted. "Run that bread, my nigga."

"Whoa! Who the fuck you think you're talking to?" Raheem shot back. "You ain't getting a dime from me if you don't learn how to talk to a nigga!"

"I should have known you were gonna be a problem by the way our phone call went… fake-ass names and all that bullshit," Neveah huffed as she reached inside her designer purse. "I don't want no problems, bro. I just want my money. I *sell* this good pussy – I don't take road-trips, burning up gas for my health! A bitch got bills to pay. I try to be a cool bitch, but I don't let anybody fuck my money up!"

Raheem observed as the young, voluptuous prostitute rifled through her purse. He took three long strides in her direction when he noticed she was gripping the handle of a pink handgun in an attempt to retrieve it from her handbag. Within seconds, Raheem was on top of the woman.

"You tryna shoot me, bitch?" Raheem growled as he grabbed the wrist Neveah had partially drawn from her purse.

The intoxicated, emotionally volatile young man slammed the palm of his other hand against the woman's throat and began to squeeze. The attractive, shapely, brown-skinned young woman gasped for air as her eyes began to tear up. Neveah struggled to pull her gun from her purse, or at least aim it in Raheem's direction and shoot him through her purse. His vice-like grip was too strong for her to combat, however. Raheem simultaneously tightened his grip against Neveah's wrist and throat. The gorgeous young escort squirmed in the chair. She panicked as she felt herself running out of air, and fought more violently with each passing moment, but to no avail.

Raheem's penis grew fully erect as he choked the woman. His bloodshot eyes grew large as the veins protruded from his forehead and his forearms. Within less than two minutes, Raheem had added another victim to his body count. The young woman stopped struggling, but Raheem maintained his vice-like grip on her wrist and neck for another minute to ensure she was not playing dead.

Raheem rose from his position bent over the woman he and Crystal were supposed to pay to have sex with. He panted heavily to catch his breath and slowly walked to the bathroom door. He glanced at himself in the mirror as he passed it, and for the first time, he thought about how he didn't even recognize himself – physically or spiritually.

"You can come out now Crystal. She's gone."

Chapter 20

"She's dead!" Crystal gasped upon exiting the bathroom and seeing the prostitute's corpse contorted in the chair.

"I told you she was gone. You told me to get rid of her," Raheem replied stoically.

"Yeah, but, I didn't mean…" Crystal stopped mid-sentence and looked at her borderline catatonic boyfriend. A surge of emotion overcame her when she saw his sullen expression. "I can't believe you did that for me! Thanks love!"

"Huh? 'Thanks?' I thought you were gonna start tripping!"

"Um, no," Crystal reluctantly objected. "I'm flattered you would go so far out of your way to make me feel better. I mean, I wish you didn't have to kill her, but she's just a hooker. It's not like we knew her or anything."

"Yeah… I did what I had to do. The bitch was reaching for her gun because I asked her if I could work something out with the seventy-five dollars."

"She has a gun?" Crystal asked, surprised. Raheem nodded as he reached into the woman's purse, retrieved her pink and black compact nine-millimeter handgun and handed it to Crystal. "That's a nice gun! She *was* a pretty girl! That's a shame."

"Yeah…"

"Well, we gotta do something about this," Crystal's voice took on a more assertive tone when she noticed Raheem beginning to zone out. "We can't leave her here like this. We need to get rid of her body."

"Yeah, but how? We already got a lot of heat on us," Raheem reminded his female companion. "We can't just carry her body out of here. We need to get rid of her car too. I need you to follow me so we can dump it somewhere."

"I don't even really drive, baby," Crystal informed Raheem matter-of-factly.

"For real? I didn't even realize that," Raheem replied in shock.

"Yeah. It's a long story. Maybe I'll tell you some other time," Crystal smiled awkwardly. "So, in the meantime, maybe you should just park her car in the back of the parking lot or in the restaurant parking lot next door. You should probably do that now. I'm gonna try to figure out what to do with the body."

"Oh, okay," Raheem complied as he grabbed the prostitute's keys from her purse and walked outside. Within five minutes he had returned. "I parked it next door in the restaurant parking lot. I left the keys in the ignition."

"Thanks love," Crystal replied as she hugged Raheem. "Um… I was thinking – we should dismember her."

"You mean, like, chopping her up?" Raheem gasped.

"I mean, what other choice do we have?" Crystal shrugged. "Unless you want to try to put her in the trunk of her car."

"Naw, that's too risky."

"Exactly," Crystal agreed. "So, if we cut her arms, her legs and you know, her head off, it will be easier to get rid of her piece-by-piece."

"That's crazy," Raheem shook his head as he let out a loud sigh.

"Yeah, it is, but what other choice do we have? None, right?"

"You're right," Raheem replied, defeated. "Honestly, I was thinking that was our only option."

"I know you were," Crystal followed. "It's only logical. Plus, I really believe we're soulmates. I don't know if the feeling is mutual, but I feel like I know what you're thinking before you say or do it. Like, I feel a really deep connection with you."

"Yeah, I feel a deep connection with you too," Raheem agreed. "I don't know what the hell you're thinking half the time, though," Raheem confessed. "I just figured that was because we just met the other day and besides – you're a woman!"

"What's that supposed to mean?" Crystal asked in a high pitch as she cut her eyes at Raheem and placed her hands on her hips.

"No offense, but y'all women are complicated!"

"Ha-ha! I understand," Crystal giggled. "Well, let's get to it. We should put her in the bathtub so we don't make a mess."

The murderous, young lovers proceeded to carry Neveah's dead body to the bathroom and carefully placed her inside the tub.

"Do you still have that Rambo knife I saw in the truck when we met?" Crystal asked without batting an eye.

"Yeah, it's in my duffle bag," Raheem replied as he walked into the suite portion of the motel room and retrieved the large hunting knife before returning to the bathroom. "We need trash bags, though."

"Oh, shit, that's right! I'll run to the store and get some in the morning," Crystal offered. "In the meantime, I'll go get some ice from the machine to put in the tub to keep her body from stinking until I can go to the store."

The couple worked in unison to cover up Raheem's most recent crime. The already tragic murder turned gruesome as the two carried out Crystal's plan to conceal the killing of the independent online escort. Raheem went about the morbid task of severing Neveah's arms, legs and head from her torso. In the meantime, Crystal made dozens of trips to the ice machines; filling the small champagne bucket from the hotel room with ice, returning to the room, dumping it into the tub and repeating the process as Raheem sawed their victim's limbs from her body. The entire process took the couple almost two hours. Crystal looked at Raheem longingly upon completing the dreadful task.

"Is it just me, or are you horny?" Crystal asked nervously.

"I've *been* horny! Why you think I called her in the first place?"

"Very funny, Raheem," Crystal contorted her face to show her displeasure. "But for real, though… not to sound crazy, but doing this with you kind of turned me on. It wasn't doing it that made me horny. I think it's the fact that we did it together. Like, there's no way you can doubt my loyalty now."

"Yeah, I feel you. You're definitely stuck with a nigga now!"

"So, let's do some more molly and fuck – right now," Crystal growled seductively as she grabbed Raheem's blood-stained hands and led him to the bed.

Raheem and Crystal engaged in adrenaline and molly-fueled, uninhibited, tantric sex for several hours after dismembering the "Chocolate Goddess's" body. They were completely wrapped up in each other spiritually, emotionally and sexually. Whether they were truly soul-mates or twin-flames remained to be seen. There was no doubt, however, that the two souls touched something deep in the other and brought extreme emotions and behaviors to the surface when they interacted.

As had become his custom, Raheem drifted into a deep sleep shortly before dawn. He was emotionally and mentally taxed from the culmination of events over the weekend. He was also physically drained after having sex with Crystal so many times that night.

Raheem abruptly woke from his slumber as the sun shone through a crack in the curtains hanging from the window. He turned to look at the clock on the nightstand. The time read "10:35" and Crystal was, once again, nowhere to be found.

"I guess I'm just gonna have to get used to this flighty broad disappearing all the time while I'm dealing with her," Raheem thought aloud. He rose from the bed and stumbled to the bathroom. As he stood in front of the toilet, swaying as he urinated, he noticed something in his peripheral vision.

"Oh shit!" Raheem jumped at the sight of the dismembered brown-skinned woman, whose body parts were soaked in the half-melted, bloody ice which surrounded her corpse. "What the fuck?"

Raheem's head spun as he suddenly recalled the events of the previous night. He immediately grew sick to his stomach and vomited violently and unexpectedly, missing the toilet and spilling liquor, half-digested food and bile on the bathroom floor.

"Oh shit! Fuck! This is too much," Raheem gasped for air. His anxiety grew to a fever pitch as the spotty, but vivid images of strangling the woman to death and dismembering her body flashed through his consciousness.

Raheem stumbled out of the bathroom and collapsed onto the bed. He began to have flashbacks of the violent events of the previous two and a half days. Images of his cousin being shot, his family being sprayed with automatic gunfire and shooting a police officer during the traffic stop played in Raheem's head like extremely short clips from a bloody action film. Raheem grew frustrated because he could not recall any of the scenarios in their entirety.

The young killer began to sob due to his grief over his losses, remorse for his actions and frustration at his inability to recollect in chronological and complete order the events of the weekend. He grew so angry with himself that he began to strike himself in his head with his fist as he cried and moaned. Raheem's emotional state was completely out of control and he knew it. He decided he needed to do something to numb his erratic emotions and troublesome thoughts but decided against snorting more molly. He could not afford to black out at the moment.

"My cousin usually kept a bottle of vodka in his trunk," Raheem thought while trying to figure out which form of escapism would be best for him to use at the time. The emotional wreck of a man slipped on his basketball shorts, grabbed the keys to the Buick and quickly ran outside to search for the bottle of liquor. He found it quickly and rushed back inside to the relative safety of his motel room.

"He must have just bought this jawn," Raheem said aloud when he noticed the bottle had never been opened. He broke the seal, removed the top, poured out a third of the bottle in memory of his recently deceased mother, wife and cousin and started chugging directly from the large bottle. "Ahhhhh!" Raheem thought the burning sensation from the liquor was a good start to the punishment he deserved for all the havoc he created over the weekend.

Raheem rolled up a blunt, smoked and continued to drink and obsess over the deaths of his family members and his inability to recall how he had murdered Sarah and her boyfriend. He could not remember what had occurred to save his life and his inability to remember agitated him to no end. Raheem also wondered about his father's condition – had he received help in enough time to survive? Even if his father was okay, Raheem was sure they would never speak again, for several reasons.

Raheem did not listen to music or even watch television for over an hour. Instead, he concentrated on his negative, self-defeating thoughts and continued to mentally torture himself for almost ninety minutes as he drank, smoked and waited for Crystal to return. As Raheem grew increasingly more intoxicated, he glanced at the clock and realized it was noon. He decided to turn the television on to watch the lunchtime local news.

"The bloody weekend seems to have carried over into the week with a shooting in Upper Darby late last night which resulted in the deaths of two women and one man on the porch of their residence. Automatic rifle fire erupted on a mostly quiet Upper Darby block near Marshall Road. Authorities believe this man; the son of the deceased homeowners was the intended target. If you have any information regarding his whereabouts, please call 9-1-1 or contact Upper Darby detectives directly."

"Oh shit! They got my picture up on the fucking TV? Fuck! It's over for a nigga. Crystal needs to get back here so we can get the fuck away from Philly!" Raheem rolled another blunt and finished drinking the last of the bottle of vodka. He was extremely intoxicated and his mind raced as he smoked. "Hold up… they said two women and one man got killed? Aw shit! Pop, no!"

Raheem once again burst into tears at the thought of his father's death. The combination of alcohol and marijuana did nothing to improve Raheem's depressed mood. The alcohol also lowered his inhibitions and caused his judgement to be even worse than it had been.

Raheem turned his cell phone on and logged onto Facebook™ for the first time in months.

"Fuck this bullshit. Everybody's gone now and I don't deserve to live. I wish one of these niggas would have killed me before it went this far. It's all good… It will happen soon enough. Somebody please just make sure you look out for my daughter. I'm sorry y'all."

After posting the ominous status to social media, Raheem slammed his phone to the floor, effortlessly shattering it into pieces. He grabbed one of the guns he had collected over the weekend, walked over to the mirror and placed the barrel to his temple as he stared into his own bloodshot eyes.

"Naw, nigga! Don't do that shit," Raheem growled at his reflection. "Don't go out like that!"

The young man once again noticed the zipper-bag of molly on the nightstand. The open mouth of the bag was shaped as if it were smiling at Raheem from across the room.

"Come on Heem! You know I'm the only thing that's gonna keep you alive right now. Just take a little bit to take the edge off..."

Raheem complied with his auditory hallucination and stumbled across the room. He sat on the bed, leaned over and snorted two lines of the crystalline powder. It was just enough molly to improve Raheem's mood – enough to prevent the young, remorseful killer from shooting himself. His mood elevated for several minutes as he lay back and collapsed onto the bed. The effects of the bottle of liquor and two blunts of marijuana overtook Raheem shortly thereafter. The young fugitive soon drifted into a deep, drug-induced coma.

Chapter 21

Raheem slept for roughly two hours. The molly circulated throughout his system as he rested and caused him to have several vivid dreams. Some of them were disturbing and frightening, others were extremely sexually graphic.

Raheem's last dream before waking up was the latter. In his dream, Raheem was laying on the very bed he was sleeping on in the motel room when Crystal returned. She undressed down to her bra and panties before joining him in bed and slipping under the sheets. Crystal then slowly and gently pulled Raheem's boxers down, placed his manhood in her mouth and began to gently administer fellatio to her twin-flame.

Raheem squirmed in his sleep. This was the most sexually graphic, realistic dream he had ever experienced. It was the type of dream he didn't want to wake up from. Raheem's consciousness was split between reality and his dream world. He knew he was asleep, but his thought process was that of a person who was alert. He savored the feeling of Crystal's wet mouth in his dream. The dream caused Raheem to eagerly anticipate Crystal's return to the motel room when he was awake, but he figured he would enjoy the dream while he could.

Raheem felt himself stirring, his body attempting to fully wake up, so he channeled all the energy he could to remain asleep until he reached the climax of his dream. As Crystal continued to suck Raheem's penis, he felt his manhood constrict and tremble slightly.

"Aw shit," Raheem groaned out loud in his sleep. "Oh, shit! I'm about to come."

"Why don't you wake your ass up, then, so you can feel it for real?" Crystal suggested after momentarily discontinuing orally servicing her boyfriend.

"Huh… what?" Raheem moved around in the bed again and slowly opened his eyes. To his surprise, Crystal was actually in the room, on the bed, wearing only her bra and panties, kneeling with her face over

Raheem's crotch. "Oh shit! I thought it was a dream, but you're really here!"

"Yes, I sure am," Crystal grinned. "You want me to finish, or what?"

"Hell yeah! Please keep going... I'm almost there!"

With that, Crystal placed her lips around Raheem's manhood and resumed enthusiastically performing oral sex on her "Clyde." Less than a minute later Raheem erupted inside of Crystal's mouth. She continued sucking until his penis stopped pulsating, then she jumped up and skipped to the bathroom.

"Feeling better now, daddy?" Crystal asked with a smile upon returning and laying on the bed next to Raheem.

"Do I? That was the best top I ever had in my life!"

"Why, thank you, my love," Crystal bashfully replied.

"No! Thank you," Raheem chuckled. "I gotta talk to you about something serious, though, ma."

"What is it, baby?" Crystal asked with a concerned expression plastered across her face. "You wanna talk about what happened last night? I bought some trash bags, duct tape and cleaning supplies while I was out so we can finish handling that situation in the bathtub."

"Kinda, but not exactly," Raheem replied, dejected. "They had my face on the news earlier."

"Oh shit! For real?"

"Yeah, for real," Raheem confirmed. "I wouldn't joke about that."

"That's not good, Raheem!"

"Who you telling?" Raheem countered. "I appreciate you riding out with me the past few days on some Bonnie and Clyde shit, but I really don't think I'm going to live if I don't get out of the Pennsylvania within the next twenty-four hours."
"Let's figure out where we're going and how we're getting there and then do it!"

"It's too dangerous," Raheem objected. "You gotta get away from me, ma. I don't want you to get locked up or killed because of fucking with me."

"Fuck that," Crystal protested. "I'm not leaving you now, Raheem."

"I appreciate you for that, sexy," Raheem continued, "but I'm just trying to do the right thing. Don't throw your life away for a nigga you just met. It's not worth it."

"I don't think you understand, Raheem," Crystal calmly replied. "When I told you I'm here for you, I really meant I'm here for *you*. I'm not going anywhere. Now that I'm here with you, I promise I'll be with you until the end – whatever that means."

"You *do* realize I killed *five* people this weekend, including a cop, right?"

"Yeah, I was there for two of them. My memory isn't messed up like that, baby," Crystal rolled her eyes.

"I'm a young, Black man with a Sunni beard; wanted for murdering a cop and also wanted for questioning regarding the murder of my own family…"

"Yeah… I'm not blind, and I'm far from slow, Raheem," Crystal huffed. "Why do you keep telling me stuff I already know?"

"Because you're acting like you don't realize that if I get pulled over, the cops are probably going to kill me and whoever is with me," Raheem snapped. "I doubt I'll ever see the inside of a jail cell."

"I'm not acting like that," Crystal objected. "I'm just not trying to focus on it. Look, Raheem… I'm ready for whatever comes out of our relationship. I'll go with you everywhere you decide to go. If that means I get locked up or killed too, then so be it."

"But Crystal…"

"No disrespect babe," Crystal interjected. "Please just respect my decision as a grown woman. I really don't want to discuss it anymore. If you really don't want me around, you're just gonna have to sneak out and leave me here one of these days!"

"If you say so," Raheem acquiesced.

"I say so," Crystal smiled and gently kissed Raheem on his forehead. "I have an idea. Why don't we handle that situation in the bathroom, then we can fuck until it gets dark outside? After the sun goes down we can go out and have some low-key fun. Didn't you say there's a casino down the street?"

"Yeah, but the casino, though, ma? My face was on the news today."

"I understand," Crystal acknowledged. "But it's Monday. Ain't nobody gonna be looking for you in there. It would be like hiding in plain sight. I'm really good at Black Jack and I win a lot of money every time I play the slots. We can use the money to get out of town."

"It sounds like a decent idea, but I'm not sure…"

"How about this – we can go to the casino, win some money and maybe even find a girl to bring back so we can finally have our threesome before we leave the city?" Crystal suggested. "It will be fun and I'm sure the casino will be worth it."

"If you say so…"

"Yaaaaay," Crystal squealed in excitement like a young child whose parents just told her she was going to Disney World for the first time. "You won't regret it, love. If we're gonna leave Philly, I think we should go out with a bang!"

"'Go out with a bang,' huh? You sound like me…" Raheem solemnly chuckled. "I'm pretty sure I've had enough 'bangs' this weekend to last us both a lifetime!"

"You're so silly, Raheem! I'm just glad you still maintained your sense of humor through all this bullshit."

"Hey…what can I say?" Raheem replied nonchalantly. "Sometimes you gotta try to laugh to keep from crying."

"Aw… I feel you baby. I feel you," Crystal reassured her boyfriend as she gently rubbed his leg. "Well, let's hurry up and handle this business in the bathroom so we can handle our business in the bed before we leave!"

The couple spent slightly less than ninety minutes securely wrapping Neveah's body parts in the trash bags, duct-taping them closed, hiding them in the motel closet and cleaning the bathroom to their satisfaction. As they finished, Crystal looked at her male companion awkwardly for close to a minute before he noticed her staring.

"You cool, ma?" Raheem asked when he noticed Crystal's gaze. "Why you looking at me like that?"

"You're covered in blood, baby! You look like a butcher!"

"I know, right?" Raheem acknowledged. "I'm over here looking crazy, huh?"

"You're reminding me of DMX on the cover of that 'Flesh of My Flesh' album," Crystal smirked. "You just have a little less blood on you than he did!"

"Yeah, I need to hop under this water with a quickness! This shit is nasty!"

"Yeah, but to tell the truth... it's kind of sexy," Crystal reluctantly admitted.

"You think so, for real?" Raheem asked, genuinely surprised. "You a real freak-body-jawn, huh, Crystal?"

"Only for you, daddy," Crystal smiled before pecking Raheem on his lips. "Let's take a shower together and get it popping!"

The couple undressed in unison and entered the shower together. While undressing, Raheem's thoughts raced. He felt Crystal's comments were in bad taste. DMX used to be one of his favorite hardcore rappers and Raheem still listened to the sophomore album Crystal had referenced. Still, her timing had been totally inappropriate in Raheem's opinion.

First, DMX was covered in blood on an album cover – Raheem was covered in blood *in real life*, after murdering and dismembering an unsuspecting prostitute, prompted by Crystal's mood swings the previous night. Yes, she had assisted him with the clean-up, but *he* was the one who had been committing the heinous acts. Raheem felt Crystal was too eager to make light of such grave circumstances. He wondered if she was a bad influence – even if only after the fact. Might she actually enjoy these types of morbid activities?

"Oh well," Raheem thought. "It doesn't really matter. I'll be locked up or dead soon anyway. I might as well enjoy Crystal's company and the sex while I still have time left."

The couple showered together, made love and exited the bathroom. As had become their routine, they parachuted more MDMA and embarked on a molly-fueled, six-hour marathon sex session.

Tuesday...

September 14, 2015

Chapter 22

The young couple remained engrossed in their sexual escapades long after the sun set, fueled by lust and large amounts of methamphetamine. Raheem and Crystal once again reached an earth-shattering mutual climax as midnight approached and Monday night transitioned into Tuesday morning.

"That was amazing, love," Crystal panted, collapsing onto the bed next to Raheem as her body stopped convulsing from riding Raheem's pole until they had both achieved explosive orgasms. "You still trying to go out?"

"I'll do anything you want to do after that," Raheem chuckled as he looked over at the digital clock on the nightstand. "Damn, it's after midnight? Time flies when you're having fun!"

"Yeah, time flies even faster when you make me come! You want to take a shower first, baby?"

"Naw… you got it," Raheem replied, dejected, as Crystal's question reminded him of the argument between him and Kim – their last argument before the fateful weekend began.

"Okay, thanks baby! I'll hurry up so you can wash all that sex-funk off you before we leave!"

Crystal exited the shower less than fifteen minutes later. Raheem showered and dressed, then the couple left the motel and made the short trip to Harrah's Casino in Chester, Pennsylvania.

Things went well for the couple as they gambled – at first. Raheem brought three-hundred dollars with him to the casino and the couple took turns playing electronic Black Jack and penny-slot machines. Raheem's winnings in Black Jack were minimal, but he was winning. By approximately four in the morning, Raheem had won about two-hundred dollars playing electronic Black Jack.

The lion's-share of their earnings came from Crystal's mastery of the penny-slot machines, however. The attractive, young woman convinced Raheem to let her try her luck on the slot machines and he was pleasantly surprised when their pot quickly grew from five-hundred dollars, to eight-hundred, to twelve-hundred, then seventeen-hundred dollars.

Raheem made his way to the restroom hourly throughout the course of the night to snort more molly before continuing to gamble. The combination of the illicit drug, the free alcohol provided by the attractive young bartenders who roamed the casino floor and the surge of adrenaline from consistently winning gave birth to a newer, darker side of Raheem's persona. The highly-addictive side of Raheem's personality reared its ugly head as a newfound gambling addiction came to the fore. After his most recent trip to the restroom to snort molly, Raheem returned sweating, his eyes bloodshot and aggressively commanded his girlfriend to allow him to take over the slot machine.

"But I'm winning, my love," Crystal innocently protested. "Look, I won two-hundred more dollars while you were in the bathroom," the young woman stated proudly.

"Yeah, that's what's up," Raheem replied dismissively. "But I'm not gonna sit up here and let my girl win all the bread. Come on, ma… move! Let me hop on."

"But baby…"

"Come on Crystal," Raheem barked as he retrieved another alcoholic beverage from a passing bartender and placed a small tip on her tray. "Let me do my thing, yo."

"Fine," Crystal acquiesced, downtrodden as she stood up and allowed Raheem to take her place seated directly in front of the machine. "You better not lose, though!"

"Why would you even say that?" Raheem growled as he cut his eyes at his smiling girlfriend. She had made the comment in jest, but Raheem's sense of humor had been temporarily disabled by his drug and adrenaline-fueled lust for the sport of gambling. "Just don't do or say anything to mess up my luck and we'll be good!"

Unfortunately, Raheem's luck was anything but good after playing the slot machine for less than thirty minutes. Their pot dropped from almost two-thousand dollars to slightly under fifteen-hundred.

"Things aren't looking too good, love," Crystal observed. "Maybe we should just take what we won and leave now."

"Naw, fuck that," Raheem barked. "It's just this machine. I gotta switch machines." Raheem quickly rose from his seated position and led the way as he marched to another penny-slot machine. He sat down, inserted his newly issued casino rewards card into the machine and started gambling again. Within fifteen minutes, however, Raheem and Crystal's total earnings had dropped from slightly under fifteen-hundred dollars to just over nine-hundred.

"Shit!" Raheem angrily exclaimed upon noticing the balance of his pot. "That's that bullshit!"

"Baby," Crystal timidly began. "Maybe we should just go…"

"Naw, you're giving me bad luck Crystal," Raheem angrily protested. "See, I've been losing ever since you said that dumb shit about losing!"

"For real, Raheem?" Crystal objected, offended. "How are you gonna blame me when I'm the one who won most of the money? Do you have a gambling problem or something?"

"My only problem is that you're making me lose," Raheem stated angrily. "I'm about to change machines because you obviously jinxed this jawn. Come on!"

Raheem once again hastily led the way to yet another slot machine, hoping his luck would change. He placed his bet, pulled the lever and his eyes lit up when he won thirty dollars on his first bet.

"See?" Raheem exclaimed with joy. "I knew they weren't gonna keep taking from me! I'm about to run to the bathroom real quick. Don't let anybody play on this machine while I'm gone!"

"Yeah, baby… I don't think you have to worry about that," Crystal slowly replied as she glanced around the casino. "There's hardly anybody here."

"Would you just do what I asked you to do, please?" Raheem snapped as he stood up. "All that talking and being opposite is gonna bring me bad vibes!"

"Okay, Raheem," Crystal replied, defeated, as she took Raheem's seat until he returned from the bathroom.

Raheem entered the bathroom stall, quickly snorted more MDMA and splashed water on his face before returning to the slot machine on the casino floor. When he returned, his eyes were crimson-red and his mood was even more aggressive than it had been moments earlier.

"Okay, get up," Raheem commanded as he approached and tapped Crystal on her shoulder. "I'm about to do my thing."

"Um… *rude*," Crystal huffed as she rolled her eyes and begrudgingly rose from the seat she had saved for her boyfriend. "I don't like this side of you, Raheem."

"Well, I don't like the side of you that's fucking up my bread and making me lose, but you don't hear me crying about it," the young man gruffly replied as he pushed past his girlfriend, sat down and placed another bet.

"For real, Raheem?" Crystal's voice cracked as tears formed in her eyes. "No, your attitude is why you're losing," the hurt young woman replied as the sound from the slot machine indicated Raheem had lost his most recent bet.

"That's exactly what I'm talking about," Raheem roared, drawing attention from the casino staff. "All these bad vibes you're giving off are fucking me up! Maybe you should wait in the car."

"I can't believe you're blaming me and acting so mean over a stupid game," Crystal sobbed before noticing two security guards and a casino manager approaching. "Um… baby, maybe we should leave."

"Not until I win my money back!"

"But baby, look," Crystal nodded in the direction of the approaching staff members. "We still have almost a thousand dollars here, plus the money you left at the motel. That's enough to help us do what we need to do for now. Let's leave the casino, go check out of the hotel and get out of Philly altogether."

"Yeah... we'll leave in a minute," Raheem frantically replied. "As soon as I get back up to two stacks we can leave."

"But baby..."

"Is everything okay, sir?" a middle-aged white man with silver-hair calmly addressed Raheem as he approached. Stocky security guards – one Black and one white – silently stood on either side of the casino manager.

"Yeah, I'm fine," Raheem abruptly replied as he focused his attention back to the slot machine.

"There's been a commotion over here for the past few minutes and it's my job to make sure everything is okay," the casino manager replied.

"I told you I'm good," Raheem aggressively dismissed the man.

"Well, sir," the middle-aged man continued. "It doesn't really seem like it..."

"How many different ways do I need to tell you to get the fuck out my face so I can concentrate?" Raheem snapped. "My girl is already nagging me, making me lose bread, now you're coming over fucking with me? Is this some type of conspiracy to make a nigga lose? Y'all dirty motherfuckers setting me up?"

The casino's floor manager exchanged perplexed glances with the two security guards before continuing.

"Excuse me, sir. I'm going to need to ask you to cash out and leave the building. You're behaving in an aggressive manner and it's making the other patrons and staff feel uncomfortable."

"What? This is bullshit!" Raheem roared. He turned to face the three men, as the manager had finally drawn his attention away from the addictive gambling machine. "What the fuck is going on here? You're coming at my neck for causing a disturbance but you're not even saying shit to her? I swear being a Black man in America sucks sometimes!"

"I'm sorry you feel that way, sir," the casino manager calmly replied. "This has nothing to do with your skin color. You seem intoxicated and are highly aggressive. You're causing a disturbance in our establishment and I need you to leave for now. I'll personally walk with you to the cashier to redeem your winnings, but this is your last chance."

"Last chance? I wish y'all would lay a hand on me," Raheem scoffed arrogantly as he slowly and defiantly rose from the chair. "It's whatever, though. I'm not trying to play on y'all bum-ass machines anymore no way!"

"Okay sir. Thank you for complying," the manager stated calmly as he motioned for the security guards to give Raheem personal space. "The cashier is this way."

"I know how the fuck to redeem my shit," Raheem aggressively replied. Crystal and the casino staff followed several steps behind the enraged young man as he walked to the cashier and handed her his ticket to cash out and receive his winnings. Raheem continued his rant as he waited to receive his cash. "It must be really nice to be a bad bitch and to always have people let you get away with whatever. But I'm a Black man, so these motherfuckers want to scape-goat me and act like I'm the problem!"

"Baby, please… don't make a scene," Crystal softly pleaded.

"Fuck that! These motherfuckers ain't gonna do shit because I didn't do shit! They call themselves kicking me out, but they really should have just checked your ass! They got the wrong one!"

Raheem continued venting as the cashier counted his winnings and handed the money to him without a word. The casino manager, security guards and the cashier exchanged puzzled glances while Raheem counted his money and continued his tirade as he walked towards the exit. The security guards and casino manager followed Raheem and Crystal to the parking garage, to the location where the young fugitive had parked Taj's Buick hours beforehand.

"Is this your vehicle, sir?" the casino floor manager inquired.

"Naw, I'm just unlocking the door for my health," Raheem sarcastically replied as he opened the driver's side door, entered the vehicle

209

and slammed the door closed without another word. Raheem waited for Crystal to enter, then started the vehicle and drove away.

"What the hell do you think was wrong with him?" the white security guard asked the casino manager.

"Well, I mean, he looked high and drunk," the casino manager replied nonchalantly. "He obviously has a problem with addiction. He can take that shit somewhere else though!"

"He looks familiar… I know him from somewhere," the Black security guard interjected.

"Is that right, Jerry?" the casino manager inquired. "What, do you know him from your neighborhood?"

"Naw," Jerry, the Black security guard hesitated as the three men watched the Buick speed down the parking garage ramp. "Naw… I don't know him like that, but I swear I saw his face somewhere recently…"

"Oh, shit," the white security guard exclaimed.

"What is it, Tom?" the older gentleman inquired.

"Isn't that the guy we saw on the news during our break, Jerry," Tom gasped.

"Oh, shit," Jerry shrieked. "That is that motherfucker! That's that 'bloody weekend in Upper Darby' motherfucker! He was on the news because they want to question him about his wife and parents' murders!"

"Jesus H. Christ," the casino manager exclaimed. "We gotta call the police!"

Chapter 23

"You really drawed on me in there, Crystal," Raheem huffed as he drove away from the casino. "We could have made so much more money if you had just kept our mouth shut!"

"So, you're just gonna keep blaming me, huh?" Crystal sighed, tearful, as she looked out the window at the sunrise while Raheem sped down Industrial Highway. "After all that money I won for us, you're still blaming me for how things went?"

"Hey... I just call it like I see it," Raheem callously replied. "Next time, do me a favor and let me be a man and handle my business without all the dumb shit!"

"You know what, Raheem?" Crystal began before changing her mind. "You know what? Never mind. You're right. I should just follow your lead... even if I think I'm helping."

"Exactly! I'm glad you finally see things my way!"

Crystal rolled her eyes and cried softly as they continued on their relatively short journey from the casino back to the motel. As they approached the motel driveway and Raheem began to turn from the main road into the parking lot, an eerie feeling overcame Crystal. She hesitated at first, but felt compelled to say something to her companion.

"Raheem... baby," Crystal began as she tapped her boyfriend's arm. "You see those two cop cars parked in front of the restaurant?"

"Yeah, so?" Raheem asked dismissively as the vehicle slowly crept down the driveway.

"What do you think they're doing here?"

"Um... why do most humans go to restaurants? They're probably eating," Raheem chuckled condescendingly. "You know most of these punk-ass business owners offer cops free food in exchange for extra protection!"

"Do you think they're here because of the hooker?"

"Come on Crystal," Raheem jeered. "How would they have found out that fast? We just left out last night!"

"If you say so…"

"Oh shit!"

The couple gasped in unison less than thirty seconds later as they caught sight of the S.W.A.T. vehicles surrounding the building where their motel room was situated.

"Oh, fuck! We gotta get out of here, baby!" Crystal exclaimed in a frenzy.

"What the fuck do you think I'm trying to do?" Raheem huffed as he quickly shifted the Buick into "reverse" and attempted to back out of the long driveway.

He was too late, however. At that very moment, two more police vehicle pulled up behind the Buick, their lights flashing and trapped the vehicle.

"Driver! Slowly place both hands out of the window, open the door from the outside and step out of the vehicle," a nasal, high-pitched voice commanded over the loud-speaker.

From their vantage point, the young, fugitive couple could see the opened door of their motel room. Raheem and Crystal watched in shock and horror as police officers exited the room with the blood-stained plastic bags containing Neveah's body parts.

"Oh my god, baby! Oh my god! What are we gonna do?"

"See? Didn't I tell you to get as far away from me as possible," Raheem chastised his girlfriend. "Now you're about to fuck around and get locked up. I tried to warn you!"

"This ain't the time for 'I told you so,' Raheem! What the fuck are we gonna do?" Crystal panicked.

"I told you I would hold you down," Raheem replied resolutely. "I promise I won't let anything bad happen to you."

Without another word, Raheem pulled his gun from under the driver's seat, rolled down the driver's side window and placed his empty hand outside. He slowly reached down and opened the door before stepping out, one foot at a time.

"But baby… the gun…"

"I don't trust these niggas," Raheem quickly replied. "I already popped a cop the other day. I'm not gonna be a sitting duck and let these motherfuckers empty their guns into me!"

"Sir! Please slowly lower your weapon and step away from the vehicle!"

"I'll surrender, but you have to promise not to hurt my girlfriend," Raheem instructed as he held his arms in the air while retaining his grip on the firearm.

"What the fuck is he talking about, sir?" the commanding officer's right-hand man asked, puzzled.

"Good question," the commanding officer replied.

"Sir… please drop your weapon. Then we can discuss your demands."

"I don't have demands," Raheem shot back. "All I'm saying is I'll drop my weapon and turn myself in if you promise not to hurt my girlfriend. I don't want anybody else to get hurt."

"We want the same thing. Who is your girlfriend, sir, and where is she? We'll make sure she's safe."

"Oh, so y'all want to play games, huh," Raheem yelled. "Y'all wanna act like you don't know what I'm talking about? Are y'all motherfuckers blind? Y'all don't see this beautiful, innocent woman in my passenger seat?"

"Sir, please remain calm. We're trying to help you. Please drop your weapon."

"Oh, these motherfuckers playing games?" Raheem growled as he cocked back his pistol while turning to address Crystal. "These pigs are trying to play me like a dummy so they can pop me!"

"Baby… what are you doing?"

"These motherfuckers are ready to kill us!" Raheem replied wildly as saliva flew from his mouth, his eyes filled with the crazed look of an intoxicated man with nothing to lose who has convinced himself that he's ready to die. "I'm not going out like a bitch, though! Get ready to be out!"

"But baby, hold on…"

"Call in a negotiator," the commanding officer urgently instructed his assistant. "This man is obviously not playing with a full-deck. We've had too many police-related shootings. I'm trying to bring him in alive."

"Sure thing, boss," the young assistant agreed as he reached for his walkie-talkie to request assistance.

"Oh, these motherfuckers calling for more back-up," Raheem growled angrily when he observed the commanding officer's assistant speaking into his walkie-talkie from across the parking lot. "Fuck that!"

Pop! Pop! Pop! Pop! Pop! Pop!

Raheem quickly pointed his gun at the officers and squeezed the trigger, unleashing a half-dozen rounds in the officers' direction.

"Oh shit! Shots fired!"

Pop! Pop! Pop! Pop! Pop! Pop! Pop!

Boom! Boom! Boom! Boom!

Crack! Crack! Crack! Crack!

Brrrrrraaaaaat! Brrrrrraaaaat! Brrrrrrraaaaaaaaaat! Brrrrraaaaaaat!

Multiple shots from several firearms echoed in the early morning quiet. The gunfire continued for almost sixty-seconds before the commanding officer's instructions to "cease-fire" were heard around the parking lot. Smoke filled the air and when the shooting had ceased,

Raheem's body, along with Taj's Buick were riddled with bullets and oozing the fluid they needed in order to remain functional. In less than a minute, both Raheem and his cousin's vehicle had ceased to exist in their previous forms.

"Wow," the commanding officer's assistant gasped as he accompanied his C.O. to examine the vehicle and Raheem's dead body. "That was absolutely crazy."

"Yeah," the commanding officer agreed. "Some way to start your first week in S.W.A.T., huh, kid?"

"No kidding," the rookie gasped. "What do you think was up with this guy?"

The commanding officer cautiously approached Raheem's lifeless body, kicked the young man's gun away and examined the contents of his pockets, retrieving the bag of molly.

"Well, I'm not quite sure, but I think this had something to do with it," the veteran S.W.A.T. officer stated as he held up the bag of crystalline powder for his colleague. "Looks like a couple ounces, but you see all that residue? I think our perp binged on this poison!"

"What is that – coke?"

"No, it doesn't look like it," the C.O. replied. "This appears to be MDMA, you know… that molly shit that has everybody acting crazy."

"But what about the girlfriend he was talking about?"

"Who fucking knows?" the veteran officer shrugged. "All I see here is his body and an empty, bullet-riddled Buick! Maybe he was talking about the girl he killed and dismembered in his motel room. The guy was obviously out of his mind!"

"So, you actually think this guy killed his own girlfriend and was so far gone that he didn't remember and wanted to bargain for her life?" the perplexed rookie asked.

"I can't say for sure, Jim," the C.O. replied honestly. "But we were obviously dealing with a mentally disturbed individual."

"Yeah, well at least that's over."

"For you... yeah," the senior S.W.A.T. officer admitted. "This is gonna lead to a whole lot of paperwork for me though! It's a shame. I gotta talk to my wife about this. Our oldest daughter just went away to college and you know all the young kids think this molly shit is fun and games. They all think the shit is just going to make them feel happy until they get a bad batch and something like this happens. My daughter suffers from chronic depression and I don't want her to get peer-pressured into taking this poison and get caught up in the madness."

"Yeah, boss. I hear you," the younger officer, Jim, replied. "So, do you think this guy was already crazy, or do you think the molly pushed him over the edge?"

"I think that's something for the Medical Examiner to try to figure out," the commanding officer replied. "I am curious though, but we can't spend too much time worrying about it. Our job here is basically done. You'll learn after you've been on the job long enough – don't take this shit home with you. You'll never survive."

"Got it, boss."

"It is a shame though. The guy probably just needed some help with his mental health and turned to drugs to make himself feel better. I wonder if anything could have been done to prevent this or if he was already psychotic. I guess we'll never know..."

Friday . . .
September 18, 2015

Outro . . .

"Come on! Stop being a baby," Jade teased her roommate.

"I'm not being a baby," Rhonda whined. "I really have work to do! I don't know what you came to college for, but my father will whoop my ass if I fail even one class!"

"Look, Rhonda... going to *one* party is not going to make you fail," Jade protested. "Your parents are all the way in Philly. This is Atlanta! You better take advantage and have fun while you still can! Why are you such a goody-goody all the time?"

"Goody-goody? That's hilarious," Rhonda chuckled. "My parents would crack up if they heard you say that! I'm just not really into partying all crazy like that. Besides... you learn to stay low-key when you're raised by a veteran S.W.A.T officer! My father might have people watching me now!"

"You sound so paranoid, Rhonda," Jade teased. "One little party isn't going to hurt anything. Besides, you've been stressing about school work all month and the semester just started. You better take a break before you get burnt-out!"

"I don't know..."

"Even if your father does have people watching you," Jade continued. "It's a freaking house-party! You think your father has never been to a house party before? How mad can he get? You're in college for God's sake!"

"I guess you're right," Rhonda replied, defeated as she sat up in her dorm room bed and closed her text books. "One party won't hurt. But I'm only gonna go for a little while so I can come back and finish studying."

"Yaaaas, bitch," Jade excitedly replied. "We're gonna turn up! I told my girlfriend about you and she's looking forward to meeting you."

"Um… cool," Rhonda hesitated. "Y'all remember I'm not into girls, though, right?"

"Bitch, I also remember you don't seem to be into anything but school work," Jade sharply replied. "The whole time we've been roommates I haven't seen you put your mouth on anything except for that pencil when you're studying! You need to bust a nut and loosen up! I don't care if it's a guy or a girl, but you definitely need to get some tonight!"

"Yeah, whatever you say," Rhonda sighed as she rolled her eyes. "I'm ready whenever you are."

"Like hell, you are! You're not going out with me dressed like somebody's grandmother!"

Jade and Rhonda arrived to the house party fashionably late, after Jade had convinced Rhonda to change into a more revealing outfit and had "beat" Rhonda's face with her unique method of applying makeup.

"Girl! Where have you been?" an attractive college, sophomore exclaimed as she ran up to Jade and kissed her passionately on the lips.

"My fault, baby," Jade answered her girlfriend as she nodded in Rhonda's direction. "I damn-near had to drag this bitch out the dorm!"

"This is your roommate you told me about?" Jade's girlfriend responded with a sly grin. "She *is* a bad bitch!"

"Hi, I'm Rhonda," the shy freshman sheepishly replied as she extended her hand and introduced herself.

"Hey girl! I'm Wendy. Nice to meet you. You ready to turn up?"

"That's what Jade said we were gonna do," Rhonda smiled naively.

"Go easy on her," Jade slyly interjected. "This is her first time! I guess they don't throw house parties in Philly!"

"Come on, now," Rhonda protested. "Of course, they have parties in Philly. I was just never allowed to go to them because my parents are overprotective."

"Oh yeah… be careful what you say around her, love," Jade instructed her girlfriend, Wendy. "Her father is a cop!"

"Oh, shit! Why'd you even bring this bitch, then?" Wendy laughed.

"Because I figured her green-ass needed to get out and learn how to have some real fun!"

"Are you trying to embarrass me, Jade?" Rhonda asked timidly with a grimace. "I think I should just go back to the dorm and study."

"Like hell you are," the two bi-sexual young women responded in unison.

"Don't feel bad," Wendy reassured Rhonda. "My girl is just teasing you. Follow me. I got something that will definitely make you feel relaxed and ready to have fun!"

Wendy led the way to an empty, furnished bedroom and sat down on the bed. She folded her legs, gestured for the two girls to accompany her on the bed and retrieved a small zipper-bag from her purse.

"You wanna snort or swallow it tonight, sexy?" Jade asked her girlfriend when she saw the young woman's bag of molly.

"Snort or swallow *what*?" an alarmed Rhonda interjected.

"You ever heard of molly before?" Wendy answered.

"Only at the end of that Kendrick Lamar video when it said, 'Death to Molly' on the screen!"

"Yeah, well, bitch don't kill my vibe!"

Jade and Wendy both laughed at Wendy's response. Rhonda shifted uneasily as she nervously watched the young women snort two lines of the drug. After doing so, they turned to her and stared in anticipation.

"Well… you ready?"

"Um, not really," Rhonda confessed. "I've never done anything like this before."

"Well, there's a first time for everything," Jade smiled. "Besides, how are you gonna get a job dancing with me if you're too shy to take a little molly?"

"I'm not *really* going to start stripping with you, Jade," Rhonda nervously confessed. "I was just stressing about money when I said that. I was just blowing smoke."

"Girl, you're tripping," Jade replied impatiently. "You better get with the program! This is ATL and you're a freshman in college with working parents. None of us are rich, so you gotta survive by any means, just like the rest of us!"

"I'm not trying to be a stripper, though," Rhonda admitted. "My father would kill me if he found out!"

"Aw, isn't that cute?" Wendy interjected. "You sound just like Jade when I met her a year ago."

"Really?" Rhonda's voice cracked. "Jade... you used to be like me?"

"Yeah, until my girl right here put me up on game," Jade confirmed. "I was a little brainwashed, goody-goody, sheltered girl just like you. I got tired of being broke and stressed out after my first semester. Me and Wendy were just friends at first. Then she introduced me to the molly and I started dancing with her at her job. Now my money is straight. I don't ask my parents for shit except for tuition. All my inhibitions about stripping go away when I take this shit. My mood gets one-hundred times better, I don't need a lot of sleep, I can go to work, go to class, get all my schoolwork done and still have energy to party! It's like a miracle drug! You really should try it..."

"Hmmmm.... For real?"

Rhonda was convinced. She followed suit and snorted two lines of molly her new friends had prepared for her. She instantly felt a rush of hormones flood her brain. Rhonda's skin tingled as the drug flooded her system.

"Wow! I feel it already! It really does feel good... it feels great!"

"See! I wouldn't steer you wrong," Jade smirked as she and Wendy observed Rhonda's demeanor drastically change. The naïve, young woman almost instantly transitioned from being tense, stiff and uptight, to behaving in a relaxed, cheerful and easy-going manner.

221

"So, everybody's on now?" Wendy asked as she looked at her female companions who replied in the affirmative. "Okay, bet! Let's go back out and show these motherfuckers how *real* bitches party!"

The three young women rose from the bed and exited the random bedroom-turned temporary drug-den. As they walked down the hallway to join the rest of the partygoers, Rhonda suddenly felt sick to her stomach and was overcome with the urge to vomit.

"Where's the bathroom? I think I'm gonna be sick," Rhonda blurted out before running off without waiting for her companions to respond.

Rhonda quickly located a spacious, vacant bathroom in the large sorority house. She ran to the toilet, knelt down and violently emptied her guts into the porcelain bowl. After vomiting several times, followed by a series of painful dry heaves, Rhonda rose and slowly walked over to the bathroom sink.

Rhonda was dizzy, off-balance and in a daze from exhaustion, dehydration and the new drug which overpowered her previously unadulterated system. She swayed as she bent over to clean her mouth and rinse her face with the cold water from the sink. She was startled when she rose to look in the mirror and saw the image of an attractive, very light-skinned young woman standing behind her apprehensively.

"Oh, shoot! You scared the mess out of me!" Rhonda gasped.

"I'm sorry sis," the young woman apologized to Rhonda. "This bathroom is so big, I thought it was for more than one person at a time. I realized it wasn't when I came in, but you seemed kind of messed up, so I wanted to make sure you're okay."

"Oh, thanks," Rhonda replied, her voice frail from exerting herself vomiting. "That was nice of you. I'm okay, now I think."

"That's cool," the light-skinned young woman replied. "Too much to drink already, huh?"

"No," Rhonda corrected her new acquaintance. "I haven't even drunk any alcohol. My roommate and her girlfriend talked me into taking molly for the first time and it got me sick!"

"Oh, that's no good," the young woman replied. "I've done it before. You gotta drink a lot of water when you take it or else you'll get dehydrated."

"You seem to know what you're talking about," Rhonda replied, her speech slightly slurred. "I wish I met you five minutes ago so you could have told me before I got sick! Do you go to school here? You might know my roommate. Her name is Jade and her girlfriend's name is Wendy."

"No," the light-skinned young woman confessed. "I don't go here. I'm actually from out of town. I was talking to this guy online. He invited me and I came all the way here and now he's nowhere to be found!"

"Aw, that sucks! Guys can be such jerks," Rhonda empathized with her new associate. "Well, why don't you hang out with me and my friends until you figure out where he is? I gotta go try to find my girls anyway. Since you know about the molly and all that, they might be willing to share…"

"That's sweet, but I really don't want to impose on y'all…"

"Girl, please," Rhonda replied emphatically. She was much more assertive with the molly in her system. "You wouldn't be imposing anyway. You just looked out for me! I'm not gonna leave you stranded at a strange party just because some dick-head-ass-nigga left you hanging! Us girls gotta stick together!"

"I guess you're right…"

"So, let's go find my girls and have some fun," Rhonda instructed. "Just be careful, though. I figured I'd warn you that they're both bisexual. You're beautiful, so they'll probably come at your neck! I don't know if you get down like that, but I already know they're gonna try to turn you out – especially with those eyes. I've never seen eyes like yours before. I don't like girls or anything, but your eyes are hypnotizing!"

"Aw, thanks honey," the young woman replied bashfully with a smile. "I don't consider myself bisexual, but I'm not opposed to having fun with some pretty women every now and then!"

"Uh-oh," Rhonda chuckled. "My first college party and y'all are gonna get me in trouble! My father is going to kill me if he finds out what I'm doing!"

"I guess you just gotta make sure he doesn't find out, then!"

"Ha! I guess you're right about that," Rhonda laughed. "Let's go find my girls, though. By the way; I'm Rhonda. What's your name?"

"Nice to meet you, Rhonda," the young woman replied. "Thanks for being so nice to me. I'll do my best to return the favor. Oh, and my name is Crystal…"

Also Available from Paper-Chase Publications:

- *Tears Behind The Veil* by Shannon Jihan Smith & J. Cerrone
- *Illegal Life: A North Philly Story Reloaded* by J. Cerrone
- *The Prodigal Son: Book One* by J. Cerrone

Available at: www.paperchasepublications.com

Coming Soon:
- *Jewels For Your Crown* by J. Cerrone
- *Hood Politics* by Jermaine Crews & J. Cerrone

For information on writing services, voice-over/narration services and speaking engagements, contact J. Cerrone Smith, owner and founder of Paper-Chase Publications, directly.

Phone: 1(888)399-0365
E-Mail: jaycerrone@paperchasepublications.com
Alternate: paperchasepublications@gmail.com

*If you aren't already doing so, please follow Paper-Chase Publications on social media to stay up-to-date with availability of products, events and new releases.

Instagram: @paperchasepublications
Facebook & YouTube: Paper-Chase Publications